STRACANDRA ISLAND

Graham Roy Swift

Second edition.
(First edition published 2016 by Diadem Books.)

All characters in this publication are fictitious and any resemblance to real persons, living or dead, is purely coincidental.

Author's Note

Stracandra Island is a work of both fact and fiction. I have tried to be as accurate as possible with the RAF details, which have been created from research and first-hand knowledge.

Place names, vehicles, roads, towns and villages within the storyline are factual, but I have also used my imagination to create fictional scenes and backdrops which fit the pace of the story.

Stracandra Island is a made-up name and supposedly lies to the south of Barra Island in the Western Isles. Certain placed landmarks, such as a lighthouse and cottages have been added, which play an important part in the story's climax.

In parts of the book, references are made to actual people, such as heads of departments like Admiral Wilhelm Canaris and Generalmajor Hans Oster, who were senior officers within Abwehr, the German intelligence service. Also, references have been made to actual aircraft designers, such as Griffith, Frank Whittle and Hans von Ohain in Germany. Apart from these, names, characters and incidents are products of the author's imagination and resemblance to persons living or dead is entirely coincidental.

Dedication

To my wife Kathleen Swift for her help and support throughout the writing of my novel.

Also to my late father; James Swift (Wireless Operator) for his invaluable knowledge of RAF Bomber Command during the Second World War.

Acknowledgements

Ian Biles for his navigation skills for which I am greatly indebted.

Michelle Emerson for help in transforming my manuscript into a published book. (www.michelleemerson.co.uk)

Chapter 1

Warrant Officer Will Madden looked down at the relentless North Sea from the confines of the bomber's rear turret. They were low. They would only have to hiccup at this height and they would be in the drink. Removing his oxygen mask, he rubbed his face where it had chafed his skin. He could make out the tops of the white-capped waves in the semi-darkness and shuddered at the thought of ditching in the sea for a second time.

It had been a long, bitterly cold fourteen hours in the dinghy until the air-sea rescue launch had finally found them. He slowly rotated the turret, his keen eyes quartering the night sky. As they came into land, crews knew that there was still a strong need to be vigilant even at this stage in the war: rogue German night fighters were prowling the skies looking for easy prey. It had been only a few nights earlier that a Lancaster had been attacked as it was coming into land, sending it cascading on to the runway in a blazing fire ball, with no survivors.

A thin wisp of black smoke trailed back from the starboard engine, a stark reminder of how close they had come to being nearly shot down. Will thought back to the aggressive manner in which the German pilot had bore down on them, flying through his own anti-aircraft fire. Twice he had come round, his first attack doing no damage as the

Lancaster was put into a 'corkscrew', the standard procedure for all bomber crews to try and evade a fighter attack.

His second attack had caught them as they tried to gain height: the fighter's cannon shells ripping into the bomber's starboard wing, damaging their fuel tanks and setting the outer engine on fire. But as Bob Roundtree fought to regain control of the damaged aircraft, the Luftwaffe pilot found he was up against a formidable adversary with Will Madden, who was on his last trip of his second tour and, when it came to air gunnery he was no pushover. With two confirmed kills under his belt already, he returned fire with devastating effect. Will felt no remorse as he watched the German fighter go down in flames and hit the ground, just a sense of relief at having achieved what he had been trained to do.

It had been an anxious time as the skipper pushed the three remaining engines to maximum power to gain as much height as possible before putting the aircraft into a shallow dive and, with the help of the engine fire extinguisher, the fire had eventually blown itself out. Then, with some clever juggling with the remaining fuel by Wes Heyburn, the flight engineer, they had been able to make it within sight of the Lincolnshire coast. But, from what Will could hear in his earphones, they were getting dangerously low on fuel and they still had to coax Z–Zebra up and over the coastline and down onto the airfield at Kelstern. He knew they would have immediate priority to land with them having contacted flying control to say that they were in trouble – if they made it that far – but whatever the outcome, they would all have to stay with the aircraft as there was no chance of bailing out from this height.

His thoughts were interrupted by the sound of Z–Zebra's remaining engines being opened up and he whistled quietly to himself when he saw the ground slip dangerously close under his turret. He had been in this position once before, when flying in a Halifax with 4 Group in Yorkshire – low on fuel and the aircraft having sustained flack damage they had just been able to make it back to their airfield. His reminiscing was abruptly curtailed by the deep African drawl of their Rhodesian bomb aimer Jerry Lennox shouting a warning of high-tension pylons and telling the skipper to 'climb'.

Will listened as the three remaining Merlin engines were pushed once again to their capacity as they lifted the huge bomber clear for a second time before settling down to a more rhythmic beat. There had still been no order for them to take up crash positions against the main spar in the centre of the aircraft, so the skipper must be fairly confident that he could get Z-Zebra down with what remaining fuel they had, he thought as he squared the turret up with the fuselage and locked it. He raised the four Brownings up to maximum elevation, his mind set on a quick exit if things didn't go according to plan, but there was only the slightest of bumps as the main wheels touched terra firma with their usual squeal followed by a second as the tail wheel came down. Will gave a little sigh of relief as he watched the tyre-scarred runway slip reassuringly behind him. Shutting down the port outer engine, they had on the two inner engines just been able to reach their dispersal before they had coughed and spluttered and slowly windmilled to a halt, starved of fuel.

Sliding back the doors, Will eased himself out of the turret and down the tunnel, collecting his parachute from its stowage position en-route. There had been the usual congratulating and back slapping as they waited for the transport to arrive. So, they had made it, the last one of their tour. Will didn't know how he felt – relief possibly, maybe sadness that the seven of them would now be broken up, each going their separate ways. He said very little as he walked towards the crew bus and even less as it took them to the operations block for a debriefing on the night's raid. He had learned to say very little at these affairs unless asked, but he did open up a little as he and the skipper walked to the mess for breakfast.

Bob Roundtree was a tall, quietly spoken Devonian who Will had taken to from their first meeting at the Operational Training Unit. He was also the only other member of the crew who had completed a previous tour of duty on Sunderland flying boats. Will watched him top up their cups with tea, after which he crossed his arms and leaned forward on the table and looked at him.

"Well, I don't know about you, Will, but I'm going to get blotto tonight."

Will sipped his tea and nodded in agreement. "What time are we meeting the rest of them?" he asked.

Before he got an answer, he saw Dusty Miller, the navigator of Flight Lieutenant Dutton's crew, head in their direction, a look on his face that Will recognised immediately.

"What's up?" Will asked, knowing full well what the answer was going to be.

"Looks like Les Mitchell and his crew bought it. Their kite was seen to take a direct hit on the run-in to the target."

"Was anybody seen to get out?" Will asked.

"No, it blew up straight away – poor sods. Anyway, I suppose you lot will be having one hell of a booze-up tonight having finished your tour, that's your second, Will, and yours as well, Bob, isn't it?"

Will looked at the two men facing him while gently stroking the rough stubble around his chin as a huge grin spread across his face.

"Yes, it is – Christ! I thought Bob and I were fighting this bloody war on our own, isn't it about time you got some time in Miller?"

* * *

He lay there half-awake, a full five minutes before sitting bolt upright in bed. What the hell had they got up to the previous evening? There was the pub crawl, the bawdy singing at the top of their voices, the climbing of the tree in the churchyard, then the gate being lifted off its hinges at the local bus depot and the joy ride around the lanes in one of their coaches. The recollection sent a shudder down his spine as he thought what would happen to them if the local constabulary found out who was responsible. Will desperately tried to remember where they had left the vehicle as he stumbled around the room, falling over discarded items of clothing and shoes, before roughly shaking his drunken room

mate who was still half-dressed, his head hanging over the foot of the bed, groaning with annoyance at the abrupt way he was being woken.

"Christ, Will, can't you let a chap die in peace?" he murmured, his eyes flickering as he slowly rolled onto his back in the hope it might give him some respite from the thumping hangover he had.

"Where did we leave that coach last night?" Will asked, a feeling of dismay sweeping over him as the previous night's events slowly started to unfold in his mind.

"In a field, I think – yes, that's right. Wes tried to turn it around, but he got the bloody thing stuck, so we abandoned it and we walked the rest of the way back to camp. I vaguely remember climbing through a hole in the hedge on the far side of the airfield and staggering around the perimeter track. That's the last thing I remember."

"Did you say Wes was driving it?"

"Yes, that's right – why?"

"He can't drive. He hasn't got a licence," Will answered, watching his skipper raise himself up on his elbows and squint at him as he tried to focus his eyes.

"Well, under the circumstances, Will, I think our best bet is to get the hell out of here before the police come sniffing around – what say you?"

"I couldn't agree more, have you got all your kit packed?"

"Yes, what about you?"

"I did most of mine yesterday. I wonder how the rest of the guys are feeling? I hope they remember what time the transport's laid on to take us to the station," he laughed before nervously attacking his face with a razor.

The conversation had been one of excitement, having survived their tour and now heading for home and loved ones as the motor transport left the sergeants' mess after collecting the other five crewmembers and made its way through the camp. The sight of the civilian police car drawing up outside the station guardroom and its two occupants getting out and entering the building did little to diminish their high spirits.

Chapter 2

With the last rounds of handshaking and goodbyes, promises of "I'll keep in touch," and "I'll drop you a line," or "I'll give you a ring," were made – promises Will knew would never be kept. They never had at the end of his last tour, so why should this one be any different?

Last to leave had been Dave Hamilton, the mid-upper gunner, whom Will had shared a room within the sergeants' quarters. He was a short and lean Scotsman, and they had become firm friends until he had been promoted to warrant officer and had to move to the officers' quarters. Fresh out of gunnery school, and a little apprehensive, he had talked to Will not just about flying but about his family and his home on the Western Isles, the trips with his sister on their father's fishing boat around the islands, and a wealth of other subjects. After Dave had left, he drank down the last of his lukewarm tea and made his way out of the cafeteria and onto the platform to catch the train for Kendal. Dropping his kit bag on an empty luggage trolley, he sat watching the hustle and bustle of Lincoln station.

After surviving a second tour of operations, he had the overwhelming feeling that he needed to be on his own for a while. He felt tired and drained of energy: this last tour had taken its toll on his war-weary body. He had started off with his usual gusto at taking the fight to the enemy, but that had now gone, and he was quite looking forward to his two weeks' leave. With no immediate family to visit, apart from two distant cousins who he had no interest in looking up, and his only sister now living in Canada with her new husband, he had decided he would like to take in the peace and quiet of the Lake District before joining his new unit. The train journey had been a delight as it meandered its way through the Yorkshire countryside, stopping en route at the market towns of Skipton and Settle before crossing the boundary into Lancashire and finally his destination, Kendal.

A local pub was his accommodation for the next two nights while he explored the town and its surrounding area before boarding the train once more for the short ride to the picturesque area of Windermere. He walked from the station, captivated by the serenity and beauty of the landscape, the early autumn sunshine reflecting off the mirror glass surface of the lake. Stone cottages, built to withstand harsh winters, bordered the road and the air was filled with the smell of wood smoke as it curled upwards from their chimneys reaching to the topmost branches of the trees, the leaves now turning gold in the autumn sun. An old inn caught his eye with its well-worn vacancy sign hanging at an acute angle in one window. As he made his entrance into the bar's cosy interior, the conversation quickly died – no doubt the local inhabitants didn't see too many airmen in best blue with an air gunner's brevet and wearing the Distinguished Flying Medal enter their local hostelry. Will was surprised at the number of people in the bar as he lowered his kit bag to the floor and propped it against the end of the bar and made inquiries about a room. The landlord told him that his other half dealt with that side of things as he quickly disappeared in search of his good lady wife.

"I'm Doris, and my husband of thirty-five years is Wilf,

that's short for Wilfred," she told him as she watched him sign the register book. "So, how do you like to be addressed? Mr Madden, or Warrant Officer Madden?" she asked as she guided him up the narrow stairway to a room at the back of the premises.

"Please, call me Will, everybody else does."

"Right! Will, it is then. Now you should be nice and quiet here, Will, no road noise, and you are well away from the bar."

"Thanks," he answered, looking around the tastefully furnished room.

"You will find everybody around here a friendly bunch," she told him as she made her way towards the door. "Oh, and is six-thirty to seven alright with you for your evening meal, that's the normal time I serve up?"

"Yes, that's fine," he replied, which earned him a smile and a nod of approval from her as she quietly closed the door behind her. The remainder of the day he spent lazily walking the quaint streets of shops and cottages. Having found a tearoom, he sat and watched the local people going about their daily tasks, untouched by the savage war which was taking place in Europe.

That evening, after a few drinks and a meal in defiance of wartime rationing, he retired to his room and once in the confines of the comfortable bed, sleep soon overcame him.

The days passed quickly amidst the breathtaking scenery of the lakes and mountains – walking lanes and wondering what may suddenly appear around the next curve in the road. During one of his walks, he came across an old wooden finger sign, ravaged with time and long overdue a coat of paint, half-hidden by leaves and pointing off to his left. Climbing over the stile, he had followed the overgrown path through a wooded area, alive with birdsong as they flew from branch to branch as though announcing his arrival in their perfect world. The path eventually led down to the lakeside where he sat for quite some time, just revelling in the sheer delight of what the day had to offer.

His last evening was meant to be a quiet drink before leaving the following day. But having got to know quite a few of the locals during his stay there, it had turned into a party, with alcohol being consumed in large quantities. As he crawled into his bed well past closing time, his ears still ringing from laughter and song, he knew he would return to the place again and savour its delights in more peaceful times.

Chapter 3

Guntram Bayer, codename *'Das Rabe',* kept perfectly still among the dense foliage that concealed his position. Focusing the camera, he took a series of photographs of the buildings of the Gloucester Aircraft Company's airfield at Moreton Valence. Intelligence gathering was Bayer's strong point; having survived for almost two years in England, he was one of Abwehr's most successful agents. Cold, ruthless and with a love for killing, he carried out his work with an air of confidence which made him feel that he was immune from being discovered.

He had covered his tracks well since coming ashore from a German submarine on a remote stretch of the Scottish coast, frequently moving between lodgings and quickly eliminating anybody he felt was a danger to his own safety. He had now taken up residence near Moreton Valence, where the new Meteor jet now resided, having moved from its former home at Newmarket Heath. He had relentlessly followed the aircraft's progress from its earliest development to the fifth prototype making its first flight in early March at RAF Cranwell.

The area along the River Severn had long been kept under close scrutiny by the German military intelligence. Abwehr paid great interest to the south of the region: to the Bristol Aeroplane Company at Filton and its shadow factory at

Weston-super-Mare. To the north, Dowty's at Staverton, near Gloucester, heavily into the design of aircraft propellers and landing gear, had also been kept under constant surveillance by the spies of the Third Reich.

Bayer's contact in the area had been Griselda Zweig, who lived in an isolated cottage near Coaley and within easy cycling distance of Moreton Valence airfield. Zweig had been recruited in 1936 by Abwehr which was under the command of Admiral Wilhelm Canaris, firstly for her good command of the English language and secondly for her known hatred of the British, going back to the First World War.

After extensive training, she had been assigned to The Central Division *'Abteilung Z'* where she had come to the notice of Generalmajor Hans Oster, head of that department. After further training in intelligence gathering and radio communication, she had travelled to Britain under the name of Lillian Gilbert eighteen months prior to the outbreak of the Second World War. Known within the intelligence service as a 'sleeper', she had quietly gone about the task of establishing herself as an upright British citizen. Her office skills and training soon secured her a secretarial position with a law firm in Gloucester, where she stayed for a short time. With war clouds looming on the distant horizon, she applied to the Bristol Aeroplane Company and was soon strategically placed where she could put her skills into practice.

Despite posing as her brother, Bayer had found Griselda attractive from their first meeting. Slightly taller than himself with an hourglass figure, her soft blue eyes had soon reciprocated his feelings and they quickly became lovers. Smirking to himself over his good fortune, he secreted the camera in a pouch on his belt, buttoned up the heavy overcoat and stealthily made his way to where his bicycle lay hidden.

Checking to make sure the lane was clear, he set off at a steady pace towards Stonehouse. On his arrival back at the cottage, he found a black motor car parked in front of the gate and stopping short, he quietly leaned the cycle against a tree then, checking the ammunition clip in his Walther P38 was full, he placed it back in his pocket as he cautiously moved towards the cottage. The elderly woman knocking on the door never heard his silent approach until he spoke.

"Good afternoon, can I help you?" he asked, smiling at the woman.

"Oh! I'm sorry to disturb you, but I seem to be lost, I'm trying to get to the village of Frocester," she answered, not realising that only inches away, a pistol was aimed directly at her. Satisfied the woman was no threat to his safety, he gave her directions to her destination, and as he watched her get into her car, he returned her wave as she drove off.

* * *

The train journey north had been a nightmare, with Will sitting in the corridor on his kit bag most of the way amidst several hundred sailors returning to their ship after leave. He had found them a friendly bunch with no animosity towards him because he was the only airman among them. In fact, he had got involved in a card game with them and won five bob for his trouble. It was after changing trains at Glasgow for the long slow ride through the Scottish Highlands to the port of Oban that he had been able to relax, with the last part of the journey being made in a compartment on his own.

The boat crossing between Oban and Tiree, most of which was done in daylight, gave him some concern as to what an easy target they made for any lurking U-boat that was looking for a 'target of opportunity', so he spent most of the passage out on deck and only ventured inside to the cafeteria for refreshments or the amenities.

He had about an hour's wait until the transport duly arrived to collect him and the conversation between himself and the bubbly WAAF driver never once lapsed until he was deposited at the entrance to the officer's quarters. After being shown to a twin-bedded room and told that he was sharing with a Pilot Officer Dennison who was on leave, he unpacked then went off in search of the bar. The room was heavy with cigarette and pipe smoke, with the usual mixture of air and ground officers milling about, some playing billiards and darts, others sat around chatting or reading, most paying him little or no attention as he entered.

Picking up his pint of beer, he found an empty table and settled down in the well-worn easy chair, listening to the noisy brigade who were propping up the bar while trying to chat up the attractive civilian barmaid with the old-hat 'line shoots', the pulling of faces and winking every time she bent down to get a bottle from the bottom shelf. Will had the distinct feeling that the place was a bit cliquey, a far cry from the boisterous goings-on at RAF Kelstern.

Bored with watching the clowning about, he was just deciding whether to have another beer or call it a night when a warrant officer flight engineer came into the bar, his well-worn uniform giving the distinct impression that he had quite a few operations under his belt. After purchasing a pint and taking a drink, Will watched him make a sweep of the room before his eyes settled on the empty chair next to him.

"Do you mind if I join you?"

"No, not at all," Will answered, gesturing to the chair.

"How long have you been here?" the warrant officer asked, taking out a packet of cigarettes and offering Will one.

"I arrived today," he replied, holding up his hand to

decline the offer.

"Oh! I came yesterday," he grinned, his Liverpudlian accent coming to the forefront as he spoke.

"Are you on ops or a rest period?" Will asked, finishing off the remainder of his beer.

"I'm starting my second tour. I put in for Bomber Command but never expected to get a Met squadron on some bloody remote island off the west coast of Scotland. Mind you, I don't suppose the 'chop' rate's so high doing meteorological flights. How about you?"

"I've just finished my second. I've to report to the armoury in the morning. So what were you flying in?"

"Stirlings, I was on 75 squadron at Mepal. I'm Keith Stanbury," he said, holding out his hand for Will to shake.

"Will Madden."

"What were you flying in, Will?"

"Lancasters – 625 squadron at Kelstern," he replied, noticing three officers who were sat together were watching them with interest.

"Well, I'll be damned, we landed there back end of forty-two, our drome was socked in with fog so we diverted there. Mind you, it was a bit of a dicey do landing, with the ground mist being so bad. But the skipper got her down without pranging it."

"I know the feeling, we've had some hairy do's with fog. The last time it happened they diverted us to Ludford Magna, which is equipped with FIDO."

"I can never remember what that stands for, it's – Fog ...?"

Will began to laugh, "Investigation and Dispersal Operation, it is a mouthful to remember, I must admit but it's good. It got us down in one piece."

"Yes, I've heard so, it's saved a lot of aircraft and lives."

"So, how did you find the old Stirlings? I've never had

anything to do with them."

"Oh! They weren't bad kites, their main problem was they couldn't get the height. At fourteen or fifteen thousand feet you were running in the flak belt all the time, even the light stuff could get at you being that low."

"Christ, that is low, we could get up to twenty thousand with the Lancs. Although we weren't safe at that height from the eighty-eights, they could reach us and bring us down."

"I know, they are bastards them things," he said, getting up from the chair. "I'll go and get us another couple of beers, Will."

The break in the conversation gave him time to run his eyes over the three wingless wonders sitting opposite. A thought crossed his mind – was one of them the armaments officer?

They chatted for over an hour, mainly about aircraft and past experiences, until time was called, to a series of "boos" from the bar brigade. After bidding his new friend "goodnight", he made his way to his room and decided to write to his sister in Canada but soon gave up on the idea through lack of interest and turned in for a good night's sleep.

It was the sound of heavy rain beating against the window that woke him; after washing and dressing, he made his way to the mess and had breakfast. There was no let-up in the rain as he arrived at the armoury in a rather bedraggled state and was shown into Flight Lieutenant Nelson's office. Coming smartly to attention he saluted, his presence provoking no response from the armaments officer who carried on reading a document before looking up and removing his glasses.

"I have just been reading your service record, Madden. Very impressive. Which makes me wonder why we have been graced with your presence?"

Will didn't answer straight away but looked at Nelson and knew it was going to be a love-hate relationship between them. "I go where I'm sent, *sir.*"

Nelson shot him a quick glance.

The rain seemed to be easing and, through the broken cloud, the faint signs of the sun began to show. Will watched a Handley Page Halifax climb steadily into the clouds, wishing he was in it as he half-listened to Nelson drone on about their work schedule and how he was a stickler for punctuality and work being carried out and finished by the allotted time, and he didn't want any cock-ups that would interfere with his promotion to squadron leader. After the meeting was over, Will was taken through to the armoury section, where he was left in the capable hands of Flight Sergeant Milroyd, who he was going to replace.

"So, how did you get on with our intrepid armaments officer?" Milroyd asked, smirking, as he showed him around the section.

"Not too well. He seems as though he has got an inferiority complex about aircrew."

"Yes, especially those that have come up through the ranks like you have," Milroyd chuckled as he showed Will the storeroom. "This is where we keep most of the bits and pieces for the turrets. The kites are Mk 5s. However, we have heard that there are some Mk 3s coming, but, as you probably know, they are both fitted with the standard Boulton Paul turrets. We also have another store around the back where we keep the new stuff if we need one, which I'll show you shortly. Well, that's about it," Milroyd told him, both men stopping momentarily to watch an aircraft as it slew its way around the perimeter track with sudden bursts of engine power. "Had anything to do with the Halifaxes?" he asked, shielding his eyes from the sun so he could see who the pilot was.

Will watched the rear gunner traverse his turret several times while depressing and elevating the four Browning machine guns before answering. "Yes! But they were the MK1 and 2s we had on 76 Squadron. We converted to the MK 5s in April forty-three."

"Oh! Now you are going back a bit with the MK 1 and 2 series, we had them at Linton-on-Ouse in 1940," Milroyd laughed.

"I see the mid-upper turret has been removed, is that to reduce its all-up weight and give it a longer endurance?" Will asked as he heard the all too familiar sound of brakes squealing as the Halifax was brought to a halt in line with the main runway.

"No! That particular aircraft came from another squadron with the turret already taken out. Fortunately, they don't come into contact with Jerry too often. The main contender up here is the weather. We've lost several aircraft since I've been here and that's in just over fourteen months."

They stood in silence as the aircraft got its permission to take off from the control tower and started to lumber its way down the runway, picking up speed as the four engines were pushed to maximum power.

Will felt a touch of envy as he watched it steadily climb into the morning sunshine, its motors giving off a mournful drone which got ever fainter until it disappeared from view.

"Well, that's another one away. Let's hope they have a good trip! I think the weather report for today is quite reasonable," Milroyd added.

"What do they actually do on these Met flights?" Will asked as they resumed their walk back to the armoury.

"I don't know the ins and outs of it. I know they fly a set course like a triangle, you know what I mean, so many nautical miles on the first leg, then on to a new heading for so many miles, then the final leg back to base. The gunners tell me they vary the height throughout the sortie to take accurate temperature measurements, which by all accounts takes some very skilful flying. They fly two of these set triangles from here, one is called *Mercer* and the other *Bismuth,* that's the longer of the two."

"So, how often do they go out?" Will enquired, pushing the door open and making his way into the armoury section.

"Four times every twenty-four hours," Milroyd told him, then started to laugh when he saw Will frowning. "I can see you are suitably impressed. I know it sounds a bit monotonous, but these Met boys take the job very seriously," he said, handing him a mug of tea, "very seriously indeed."

Will smiled to himself as he thought back to past operations, too many to remember, where the Met briefing had been totally different to what they had encountered, going to and returning from the target with one particular sortie to Nuremberg, which was etched firmly in his mind when Bomber Command had lost ninety-five aircraft in one night partially due to the Met forecast being wrong.

"So, Flight, when are you due to leave?"

"I was supposed to be going at the end of the week to do an air gunnery course at Pembrey, but I've been informed that it's been cancelled. By all accounts, the course is full at the moment," Milroyd replied with a look of disappointment.

Chapter 4

Approaching footsteps coming along the corridor quickly made Griselda Zweig replace the files she had been photographing back into their folder, re-lock the filing cabinet drawer and make it back to her desk before the burly form of Wendell Priestly, the office cleaner, appeared.

"Hello Wendell, you timed that just right, I've just finished," she announced, switching out the desk light. She smiled to herself as his eyes lit up when he saw her skirt ride up, showing off her shapely legs and nylon stockings as they came out from under the desk.

"You are working late, Lillian," he grinned, the thought of catching her on her own foremost in his mind.

"Oh! You know what it's like working here, always lots to do and work to be caught up on. That's the aircraft industry for you," she replied, making for the stand that held her coat.

"Would you like me to make you a cup of tea before you go?" he suggested.

"That's very kind of you, Wendell, but maybe some other time. I'll miss my train if I don't hurry," she answered, knowing full well what he had in mind. She squeezed his arm in a friendly gesture as she passed him. Lifting her eyes, she compared him with Guntram, who was giving her everything she needed.

The distance from the aircraft company's main gate to the railway station was only a short walk, but all the same, she felt apprehensive being so late and several times turned around to see if she was being followed. The station offered little comfort, with only a handful of passengers spread along the length of its platform. Taking a cigarette from the packet in her bag, she inadvertently touched the smooth barrel of the P38 Walther which gave her some reassurance as she thought of the secret film she was carrying.

After the train left Yate, she found herself alone in the compartment. Content with her own company, she felt a little easier and relaxed, leaning her head back and closing her eyes for a few moments only to reopen them as she felt the train come to a halt. Looking at her watch, she estimated they must be near the Wickwar tunnel. It was the opening and closing of a door along the corridor, followed by footsteps, which made her automatically reach for her shoulder bag, so its contents were near to hand if she needed it. The man's features were not discernible in the corridor's subdued lighting as he stood opposite her compartment, peering through the peephole of the blacked-out window to see what the holdup was.

Griselda's mind was fully alert. It may be nothing, but the uneasy feeling she'd had earlier when walking to the station still niggled away at the back of her mind – were MI5 on to her and was this one of their operatives following her or was she worrying unduly? She had survived over five years without any problems, she thought, but even so, caution and vigilance had to be heeded at whatever cost. The British were no fools when it came to counter-intelligence, she knew that by the number of German operatives that had been caught, tried and executed.

The compartment suddenly had a sinister feel about it,

the stale smell of tobacco smoke added to its confinement, giving her a feeling of being trapped like an animal in a cage with only one way out, which was blocked by this faceless figure. Sliding her hand inside her bag, she tightened her grip on the Walther and took stock of her options. The distance between them wasn't much, but it was enough for her to kill him if necessary and, with the train now at a standstill, she could quickly leave by the carriage door one compartment down to her left. Minutes seemed to tick by painfully slow as she watched her adversary for any kind of movement as to what he might do next. The unexpected jolt of the train moving off, followed by "Tickets please", eased the tension as she watched him fumble in his inside pocket for his ticket. Releasing her hold on the pistol and taking out her ticket, she did manage to catch a quick glimpse of the man's dark features from the inspector's torch before he moved off along the corridor.

"What was the holdup?" she enquired, holding out the ticket as the inspector came into the compartment.

"I don't know, ma'am. We had a red light against us so we had to wait. It shouldn't be too long now before we reach Coaley Junction," he said, clipping the ticket and handing it back to her.

"Thank you," she said, smiling as she watched him close the door behind him. Waiting a few seconds, she quickly transferred to the corner seat near the door so she could see into the corridor and took particular notice that he bypassed the adjacent compartment to her left that she now knew must be unoccupied.

Steadying herself against the swaying carriage, she slowly slid back the compartment door and made her way forward to the front of the carriage and, with her back against the polished woodwork, she now had a clear view down the entire length of the corridor. There was no further sign of the mysterious figure as the train rattled on towards its destination and when it finally slowed and came to a shuddering halt, she took note that nobody left any of the other compartments in the carriage before she opened the door and stepped out onto the platform.

Stations such as Coaley were ominous places in wartime; small and poorly lit by lanterns; dark shadows seemed to lurk everywhere. Walking briskly towards the ticket hall, she stopped briefly to look along the platform to see if anybody else was alighting and, standing to one side to light a cigarette, she acknowledged a young couple's gesture as they emerged out of the darkness.

The ticket hall felt warm, remnants of a fire's dying embers still glowed amidst the grey ash that spilt over onto the tiles below. Using the light from the solitary lantern, she rummaged through her bag until she found her torch. Passing the ticket office window, Griselda returned the nod from the ticket clerk, who she noticed was far younger than the regular older man who was normally on duty when she came home on the earlier train.

There was no sign of the couple when she emerged from the ticket office entrance. How could they have vanished so quickly? she thought, straining her eyes in the direction of the lane that would take her to the main Dursley road. A loud hiss of steam startled her as the train started to move off and slowly disappeared into the night; the silence after it had gone left an eeriness that was made worse by the soft rustle of the trees as they shivered in the late evening breeze. At the end of the lane, she turned right onto Draycott Road and, on reaching the railway bridge, was enveloped in smoke from a southbound express, its whistle screaming as it thundered through the station.

Cursing out loud at her misfortune, she was partway across the bridge when she thought she heard the sound of footsteps behind her. Switching off her torch she stood and listened but the sound of another approaching train made hearing difficult.

Quickening her pace to reach the far side of the bridge, she took out the Walther and receded back into the bushes to wait. The sound of voices and laughing coming from the direction of Dursley and heading towards the railway station made her breathe more easily, all the same she waited until the revelry had died away in the distance before breaking cover. A further fifteen minutes walking found her rounding the bend in the lane where she could just make out the dark outline of the roof and chimney of the cottage against the night sky.

Opening and closing the gate behind her she made her way around to the side to let herself in via the kitchen door. What met her as she pushed open the door was a dark empty room and Guntram nowhere to be seen, which did not worry her unduly. What did was finding the kitchen door unlocked and a roll of film on the kitchen table when she switched on the light. Once again taking the Walther from her bag, she stood quite still and cast a careful eye around the contents of the room. Nothing seemed to be out of place, and, knowing Guntram's temperament, it would have been. He wouldn't have given up without a fight if something unexpected had happened.

Moving towards the door that led through to the front of the house, she had just put her hand on the door handle when she felt the cold feel of a gun barrel pressed firmly against her neck. Pushed roughly against the door and her right arm pulled quickly around her back, the Walther was taken from her. Griselda found herself breathing hard as the seconds ticked by, wondering what the opposition's next move would be. Was she going to be arrested? Or even shot? Where the hell was Guntram when she needed him? Had he escaped the trap and left her to face the consequences? All this had been flashing through her mind when she felt her hair on her shoulders being gently pushed up and a kiss planted tenderly on her neck.

"You're late!" a voice whispered in her ear.

She tried to twist around to face him but found she was still being held firmly as he pressed against her and slowly slid his left hand under her skirt until he reached the top of her stockings. Griselda was annoyed with herself for being caught like she was and, twisting and wriggling, tried to show her annoyance, but to no avail. Guntram was skilful at whatever he did, she'd known that since the first night they had slept together. His masterfulness and constant appetite to make love soon melted away any resistance she had towards him.

"I'll deal with you later," he said, releasing his hold on her.

Straightening her ruffled skirt, she watched him take a seat at the table and pick up the roll of film. "How did you know I was coming?" she asked.

"You'll have to learn to close the gate more quietly in future, I heard you close it from here. If I had been MI5, you know where you would have been now? Arrested," he said sharply, without looking up.

"Where were you hiding?"

"In the first place, you should have thought of when you came in and saw that the room was empty … the pantry," he replied coldly.

"Oh! I'd forgotten about there."

"Well, you don't forget, you stupid bitch. Mistakes like that will get you taken – or killed," he snapped angrily, pushing back the chair which tipped over as he stood up.

His outburst and the way he was looking frightened her; this was a side to him she hadn't seen before and, for a brief moment, she wasn't sure what he was going to do to her until she saw his eyes soften and he picked up the overturned chair.

"Did you manage to photograph the documents Berlin asked for?" he asked, crossing the room to lock the door.

"Yes. That's why I'm late home, I had to wait until everyone had gone," she answered, taking the camera from her bag and handing it to him.

The makings of a smile spread across his face as he removed the film from the camera. "Right, I'll go down to the basement and develop these while you get some food ready. After we have eaten, we will contact Berlin for further instructions."

* * *

Henry Maynard picked up his pipe from his desk before closing the office door behind him. Too old for active service but, with a razor-sharp mind acquired from his days in commercial banking, he had been recruited by Military Intelligence at the War Office in the spring of 1940. The door to Clifford Granville's office was ajar when he got there and he smiled to himself when he saw his old friend surrounded in the usual halo of cigar smoke staring out through the window.

"Morning, Clifford," he said, tapping on the door out of courtesy as he entered.

"Morning, Henry, close the door and have a seat."

Maynard could see the closed file on Granville's desk. "Is that the Filton file?" he asked as he watched Granville retake his seat and stub out the cigar butt into the half-filled ashtray.

"Yes! Here, take a look," he replied, sliding the folder towards him. "Information is getting to the Germans somehow, Henry. And we've been given the task of finding out how and by whom."

Maynard carefully went through the documents, which were all to do with modifications that had been carried out on the radar that was fitted into the Bristol Beaufighter.

"Disturbing reading, isn't it, Henry?"

"Yes, it is. So our boys haven't been able to get a fix on where the information is being sent from?"

"No! Whoever he or she is, they are professional. When transmitting they never stay on long enough for us to get a fix on the position. But, this is the most interesting part, when the Germans replied they used the code name '*Das Rabe*'. At least we have a name to work with now."

Maynard sat quietly for a few moments while he filled his pipe. Lighting it, he sat back in the chair to savour the aroma. "So, we are looking for somebody called *The Raven,*" he answered, studying the fragments of the messages they had at their disposal. "There's not a lot to go on here, Clifford, the chances of catching who is getting this information out and sending it is very slim with what we've got."

"Yes, I know. But we might have had a breakthrough, Henry, albeit a small one but worth looking into. Read this," Granville said, handing him part of a message that had been picked up.

"Hell's bells, they have been watching and photographing the test flights of the Meteor! When was this intercepted?" Maynard asked, handing back the paper and relighting his pipe.

"Late last night. But again the sender didn't stay on long enough for our chaps to get a fix. What the message does tell us is what area it's being sent from."

"And that is?" Maynard queried.

Granville sat back in his chair and lit another cigar, and took a long draw before answering. "The Gloucester area, because that is where the Meteor is now being made ready to undergo test trials at Moreton Valence airfield. So, whoever he or she is, they must now be operating from around that area."

Maynard blew a cloud of tobacco smoke towards the ceiling before leaning forward and tapping the Filton file with the end of his pipe. "But that still doesn't help us with how they've managed to get hold of the radar information – that's top-secret stuff, Clifford. The Germans now know how the RAF is carrying out these all-weather and night-time attacks with such precision. The torpedo Beaufighters have had great success with their low-level attacks on German shipping since they adopted the practice."

"Yes, I know, Henry, that's why I want you to go across to Filton and have a quiet nose about. It's been arranged with their top people over there. They've agreed to fix you up with an office within the personnel department so you can go through their staff files and see what you can dig up. There may be something you pick up on that their people have missed."

"Alright. When do you want me to go?"

"There is a train leaving Paddington early tomorrow morning for Bristol. See Amy next door, she has all the details. Filton will have transport waiting for you when you arrive. I know it's a bit short notice, Henry, but the sooner we can nail this sod, the better."

"I couldn't agree more. So what are you going to do about Moreton Valence?"

"Well, by all accounts, the airfield is fairly well-guarded, but from what we now know, it looks like we are going to have to increase it. This *Raven* character might well be bold enough to try and get onto the place under cover of darkness and try a bit of sabotage now he knows the layout."

"It's possible, I suppose. But you know, Clifford, my gut feeling tells me that *The Raven* is a man and that there are two separate incidents going on here," Maynard suggested, abruptly breaking off the conversation when there was a tap on the door.

"Come in!" Granville said sharply, annoyed at the timing.

Silence fell across the room as a young girl appeared carrying a tray with two cups of tea on it.

After she had left the room, Granville took a drink before speaking. "So what you are really saying, Henry, is that there are two separate agents at large in close proximity to one another?"

Maynard nodded as he put his cup back on the saucer. "Yes. And I wouldn't mind betting that one is a permanent fixture at Filton, the other is a field agent, an information gatherer. If he is, it is unlikely he will try his hand at sabotage if he is attached to the counter-intelligence division."

Chapter 5

Isobel Hamilton followed the windswept path that ran along the cliff edge, stopping to admire the view out to sea. The stiff breeze ruffled her jet-black hair across her shoulders and forehead. Of medium build with fine features and sparkling blue eyes, she had all the attributes men found attractive in a woman and one such person was Sergeant Trevor Roach, their relationship having blossomed during his time with the air-sea rescue unit which was stationed in the bay.

Slipping her hand into her coat pocket, she felt the letter. Taking it out, she unfolded it and read it through for the fourth time, its contents short but to the point. He had met someone else at his new station and he had written to tell her he was ending their relationship.

Wiping away the tears from her cheeks with the back of her hand, she screwed the letter up and thrust it back in her pocket. "To hell with you, Trevor Roach," she shouted, her words carried away on the wind.

Reaching the point where the footpath turned back towards the town, she stood and took in the beauty of the picturesque bay and its harbour. Her father's fishing boat rode gently against the quay amidst the array of the other colourful boats; how she loved the remoteness and beauty of the Western Isles.

It was the sound of powerful engines starting that drew

her attention to the opposite side of the bay where the Royal Air Force had commandeered a section to moor their air-sea rescue boats, which were on detachment from their main base at Stornoway. She couldn't make out its number behind the RAF roundel as it was slowly manoeuvred away from the one adjacent to it. Once clear, its three Napier engines were opened up as it glided smoothly away from its mooring, its speed increasing as it headed out to sea.

She cut through the narrow streets of stone cottages that were built to withstand the harsh Atlantic gales to where her parents' shop was.

"Oh! There you are. Had a good walk?" her mother asked, coming from behind the meagre display.

"Yes, thanks. It's a bit wild up on the cliff path," she answered, lifting up the counter flap and making her way into the kitchen. "Where's David?" she asked while going through the motions of making some tea.

"He's gone down to the boat with your father. Helping him put on a new part that it's been waiting for since I don't know when. Something to do with the winch, I believe," her mother told her as she came through to join her.

"Are you okay here if I go down to the boat after I've had this drink? It will be nice to spend a bit more time with that brother of mine before he leaves on Friday. Is he still determined to put in a request to join the marine craft unit here when he gets to his new camp?" she asked, handing her mother a cup of tea.

"Oh! I'll be okay on my own, it's not been very busy this morning. And yes, he seems very keen on the idea of the air-sea rescue boats, but you know yourself, Isobel, both of you have had a love of the sea since you were youngsters. That's what comes with having a father who's a fisherman."

She looked at her mother and nodded in agreement. "Yes,

I suppose it is. I never understood him joining the RAF as against the navy."

"That took us all by surprise! Where the love of wanting to fly came from, I've no idea. And in those big bombers as well."

"I asked him that, the other night when we were walking down to the pub together; he told me after seeing what the Germans were doing to our cities on the Pathé News in the cinema he felt flying in the Royal Air Force would be a good way of hitting back at them."

Aileen Hamilton frowned at her daughter's remark. "Is that what he thought!" she said softly, replacing the cup back on its saucer.

Isobel smiled at her mother's shrewdness before changing the subject. "He seemed to get on very well with the rear gunner in his crew, this Will Madden? By what David was telling me, he has completed two tours of duty on Bomber Command and shot down several German aircraft in the process."

"Yes, your father did mention something about it a couple of days ago, and by all accounts this Will Madden is stationed up here on Tiree but, like David, he's not flying."

Isobel studied her mother's expression for a few moments. "Has David told you that after he has had this rest period he can be called back to do a second tour of duty?"

Aileen looked at her daughter. "Yes, I did know that. It wasn't David who told me though, it was Trevor who mentioned it one evening while he was waiting for you to get ready to go out for a drink."

Isobel pulled a face at the mention of Roach's name, which was seen by her mother.

"What's the matter, have you and Trevor had a falling out?" she asked.

"A little bit more than that," she answered, taking the screwed up bundle from her coat pocket and giving it to her mother to read.

After straightening it out, Aileen read it through slowly until coming to the part about him meeting someone else and ending their relationship. "Oh! I see," she said quietly, lowering the letter and looking at her daughter. "I'm so sorry, love, I know you had grown very fond of him but, as they say, there's plenty more fish in the sea and I'm sure some nice young man will eventually come along and steal your heart, you mark my words."

"Thanks, Mum."

"Now away with you and get yourself down to that boat if you're going before I find you something here to do."

Leaving her mother to manage the shop, she made her way down to the quay. "How's it going?" she asked, climbing down the steel ladder onto the fishing boat's rear deck.

"Just about finished, lass," her father answered, with the makings of a smile on his weather-beaten face.

"Did you see the rescue boat go out, Issy?" her brother asked, wiping his oily hands on a piece of dirty rag.

"Yes, I watched it from the cliff path. You're putting more on than taking off with that. And don't call me Issy, you know I don't like it," she told him.

"Get some clean stuff from the wheelhouse, David," her father suggested, winking at his daughter.

"So, have you heard what the emergency is?" she enquired, sitting down on an upturned fishing box.

"No, nary a word, lass. But you know how tight-lipped the RAF can be about what they are up to, especially when they have a rescue on. Your laddie Trevor would only tell you what he wanted you to know," her father said, taking the waste rag from his son.

"He sounds a nice chap, Isobel, I would have liked to have met him; has he written to you to let you know how he's getting on at his new camp?" her brother asked, sitting down next to her.

She went quiet for a few moments. "Well, you might as well both know because if I don't tell you, mother will. He wrote and told me he has met someone else and he has ended the relationship between us, so that's the end of that," she sighed.

"Oh! I'm sorry to hear that, lass, you both seemed to be getting on quite well together."

"I thought so too, Dad."

"He sent you a '*Dear John*' did he, the bastard?"

"Now David, I don't like to hear language like that in front of your sister."

"Anyway, what is a '*Dear John*'?" she asked, turning to look at her brother.

"It's RAF terminology for the type of letter that you have had from Roach, it means he or she is ending the relationship."

"Oh, I see. So girls are quite often sent these when you airmen are sent elsewhere. Have you sent one?" she asked sharply, giving her brother a withering look of disapproval.

"No. Not as yet," he laughed, giving her a nudge with his shoulder.

"You'll tell me anything to keep me quiet, David Hamilton! But I will tell you one thing, I'll not be having anything to do with airmen anymore, that's for sure," she snapped, getting up and making for the ladder.

Duncan Hamilton looked at his son and lifted his eyes. "That's enough said on that subject," he said as he watched his daughter skilfully climb the steel rungs up to the quayside.

"She can be a fiery one, that sister of mine at times!"

"Aye! She gets that from her mother, but I wouldn't change either of them. Fancy a pint son on the way back? The Castlebay should just about be opening by the time we get there."

"Sounds good to me," he answered.

Thinking about the letter she had received, Isobel became tearful as she walked along the quay back home. Stopping briefly to wipe her eyes, she forced a smile as she caught sight of her father and brother entering the Castlebay Bar.

"I suppose those two have stopped off for a drink?" her mother asked as she finished serving Helen McAlister.

"They were heading in that direction the last I saw of them," Isobel replied as she came in, closing the shop door behind her.

"So how is that lovely young man of yours, Isobel, I hope he's well?"

Isobel looked at the elderly spinster and smiled. "As a matter of fact, Miss McAlister, we have ended our relationship, if you must know," she told her, knowing full well it would be all around the town by the following morning.

"Well, it's probably for the best with him being so far away now," her face lighting up as she made for the door with her new-found gossip.

Isobel saw her mother looking at her from behind the counter. "It will come out sooner or later, so why not now? It will give them something to talk about over the next day or two until they light on their next victim," she laughed, going through to the rear of the premises.

In The Castlebay, Robbie, the landlord, greeted them in his customary manner and put two pint glasses on the counter, one of which he began to fill. "So, how much longer have you got, Dave?"

"I go back on Friday."

"But you're not flying, are you?"

"No, I'm on my rest period," he told him, making eye contact with his father who was beckoning towards an empty table.

"That's the trouble with living in a small community like this place – everybody wants to know your business," his father said quietly as they sat down. "So, this new camp you are going to, son, you say it's in Dumfries and Galloway and it's a gunnery school?"

"Yes, that's right. It's the No 3 Air Gunnery School at Castle Kennedy, it sounds as though I will be teaching sprog gunners."

"Well, there is one thing, lad, you'll be well out of harm's way over there."

Dave took a long drink of beer and stared at the fire, his mind going back to their last sortie.

"What is it, David?" his father asked quietly.

"Don't say anything back home, Dad, but we had a dicey do on this last trip."

Duncan could see the strain on his son's face but also sensed he wanted to talk about it. "What was it, anti-aircraft fire?"

"No, a night fighter. Twice he came round, the second time he hit our starboard wing and outer engine. Fortunately, Will put a long burst into him and shot him down but even so, we only just made it back on three engines."

"You liked Will didn't you, son?"

"Aye, he was a good friend, even though he was a *Sassenach,*" he laughed.

"Have you got his address?"

"Yes! We said we would keep in touch with one another."

"What you will have to do is next time you get some leave,

drop this Will a line, or if you can, phone him and arrange to have your leave together, he's not far away being stationed on Tiree. He can use the spare bedroom while he's here. We'll have a word with your mother about it when we get back."

"Thanks, Dad, that's a great idea."

"Right! That's sorted then. Drink up lad, we'll have one more before we go."

Chapter 6

Will did his best to settle into his new job in the armoury but found it hard. He missed the buzz and camaraderie of an operational bomber station, and he had also soon come to realise that there was never going to be any love lost between Nelson and himself; they were poles apart, and that would never alter. His friendship with Keith Stanbury and the other members of his crew seemed to irritate Nelson, which Will exploited for his own amusement. Word had also spread among the other flight crews that he had survived two tours of duty on Bomber Command, which didn't help the situation and made him a bit of a celebrity which he didn't like, being of a reserved nature.

Mixing with the Met crews, he did pick up quite a lot of gen as to what was involved in flying these meteorological flights and the atrocious weather conditions the crews had to endure to bring back their reports. The bomber crews had quite often taken the Met briefings with a pinch of salt as weather conditions that had been predicted were often wrong, but he had secretly admitted to himself the more he listened, that the cost had been high in some cases to get those reports to the bomber squadrons.

He had been in the mess after being on duty over the weekend when he saw Squadron Leader Barfield Walker heading in his direction. Barfield Walker was the officer in charge of flying. Of a jovial disposition, sporting a huge handlebar moustache, he was very seldom seen without a large glass of whisky in his hand when off-duty in pre-war days – hence he soon acquired the name 'Johnny', after a certain brand of well-known Scottish Whisky. Intrigued as to what was on, Will eyed him cautiously as Barfield Walker pulled back a chair and sat down opposite him, then leant forward so as to keep their conversation out of earshot of others who may be listening.

"I've heard, through the grapevine, that you want to get back to flying and also that you've been on duty over the weekend?" Walker asked, holding Will's gaze.

"You are correct on both counts, sir," he replied, drinking down the remainder of his tea.

"So, are you on stand down for a couple of days?"

Will nodded before answering. "Yes, sir."

"If I square it with the armaments officer, would you undertake a Bismuth operation for me tomorrow morning with Flight Sergeant Lambert and his crew? They are short of a rear gunner."

"Yes, I would, sir."

Take-off was rescheduled for 09.00 hours, due to a problem with one of the engines. After a good breakfast and attending the briefing, Will made his way to the safety equipment section and put on his Taylor suit, collected his parachute and survival rations, then made his way out to the waiting transport to take them out to the dispersal where their aircraft, T–Tommy, stood waiting. Settling himself into the familiar surroundings of the Halifax's rear turret, he went through the general procedure laid down for all air gunners before take-off. Satisfied all was as it should be, he sat back against the turret doors and looked out at the lush green landscape behind him. He wondered how many times he would see again the all too familiar scenes – a hedgerow with its well-worn gate, a farmer working his land, a distant village with its church spire – all the things Will took for granted but which could suddenly be ended by an accurate burst of flak or the guns of a German night fighter. Even so, it felt good to be doing again what he loved best: flying. Reporting back, he told the skipper that everything was on top line as the aircraft slowly started to move from its dispersal point onto the perimeter track for its journey round to the runway.

There was the usual wait until they got permission to take off, and Will used the time to regulate the heat to his flying suit. With a loud hiss from the brakes being released, the Halifax started to gather speed; Will noticed that there wasn't a gathering of well-wishers by the side of the runway like there normally was on a bomber station. The four engines made easy work of the climb, being devoid of a heavy bomb load, and they were soon out over the sea turning onto their course, due west. Once clear of the coast and checking there was nothing below them, Will asked permission to test-fire the guns; he gave the four Brownings a short burst and reported back that they were all okay, then settled down to the lonely vigil of quartering the sky for any signs of the enemy.

The outward leg was uneventful and after they had turned on to their northeast heading, he had done a changeover with the wireless operator and was sat in the rest position tucking into his flight rations when he felt the start of the turbulence. By the time he had returned to his turret, the weather had deteriorated from the earlier blue skies. The descent down to sea level to check the sea-level pressure was an uncomfortable affair, but climbing back to their operating height of nineteen thousand feet gave them some respite from the constant buffeting. Rain had streaked down the front of the turret making visibility difficult. It was much colder at this altitude, forcing him to turn up the heat on his flying suit, while all the time his experienced eyes constantly searched the black clouds for any sign of aircraft movement.

They landed back at base just after seven o'clock, having been airborne for ten hours, with a large proportion of the flight being flown in atrocious weather. Emerging from the aircraft's dark interior and carrying their respective equipment, they climbed aboard the waiting transport and Will found himself next to the skipper.

"So, what did you think of your first Met flight?" Lambert asked, offering him a cigarette which Will declined.

"I enjoyed it, beats being stuck in the bloody armoury all day."

Lambert gave him the makings of a smile. "Yes, I suppose it does."

"What happens to the data we have collected?" Will asked.

"It's sent around the airfields and used for weather forecasting for the next twelve hours."

"I never realised there was so much involved in these Meteorological flights. It's quite a complicated procedure, isn't it?"

"It can be. There is a more complex flight called a Bismuth O. Tracks are flown at low levels with a number of sounding ascents. That takes some accurate flying and time-keeping during the flight," Lambert answered.

Will was suitably impressed as the crew bus came to a halt outside the debriefing section. Clutching his parachute as he waited his turn to alight, he thought he had better curtail in future the rude comments he had made about the forecasting and how often they had been wrong.

After a meal in the mess, he made his way back to his

room, thoughts of a shower and an early night foremost in his mind, only to find Colin, his roommate, hastily packing.

"Where are you off to all in a hurry?" he asked, rolling onto his bed.

"I'm posted, Will, to Pembroke Dock in South Wales – a Sunderland squadron, I'm off in the morning."

Will could see the excitement in the young navigator's eyes, he had been through the same youthful enthusiasm at the start of his first tour.

"Have you ever flown in a Sunderland, Will? They say they are a lovely aircraft to fly in. Dead reliable and bags of room in them. And a galley, by all accounts. I'm really looking forward to it."

"No, I've never had anything to do with flying boats," Will said, his eyes closed. "Is that what you put in for – Coastal Command?"

"Actually, I put in for either Bomber or Coastal Command, I wasn't bothered, which I got as long as I got on Ops."

"Well, I think you've got the best bet out of the two with Coastal Command. You have a better chance of marrying that Nottingham girl you keep on about, the odds on you completing a tour on Bomber Command aren't all that great," he laughed.

"You survived two tours, Will?"

"Yes, I know. But I'm a bloody good air gunner. Think of all the poor sods who aren't!" his pretentious remark started them both off laughing.

"Anyway, are you going to have a drink with me after you get cleaned up?"

"Of course I will, give me half an hour and I'll see you in the bar, okay?"

The party was well underway when he arrived and a pint

was immediately thrust into his hand. He had just got into conversation with Daphne, a pretty WAAF officer who had caught his eye when he was confronted by Flight Lieutenant Nelson.

"Ha! Madden, back from our little soiree, are we?" he said sarcastically with a smirk on his face.

"Well, we have to know when the odd shower is coming, so you don't get wet between the officer's mess and your office, don't we, sir?" he fired back, his remark having the desired effect as he watched the smirk suddenly disappear from Nelson's face.

"I'll expect you in the armaments section on time tomorrow morning, Madden. Is that understood?"

Will let the remnants of a smile spread across his face. "I'll be there," he answered quietly as he watched Nelson turn on his heels and head off in the direction of his two drinking companions.

Daphne took a long draw on her cigarette from the corner of her mouth. "Aren't you two getting on?" she enquired, holding her cigarette upwards and stroking the underside of her chin with the palm of her thumb.

Will grinned at her observation. "You could say that. Let's put it this way, I don't think we will ever be bosom buddies," he answered, trying to catch the barmaid's eye for another round of drinks.

"What's the problem?" she asked quietly.

"It seems as though he doesn't care much for aircrew who have come up through the ranks."

She started to laugh. "Especially one who has done as many operations as you have. Two tours, isn't it?"

"Word gets around fast!" he answered, fixing her with a steely gaze at how well-informed she was.

"Not really. I work in the section that deals with the

movement of personnel so I get to see a lot of records."

"Oh! I see," he smiled, becoming aware of how close she was to him.

They had kissed quite passionately outside her quarters before parting with a promise he would ring her the following day.

He had been in the armaments section inspecting the firing mechanism of a stripped-down Browning machine gun, which the gunner said kept jamming when fired, when Nelson came in. Before entering his office, he called Will over. "Madden, I would like you to do the air test in P–Peter this afternoon; since that run-in she had with that Junkers she has had a fair amount of work done on her, which included a new rear turret, so they want an air gunner to check it out when she's airborne – take-off time is scheduled for 1430 hours, so you had better take early lunch, okay?"

"Yes, sir. But as far as I know, Sergeant Milroyd had put his name down to do that air test?" Will answered, with caution in his tone.

Nelson looked at him for a few moments.

Will thought there was going to be another confrontation between them but was surprised at the soft-spoken reply he received.

"Yes, I know he was, but he was feeling unwell early this morning so was taken to the sick quarters and they have kept him in for observation until tomorrow morning."

"It's nothing serious, is it, sir?" he questioned.

"I hope not," Nelson concluded, entering his office and closing the door quietly behind him.

He tried to contact Daphne before lunch, but was told she wasn't available as she was out of the section. So, after leaving a message to say he would see her later that evening, he made his way to the mess. It was only a short walk to where the aircraft stood waiting in front of number two hangar where the repairs had been carried out. Once aboard, he sat in the crew rest position, trying to make conversation with a ground radio bod who was also going aloft to check the wireless equipment.

"This should while away a couple of hours," he shouted, over the noise of the four engines being opened up for take-off, but only getting a sickly nod of acknowledgement. Once airborne, he left the company of his not-so-overtalkative friend and made his way to the rear turret, checking everything was in working order and reporting it so. He slowly traversed the turret from side to side, keeping a wary eye on all around him as he listened to the cross chatter between the other crewmembers.

They were an hour into the air test when he heard the flight engineer raise concerns about number two engine running rough and it starting to overheat. After a lengthy discussion with ground control, a decision was made to abort the remainder of the air test and return to base, the pilot bringing the aircraft down safely on three engines with a strong cross-wind blowing.

He was leaving the squadron office when he bumped into Squadron Leader Walker and seized the opportunity to have a word about any further flights that may be in the offing, and if so, "he would be up for it."

"I'll bear it in mind," Walker winked, squeezing Will's elbow as he went past.

That evening he met Daphne for a drink, but their privacy was short-lived, interrupted by returning aircrew crowding into the bar. Keith and some of his crew were among them, pushing several tables together; the beer soon started to flow.

"We have just heard about the air test on P–Peter. You

had a bit of a shaky do, Will. Landed on three by all accounts?" his remark made Daphne shoot both men a long questioning look.

He grimaced at Keith's untimely comment and stroked his forehead.

"You never mentioned that?" she said.

"Sorry, Will, thought she knew."

"I was just about to tell her when you noisy sods came in," he answered, hoping his reason would suffice.

The evening turned into a bawdy affair, with Daphne being paid a lot of attention as the only female there. It wasn't until later in the evening when two more WAAF officers joined the group that he was able to explain in more detail what had happened during the air test.

Daphne studied him with a fixed expression. "Apart from doing air tests, which I know you have to do, why are you volunteering for these Met flights, Will. When you are supposed to be on your rest period?" she asked.

"Squadron Leader Walker asked me if I could do it. They needed a rear gunner," he said as he watched the main bulk of the party head for the billiard table, where the two girls were being given some tuition on the best way to hold a cue.

"You could have turned him down, and if you want my opinion, Will, you should have done. I think you've done enough with two tours."

"Yes, I suppose I could," he replied, subdued.

"But you didn't want to, did you? All the same, you flyers. You never know when you've had enough, keep pushing and pushing until the inevitable happens – like it did with Pa–" her words trailing off as she turned and looked away from him.

"I'm sorry, I didn't know you had lost somebody close."

"Shall we get out of here?" she said quietly, "I'm not

really in the mood for this in here tonight."

Will smiled at her. "Neither am I."

Although it was only their second time together, she felt at ease with Will, like he had always been there. Maybe it was because he oozed strength and confidence, qualities she liked in a man. "It's a lovely evening," she said, looking up at the canopy of stars above them as they started to slowly walk back to her quarters.

Will felt she wanted to talk about her lost love but didn't pursue the matter, and it was only as they were nearing her quarters that she stopped walking and turned to face him.

"He was a navigator on Bomber Command. I met him at a dance in Huntingdon and it became serious between us. We got engaged. He had just finished his first tour and we were all set to spend some quality time together in a cottage in Wales."

"And what happened?"

"He volunteered to do one more trip and never came back," she sighed, taking out her handkerchief to wipe her eyes.

"You must have loved him very much?"

"Yes, I did. He was only twenty-two years old."

"When did it happen?"

"Eleven months ago, and I know what you are going to say now, Will, that there's a chance that he may have bailed out and be in a prison of war camp – but surely we would have heard by now if that's what happened?"

"Well, I would have thought so. It's strange though that you've not heard anything one way or the other by now, which makes me wonder if he hasn't been caught and he's on the run."

"But how often does that happen?"

"I don't know. We did have an air gunner at Kelstern who

had made a home run, it took him nearly twelve months to get back."

She looked at him a few moments with the makings of a smile on her face. "I suppose there is a slim chance he could still be alive, but I'm not holding my breath. I'm coming to terms that he's gone but thanks for trying to be reassuring anyway," she answered, leaning forward to kiss him tenderly. "Will I see you tomorrow evening? There is a good film on at the camp cinema if you're interested, if you are, give me a ring about lunchtime?"

* * *

Atlantic storms battered the islands and the west coast of Scotland. Will wondered if he had done the right thing, volunteering for the flight as he slid into the cold interior of the rear turret and went through the preliminary pre-flight checks.

The airframe shuddered and flexed as they made the perilous journey around the perimeter track, with the constant fear of running off the hard concrete onto the wet grass and getting bogged down. Heavy rain streaked down the Perspex in front of him as he felt the engines taken up to full power and the aircraft start to move down the rain-soaked runway. Sheets of spray, thrown up by the huge smooth tyres, swept back over the tailplane and down either side of the turret, disappearing into a swirling mass behind them. A constant stream of obscenities came from the pilot as he fought with the controls until they got airborne.

Will had seen his fair share of bad weather over the continent but this was shaping up to be a storm of mammoth proportions as they climbed steadily through the dense grey cloud that enshrouded them. Partway into the first leg of the flight they encountered severe turbulence with strong headwinds and visibility down to zero. Will knew from past experience that the Halifax was a well-made aircraft and could take a hell of a lot of punishment. Just how much, he wondered, as a heavy rumble of thunder followed by a flash of lightning lit up the sky off to his right, making him temporarily turn away.

Concern in the voices of the other crewmembers grew as the weather intensified as they pushed on further out into the Atlantic. The ghostly glow of St Elmo's Fire was seen on the propeller blades and wing tips and the wireless operator reported that he could hear a kind of singing or hissing sound like running up and down the musical scale on the aircraft's radio.

Finally, they reached their first turning point that would put them onto a northeast track. The winds had now increased and were hitting the aircraft fully on the port side, making it a constant battle for the pilot and navigator to keep on course. The thunder and lightning had intensified, while the rain – which had turned to hail – pelted the fuselage with such ferocity that it was difficult to hear what the other members of the crew were saying. They battled on for what seemed an eternity, going through the procedures to get the data that was expected of them as a Met crew and they had been at their operational height when they reached their second turning point, which would take them on a course due south back to base.

He breathed steadily on the oxygen, thankful for once that the turret had not had the centre section cut away by a previous gunner to aid better visibility, as it was now taking the full impact of the storm's fury. Will peered out over the barrels of the four machine guns and shook his head. "There's not a cat in hell's chance of seeing anything stalking us in this bloody stuff," he said quietly to himself as they descended down to a lower height and the order came: "Oxygen off".

Listening to the cross chat between the pilot and the navigator, it soon became clear that they were off course by several degrees, which put them further east than they should have been. Will smiled to himself as he listened to the sharp exchange of words between the two men. Distant thoughts came flooding back to a certain cross-country night flight over the mountains of Wales in a Vicker's Wellington, when they had been nearly forty miles off course due to poor navigation but they had, eventually, bonded as a crew and gone on to complete fifteen operational sorties together before his crewmates had finally gone missing on a raid to Duisburg while he was grounded with a severe bout of tonsillitis.

With the aircraft now on its sea-level run and some respite from the constant buffeting and hailstones, Will decided he would try to drink some of his coffee. Relaxing slightly as he drank, but still vigilant, he was surprised to see as they began to climb a break in the cloud appear, if only for a brief period, but enough time for him to make out the distinct features of an island, its sheer cliffs and rocky shoreline taking a merciless pounding from the sea's fury. Reporting his sighting, he wondered what island it was as it reappeared, his eyes drawn to the tall grey structure of a lighthouse lit up by a flash of lightning, standing defiantly against the elements on the island's headland. As he looked down at the weather-beaten tower and cottages adjacent to it, he was surprised to see it emit two quick flashes of light, followed by one long flash then nothing more – total darkness, just as though it had been an intermittent signal of some kind.

"What the hell?" he said sharply as he recollected something Bob Roundtree had told him one evening over a drink in the bar at Kelstern. Many of the lighthouse lights, he said, had been switched off for the duration of the war so they did not aid the enemy, so what the hell was this one doing flashing?

"Everything okay back there, rear gunner?" a voice asked in a calm but direct tone.

Will told the skipper what he'd seen but he made very little of it, being still in discussion with the navigator about their position. With two more course corrections they were finally lined up with the main runway and touched down nine hours and fifty minutes after take-off. The long and strenuous flight had taken its toll and showed on each man's face as they stood around weighed down in heavy flying gear and carrying equipment, cursing impatiently in the cold evening air as they waited for the transport.

On the way back to debriefing, he managed to have a word with Bryant, the navigator about the lighthouse incident, but in his tired state, said he didn't know what the island was called and most probably the three flashes he saw was lightning reflecting off the lens glass. Will wasn't satisfied, he knew what he had seen and it wasn't any reflection, so he decided he would try and find out where their course had taken them with help coming from their Met Operator, Flying Officer Yates while having their evening meal.

"It sounds to me like the lighthouse on Stracandra Island by the way you've described the tower and the buildings around it."

"Do you know if there's anybody living there – like keepers who tend the light?" Will asked, pushing his empty plate to one side.

"It's quite possible there is, just to keep an eye on things, as regards the flashes that you saw, it most likely was the reflection from the lightning," Yates replied wearily.

Will sat back in his chair and looked at him. "Maybe," he answered quietly.

Yates began to laugh. "You're still not convinced, are you, Will?"

"No, I'm not!"

"I have seen some strange things happen while I've been doing these Met flights. I remember one particular Bismuth sortie; we had climbed up and levelled off when we saw this electric lightning running through the clouds below us which made like a ripple effect, you know what I mean?"

Will nodded in agreement as he watched Yates go through the motions with the palm of his hand before continuing.

"There was no sound to it, but the weirdest part was if you looked upwards, you got a complete mirror image of the aircraft silhouetted against the clouds above you – it was spooky. We eventually ran out of it as we came down to a lower height, so you see, you get some strange things happen with electrical storms."

"Yes, I know what you mean. I've seen the searchlights throw off a shadow of the cloud base above us, and it looks as though there's another aircraft directly above you; it's a bit off-putting if you're over the target and you think there may be a bloody load of bombs going to be unloaded on top of you."

"Yes, I'll bet it is," Yates answered, with a serious look on his face.

"One particular night over Duisburg, the mid-upper gunner and myself both shouted simultaneously a warning of an aircraft above us which made the skipper kick her over to port, which in turn buggered up the bombing run, and we had to go round again to get lined up to the moans and groans of the rest of the crew. We weren't very popular!" Will laughed, recalling the incident.

"I suppose that must happen a lot, aircraft being hit by bombs dropped from above."

"I don't reckon we will ever know how many aircraft have been lost that way," Will said quietly, recollecting a previous raid on Essen when he had seen the tailplane and rear turret completely ripped off a Halifax by the bombs dropped from a Lancaster above. He had watched in horror as the aircraft turned over and spiralled down onto the burning city below with no one getting out of the stricken bomber.

Chapter 7

Bayer felt uneasy about the instructions he had received from Abwehr headquarters. They wanted photographic details of the Meteor's jet engine, which could only be obtained by gaining access to the airfield at Moreton Valence. He wondered if this was achievable, feeling the cold penetrate the clothing he was wearing as he waited for the time he planned to make his assault on the airfield's perimeter fence.

The sound of someone approaching, whistling, made him retreat further into the bushes. He watched the sentry, attired in a heavy greatcoat, appear out of the darkness on the inside of the fence, stop almost directly in front of him then, taking a cigarette from behind his ear, light it before moving off, humming the tune he had previously been whistling.

Bayer patiently watched the moon slip behind a mass of dark clouds. Seizing his opportunity, he moved in close to the fence and, working quickly, cut a hole big enough for him to get through. Once inside, he repositioned the wire back neatly, fastening it with two small strands of thin wire. To a passing sentry, the cut was unnoticeable. Pleased with his handiwork, he set off at a steady pace, working his way along the inside of the fence until it brought him in line with the building he had kept under surveillance and where he had seen the new jet aircraft being housed.

It was only a few metres of open ground, but it was across

a pathway that the guards used to make their patrols around the complex. Keeping a wary eye on the reappearing moon, he sprinted across to the corner of the building and flattened himself against the structure to listen. The sound of a vehicle being started in the distance made him immediately crouch closer to the ground. Who the hell was driving around at this time of night, he thought, looking at the luminous hands of his watch that showed 00.35. Satisfied all seemed as it should be, he edged his way along the side of the hangar until he saw the shape of a blacked-out window.

On closer inspection, Bayer saw that a piece of the bottom right-hand pane was missing; a crude attempt had been made to repair it by taping over the offending hole to stop the light showing through from the inside. Taking out his switchblade, he eased away the tape then, with the point of the blade, gently pushed to one side a discarded paint tin. The hangar to his left was in total darkness, albeit for a solitary workbench light that had been left on. To his right, several lights glowed from what looked like an office and stores section. The sound of a wireless playing light music carried across the room.

Leaning against the hangar wall, Bayer checked his watch, 00.43, then contemplated the situation. He had come this far, so there was no turning back now. The guard could well turn up at any time, he thought, turning towards the window. Sliding his arm in through the broken glass, he unfastened the bottom latch then, using his knife for added length, he prised apart the central catch from its securing recess, and the window swung open. Making sure there were no obstacles in the way that might fall and give the game away, he climbed in.

The building had the usual smell of oil and grease, accompanied by an unusual odour which Bayer attributed to the fuel that the jet engine ran on. With the help of the lights from the adjacent rooms, he ran a careful eye around the hangar's dark interior until he saw what he was looking for: the dark shape of an aircraft. Slowly but ever vigilant for any would-be obstacles on the floor that could give away his presence, he made his way towards the aeroplane. As Bayer got nearer, he recognised it as one of the new jets and made a close inspection of its graceful lines. The outer panels had been removed, exposing the jet engines and all their details.

Bayer was puzzled as to why he had seen no movement of personnel from within the office and, knowing he would have to use a flash attachment on the Leica camera to get the photographs Berlin wanted, he needed not to be disturbed.

Crossing the open floor towards the smaller inner building, he positioned himself near the half-opened door and, with the knife at the ready, cast a cautious eye around the room. Finding the place empty, he pushed the door fully open with the point of the blade and waited a few moments before entering. He checked each of the other rooms in turn and found them empty too.

Retracing his steps, he checked the hangar side doors and found them locked. Lady luck was certainly smiling down on him this night, he thought, as he made his way back to where the jet stood in the darkness, unconcerned that its secrets were now to be stolen.

Taking out the Leica from its case, he inserted a flash, and positioning the camera, took a frontal picture of the aircraft and its engines. Working quickly, he stepped to one side to take a shot of the jet engine from a different angle, but in doing so his left leg brushed against something solid. In the beam of his torch was the offending object. He was amazed to see, sat neatly on a cradle, a complete Welland jet engine, its details just begging to be photographed. After taking several shots of the engine, he turned his attention to the aircraft's airframe, cockpit interior and lastly, the undercarriage.

Satisfied with his work, he replaced the camera back in its case and then, retracing his footsteps, made for the window. Climbing onto the workbench, he carefully pushed open the window and had just been about to lower himself to the ground when he saw the beam of light picking out the path from an approaching sentry. Receding into the darkness, he realised he had made a fatal mistake by leaving the window open. Feeling in his coat pocket for his switchblade, he cushioned the broadside of the blade against the palm of his hand so the blade would open slowly and quietly. Bayer could hear his own ragged breathing as he listened to the crunching of boots on the gravel. They got nearer; the eventual dark shape of a figure emerged from the corner of the building and, to his relief, carried on walking.

Shifting his weight to take the pressure off his knee, his foot inadvertently caught a glass jar which overturned, spilling out its contents of paint brushes and fluid. Bayer quietly let out a string of obscenities as he watched the glass jar crash to the floor, the noise instantly bringing the guard's beam to bear on the open window. Strangely he felt composed, at ease with what he had to do. He waited for his victim to come within striking distance. Shining his torch at the half-open window, the sentry gently nudged it fully open with the barrel of his rifle. Then did what Bayer hoped he would do; look in.

With lightning speed, he grabbed the man behind his head and smashed his face down hard against the window ledge. Then, with one swift blow, drove the knife deep into the base of the man's neck. Reeling backwards, his face covered in blood, the guard fell heavily onto the ground.

Bayer couldn't help but admire the soldier's bravery as he dropped on the ground beside him. He watched as the guard desperately tried to reach for his weapon but, kicking him hard in his side, Bayer then drove the knife inwards to the area of the heart.

After wiping the man's blood from the blade on his greatcoat, he put the knife back in his pocket then set about putting things back as he had found them before closing the window. How long it took the guards to make their patrols, he had no way of knowing. But he knew that time was of the essence.

He dragged the lifeless body with both hands to a shallow ditch and rolled it in. Walking back to the path, he turned and smiled to himself when he saw the body couldn't be seen; at least it might buy him some time to make good his escape. Finding the cut in the perimeter fence, he undid his handiwork and slipped through. After rewiring it, he picked up his pace, quickly reaching the opening in the hedgerow where he had concealed his bicycle from any inquisitive eyes.

He began to whistle softly to himself as he pedalled along the deserted lanes back to the cottage. For what he had achieved tonight, he surely would come to the attention of Adolf Hitler, maybe even be decorated by him personally, what a great honour that would be for both for him and his family! The cold was beginning to take its toll on his tired body as he pedalled hard to cover the last mile, his thoughts of glory and medals being pushed to the back of his mind as he thought of Griselda's shapely body in the confines of a warm bed.

* * *

The phone had been ringing for some time when Maynard

reached the small office he was using to check the personnel files. Reaching across the desk from the wrong side, he quickly grabbed the receiver. "Maynard!" he snapped.

"Morning, Henry! Caught you on the hop, did I?" a voice said in a droll tone.

"Yes, you did rather, Clifford. I was just collecting some files from the other office," he answered, recognising his old friend's voice.

"So how are you getting on over there at Filton, Henry. Made any progress?"

"I was just collecting the last batch of files on the manual workers who work on the shop floor building the aircraft when you rang, but up to now, I haven't come across anything that we should be concerned over. Once I've got them out of the way, I'll make a start on the clerical staff and see if that turns up anything. So how are things with our German bird – has there been any further communiqué from him since I left?"

"That's why I've actually rung you, Henry. Things have taken a turn for the worse at *you know where.* They had a visitor last night, with grave consequences."

"How grave?" Maynard asked, pushing the office door shut with his foot while leaning against the desk.

"We have one of the guards in the mortuary, rather a nasty business," Granville replied.

"I see, that is serious, are the police involved?"

"Yes. The investigation is in the hands of a Detective Chief Inspector Barrett, good man by all accounts when it comes to standard detective work but a little out of his depth when it comes to our kind of stuff. So I'd like you to go up there and put Barrett in the picture as to what he's up against. I'll arrange for the police to pick you up when you get there and take you to the airfield. How soon can you be ready?"

"Say an hour. That will give me time to sort things out here and have a word with Sam."

"Who is Sam?" Granville enquired.

Maynard began to chuckle. "Sam, or should I say, Samantha, is a young lady from the personnel department who has been giving me a hand to go through the files. Don't worry, Clifford. She was the first one I ran a check on when it was proposed that she come and work with me. She's a bright girl, and I've brought her up to speed as to what we are looking for. She can carry on going through the files until I get back."

"Okay. As long as she doesn't miss anything of importance," Granville answered.

Maynard detected some concern in his tone. "She won't do that. I'll tell her to ring me straight away if she finds anything that's out of the ordinary."

* * *

It was early afternoon by the time Maynard reached Moreton Valence and was shown into a medium-sized room that the police were using as an incident room. Shaking the Chief Inspector's hand, Maynard noticed how Barrett's steely brown eyes held his, as though reading his every thought.

"Thank you for your help on this one, Chief Inspector," he said, hoping his friendly approach would break the ice and get Barrett onside. "We need to catch this character as soon as possible. How much has London told you?" he asked, taking off his overcoat and laying it over the back of an empty chair.

"Nothing. I was told to wait with my investigation until you arrived from Filton and you would put me in the picture as to what is going on. Then afterwards give you all the police cooperation to apprehend this man. I have been told on the quiet that you are with MI5, is that correct, sir?" Barrett asked in a broad West Country accent.

Maynard gave him a shrewd look. "Yes, that's correct," he answered quietly.

"So, is this incident last night to do with the new aircraft they have here?"

Maynard nodded in acknowledgement. "Let's take a walk, shall we, and I'll give you the details of what we know so far."

Barrett felt a touch of excitement to be working with military intelligence as he walked and listened to what Maynard had to say. German spies, espionage, all a far cry from the normal police business, Barrett thought, as they reached the road that ran between the buildings that housed the new aircraft. "So you have no idea what this *Raven* chappie looks like?" Barrett asked as they waited for a slow-moving vehicle to pass before resuming their walk.

"No, we don't. And I must admit, what we have on him so far is very sketchy. But he is very proficient in everything he does. All we can say with some certainty is that he must be operating from somewhere close by and is lodging in a hotel, guesthouse, hostel or rented cottage. Someplace where he is reasonably safe to transmit from without being discovered. Can you get your people organised to check out such places, let's say within a five-mile radius of the airfield?"

"Right. I'll put that in motion as soon as we get back. So, what do you want to see first? Inside the hangar or the place where the body was found? If so, that's the building over there to your left. The guard's body was found in a shallow ditch behind the place. It looks like it had been dragged from where the killing took place, his boots had left indentations on the ground and there were scuff marks on the heels."

Maynard didn't answer straight away but stood a few

moments to take in the general layout of the place and the surrounding area. He tried to visualize what line of approach *The Raven* might have taken to reach his objective. "Have you checked for any cuts in the perimeter wire?" he asked, trying not to sound as though he was telling Barrett his job.

"No, I haven't. From the outset, I was just treating it as an ordinary murder case. It was only after I was told to await your arrival and that you were from military intelligence that I realised it was more serious than I first anticipated, I'm sorry about that."

"That's quite alright, Chief Inspector. You weren't to know. Let's start with taking a look at the murder scene, shall we and take it from there?"

A solitary constable on duty bid his superior "good afternoon, sir" when they arrived, to which Barrett responded by telling the constable to go and get himself a cup of tea. Maynard studied the crime scene, his eyes following the dead man's boot tracks to the ditch where he was found.

"This is where he was killed, you can see the bloodstains on the grass and his rifle was over there. It looks like the killer, or *The Raven* as you call him, heard him coming, hid around the corner of the building there and took the poor sod by surprise and knifed him."

"But that's quite a way from where he was killed. How do you explain that?" Maynard asked, taking out his pipe and filling it.

"Briggs. That's the guard's name. Had two knife wounds, one to the base of the neck, the second to the heart was the fatal one. It looks like, although being seriously hurt from the first stab, Briggs must have tried to make a run for it and raise the alarm. But he was caught and stabbed a second time, in the heart, which finished him off. There is also a large bruise on the right side of the body, most likely from being kicked."

Listening carefully to what Barrett was saying, Maynard's eyes were drawn to the window. "What's behind this window, Inspector?" he asked, walking over to take a closer look.

"Just a workbench with tools and accessories on it. Paint tins, brushes, bottles, you know the kind of things. But the window was securely locked," Barrett gestured to the two locks.

"Was there anything out of the ordinary on the inside when you examined it?" Maynard asked and could tell by Barrett's expression that there was something.

"There was a broken glass jar on the floor. It looked as though it had been there a day or two, so I didn't think much of it with the window not being tampered with … So what are you thinking? That this *Raven* fellow has got in and out through the window and knocked over the jar?"

"Could be, but I'll reserve judgment on that until we take a look inside. But first, let's take a walk around the perimeter fence and see what that turns up there, shall we?"

* * *

Maynard thanked the young WPC for the steaming mug of tea.

"Right! That's all organised," Barrett said, replacing the receiver and walking over to where Maynard stood pondering over a detailed map of the surrounding area.

"What's that?" Maynard asked without looking up.

"The checking of all hotels and so forth. I've got my people visiting all known places within a five-mile radius like you asked for. The trouble is, without a description of this man, it's going to be a long shot as to whether we turn up anything," Barrett replied.

"Yes, I know it is. But you never know, Chief Inspector, it may just jog a memory. It could be they are uneasy about a guest who has a slight or foreign accent, staying in their room for long periods, coming and going at odd times, things they hadn't thought too much about until they get a visit from the police. We caught one in London earlier this year after a tip-off. A landlord of a public house heard what he thought was, as he put it, a whistling sound coming from one of the bedrooms. To begin with, he thought it was someone tuning in a wireless set but got a little suspicious when it happened at the same time over several nights. We kept the place under close surveillance for a time and it turned out it was someone we had been after for quite some time. So you see, you never know what it might turn up."

"Well, let's hope so," Barrett responded, knowing from past experience that detective work was never normally that easy. "Mr Maynard, what are your thoughts on what you have seen today?"

Maynard sat down and commenced pushing down the tobacco into the bowl of his pipe, lighting it, then sitting back, he took a couple of puffs. "There's no doubt in my mind that *The Raven* has achieved what he set out to do. That was to photograph the new jet fighter, and it was handed to him on a plate. Easy access through a window with a broken pane, a building with no personnel working in it and an aircraft stripped of its engine coverings and last, but not least, a jet engine sat on a cradle, what more could a spy ask for? I would think our German bird is feeling very pleased with himself at the moment. Very pleased indeed."

"And Private Briggs' murder?" Barrett asked, folding his arms across his chest.

"Done on the way out, I should say. Either Briggs saw

the window open, or he heard the glass jar break and went to investigate. Whichever way it was, *The Raven* had the advantage of both height and surprise and, after the killing, he had time to put things back as he found them. That's why I'm convinced the murder was committed on the way out."

There was silence for a few moments between the two men, eventually broken by Barrett. "Where does that leave the investigation now?"

"Well, there is not a lot more I can do here now. I'll return to Filton and see if we can come up with anything there and leave you to carry on with your police work here. You have my number. Will you keep me informed as to how your investigation is going? And I will, of course, do the same if we dig up anything new at our end. But until we can get identification on this murdering sod, I think we are both going to be running a little bit in the dark for the time being, don't you?"

"Yes, I do," Barrett acknowledged, helping Maynard on with his topcoat and walking with him to the waiting car.

"You know, Chief Inspector, I've been convinced all along that the information we need to crack this case is at the Bristol Aeroplane Company if we could just shed light on it," Maynard concluded, shaking hands before getting into the rear passenger seat and closing the door.

Barrett watched the vehicle disappear into the darkness. "Let's hope so before some other poor devil gets murdered," he said quietly to himself.

Chapter 8

Tiree looked to be a beautiful island from what Will had seen of it, and that had only been from the air. But as autumn gave way to winter, it was obvious that the weather was the main obstacle for both the ground and aircrew alike. Biting cold winds swept across the open expanse of the airfield, bringing with it heavy rain, hail and occasional snow flurries. Will lay in the dark listening to the steady beat of the rain against the windows and the constant moan of the wind as it tried to force itself in through a crack in the weather-beaten window frame.

He was down to fly today; it had been almost a week since his last flight and the encounter with the mysterious lighthouse. He hadn't been convinced by the theory that it had been the reflection from a flash of lightning. He knew what he'd seen and it certainly wasn't that. He felt warm and comfortable within the confines of the bed; slipping his arm out from under the blankets, he looked at the luminous hands on his watch – five past three, plenty of time yet, he thought, as he snuggled down and tried to sleep.

His alarm roused him. After washing and shaving, he dressed warmly for the long flight ahead, which brought a smile to his face as he remembered the look on Nelson's face after being told by the commanding officer that he had to release him for flying duty as the Met flights took priority over everything else. "Do I make myself clear, Nelson?" the CO had said, rather sharply, the confrontation arising after the flight lieutenant had put a stop to his flying "jollies", as he called them. But a bad bout of influenza had taken its toll on many sections of the camp and, with the aircrew also badly affected, they needed all the fit personnel they could muster for flying duty. Taking off a little after eight, they had climbed steadily out into the cold, grey light of day on a westerly heading. With the bulk of the heavy rain having passed through during the night, breaks in the cloud started to appear. Their outward track was uneventful and, at their turning point, the weather had steadily improved with heaped masses of cumulus cloud which, from a distance, looked like snow-covered mountains, intermingled with large patches of clear blue sky.

They were on the final leg back to base when Will first caught a fleeting glimpse of what looked like an aircraft. Quickly bringing the turret to bear, he searched the clouds below in the general direction that he thought the aircraft would appear, while informing the skipper, Pilot Officer Bingham, of a possible sighting.

He didn't have to wait long before the aircraft reappeared, which he recognised as a German long-range flying boat. Not having come up against one before, but knowing the possibility it could happen, he had studied the aircraft's profile in the gunnery section. They were slower and lacked the height the Halifax had, but they were heavily armed with two cannons in powered turrets, one in the nose and one in the rear of the hull, as well as a machine gun in a position behind the central engine.

After reporting the enemy aircraft, he ran a careful eye over its defences. With the flying boat keeping as low as possible, close to sea level, whichever way they went in for the attack, their height advantage was going to be no help in taking on all its defensive armament.

The flying boat seemed to be keeping to its intended course and taking no evasive action, which made Will wonder if the gunners hadn't seen them yet, but without the firepower from a mid-upper turret it was going to be a hard fight. Giving Bingham a running commentary, he felt the aircraft bank into a shallow turning dive, putting the sun to their advantage. He could only listen and wait as the Halifax dived on its unsuspecting prey, closely followed by the sound of the front Vickers gun being fired and the shout of, "I think I've hit him and he's turning to port, skipper."

Will felt the pilot bank the Halifax round in a tight turn, putting the enemy aircraft on his starboard side and below him, making the flying boat a perfect target. What he hadn't expected was how accurate the return fire was from the German gunner manning the machine gun, its arc of fire passing dangerously close over his turret before hitting the starboard tailfin and punching a line of holes through the Halifax's fuselage forward of the tailplane. Returning fire at the gunner's position with a five-second burst, the rounds fell short as the flying boat's pilot took evasive action. Realigning his fire, he saw a steady stream of hits behind the gunner's position and the central engine. He managed to get in another quick burst, but they missed the target, sending up a line of splashes across the surface of the ocean, as the flying boat suddenly made a sharp turn to starboard, passing under the Halifax, the German pilot no doubt trying to manoeuvre his aircraft into a position so he could bring the two deadly cannons to bear.

Will tried to anticipate what the German's next move would be as the flying boat disappeared from his view and a long stream of fire from its top turret gunner arched over the

Halifax's tailplane. Will shouted to the skipper to turn to port. Banking hard, Bingham brought the aircraft around in a tight turn as another burst of fire found its mark, hitting the Halifax's starboard wingtip.

He's a tricky sod is this one, Will thought, as he quickly tracked the turret round onto his starboard side as the flying boat came out from underneath them, on a south-easterly heading. He fired a long burst – longer than the recommended five seconds – aiming at the gunner's position and central engine. He knew he'd found his mark when he saw Perspex fly upwards and the gunner abruptly stop firing while black smoke and flames trailed out from its number two motor. Informing the skipper that he had seriously damaged it, he watched it make a sharp turn to port, then drop rapidly, striking the sea at a nose-down angle, ripping off its port float, which lifted the aircraft tail high into the air before falling back in a shower of spray.

"Poor buggers," he whispered quietly to himself as they circled around the downed aircraft, his mind recollecting his own ditching in the North Sea. He didn't think he had ever been so cold before they had been picked up, given dry clothes, a hot drink and food. Nothing had ever sounded so good as the boat engines taking them back to Blighty.

A couple of bangs on the turret made him square the turret up with the fuselage and slide back the doors.

"You okay?" Tom Fielding, the flight engineer, shouted, patting him on the arm.

"Yes, I'm fine," he acknowledged, giving him the thumbs up.

"I have just been going around the crew positions to make sure everybody's alright and see what damage has been done."

"Is everybody okay?" Will asked.

"Yes, but we've got some bloody great holes through the fuselage. Fortunately, Jerry's fire didn't hit anything vital. It will give the ground crew bods something to do when we get back," Fielding said, laughing.

"Chiefy Baker's face will be a picture when he sees we've bent his aircraft for him. So what's happening about these chaps below, Flight?"

"Air-sea rescue is on the way out to pick them up. We've told them that we'll circle them for as long as our fuel will allow."

"And how long will that be?"

Fielding looked at his watch. "Thirty minutes, then we'll have to start heading back. Oh! Nice bit of shooting, by the way," he remarked, grinning.

"Thanks, it got a bit hairy at times though, he wasn't going to go down without a fight. He was a good pilot that Jerry, whoever he is!"

"Well, he won't be doing any more flying when the rescue boys get hold of him."

"No, that's him and his crew in the bag for the remainder of the war."

"Anyway, I'd better get back. If you want to get out and have a stretch for a while and a cup of coffee, I can send Benny back to man the turret?"

"No, I'm okay," he answered, content to sit back and watch proceedings unfold below.

They had been circling for thirty minutes and were just about to head for home when the small speck of the air-sea rescue launch was seen heading in their direction. So after a discussion between Bingham and Tom Fielding about their fuel state, it was decided to circle for five minutes more to vector the launch to the survivors.

Chapter 9

Griselda sat back in the chair and watched Guntram finish transmitting then pack away the equipment neatly in its case. "What did they say?" she asked, taking two cigarettes from a packet, lighting them both and handing him one.

"We will get further instructions in twenty-four hours. So all we can do is wait," he answered, concealing the transmitter behind a false panel in the cupboard under the stairs.

Griselda shook her head and stared at her lover. "Don't they realise how dangerous it is for us to remain here after what happened on the airfield? The police, MI5, they will all be searching the area for any clues to our whereabouts," she said, drawing hard on the cigarette.

Bayer stood and looked at her; he could see the fear in her eyes and knew what had to be done if things should take a turn for the worse. It would be a tragedy to have to kill her as he had grown quite fond of her over the past few weeks, but he could see she was going to be a liability and a threat to his own safety if the net started to close in around them. He stroked her cheek tenderly and smiled at her before sitting down – he would make it as quick as possible when the time came to take her life.

* * *

Laying on his back, Bayer watched the grey clouds of dawn through the bedroom window. Rolling over onto his side, he propped himself up on one elbow and watched Griselda brush her hair in front of the mirror. "You look tired!" he remarked casually, reaching for the cigarettes on the bedside table.

"What do you expect?" Her voice was husky, and she looked back at him through the dressing table mirror. "We were making love until God knows what time." Getting up, she walked over to the bed. "Zip me up, will you?" she said, checking the time for her walk to the railway station.

After Griselda had left, he lay for a while turning over the events of the past few days, but his thoughts still kept coming back to the photographs he had of the new jet fighter and its engines; they would now be top priority and needed to be got back to Germany as soon as possible.

After washing and dressing, he ate a light breakfast, after which he got out the bicycle from the shed and, using the lanes, set off at a steady pace in the general direction of Stonehouse. After further deliberation, he decided against it because of its close proximity to the airfield at Moreton Valence. Turning back towards Nympsfield, he eventually came across a public house where he spent an enjoyable two hours listening to the banter of the locals and occasionally joining in. It had been the last thing on his mind that he would meet a police car down one of the narrow lanes as he cycled back, rather unsteadily due to the large amount of alcohol in his system.

"You seemed to be riding very erratically, sir, have you a problem with your bike?" the officer asked from the confines of his police vehicle.

Bayer had to think fast. "A friend of mine lent me the cycle and the brakes aren't as good as I thought they were," he lied while trying to look apologetic.

"Well, be more careful in future, and get that friend of yours to sort those brakes out," the officer said, winding up his window before driving off.

Bayer grinned to himself as he watched the car disappear down the lane and out of sight. "And balls to you, you English bastard," he said quietly to himself while holding the switchblade in his pocket.

The sound of a key being inserted and a door being opened woke him, then Griselda called his name. "I must have fallen asleep," he answered as she came into the room and he got clumsily to his feet.

She moved to kiss him but immediately pulled away. "You stink of drink!"

"I went for a cycle ride this morning to think things over and stopped and had a few at a local pub," he said, following her into the kitchen.

"It was more than a few, Guntram. You reek of the stuff."

"What have we got to eat?" he asked, leaning over the sink to splash his face with cold water.

"I'll see what I can find. You'd better do the blackout," she smirked, pleased with his suffering.

The last two hours dragged by painfully slowly until it was time to make the callsign to Berlin. After acknowledging the orders he had been given, Bayer switched off the radio transmitter and sat back in the chair, turning over in his mind the message he had received.

"What do they want us to do?"

"I've to be at 'location seven' tomorrow afternoon between one and two o'clock to make contact with one of our agents who will give me further instructions."

"Where is 'location seven'?"

"If I told you that, my little lovebird, I'd have to eliminate you afterwards," he grinned.

Griselda was shocked by his forthright remark. "Okay," she said quietly, "but how will you recognise each other?"

Bayer got to his feet and went over and gently stroked her hair. "You are too inquisitive for your own good, sometimes," he said, kissing her. "Now, I have a long day tomorrow so I need to get some rest, but first I have plans for you before I do, so you go up and get undressed while I take care of things down here."

After their lovemaking, Griselda lay listening to Guntram sleeping; he was beginning to frighten her with some of the remarks he had been making of late. Unable to sleep, she eased herself quietly out of bed and, putting on her dressing gown, went down to the kitchen. The warmth from the fire, coupled with the drink she had made, lulled her into a state of drowsiness and finally to sleep. It was Guntram shaking her that woke her with a stern look on his face.

"What are you doing down here?"

"I couldn't sleep, so I came down to make a hot drink. I must have fallen asleep," she answered, getting up but conscious of his eyes following her every move. "What time is it?"

"Quarter to six."

"Oh! There's not much point in going back to bed now. I might as well get ready for work," she smiled, heading for the stairs.

He got ready at a leisurely pace after Griselda had left. There was no need to rush as he could catch the later train. Checking the Walther was fully loaded and his favoured way of killing, the knife, was in his pocket, Bayer put on his topcoat and made for the door, checking that everything in the room was as it should be. He quietly closed the door behind him and, walking steadily, soon covered the distance to the station. The train was surprisingly crowded when it arrived, and he stood in the corridor for the entire journey to Bristol Temple Meads station. Holding back as he walked along the platform to give the alighting passengers time to thin out, he made a necessary stop at the paper stand to buy the *Daily Mail*, the paper to be folded in such a way that it displayed *Mail* from his left coat pocket, his contact to do the same with his paper showing *Daily* from his right pocket.

Bayer knew nothing about his contact, but even so, experience had taught him never to throw caution to the wind, and he decided as he walked down the road that he would take an indirect route to the rendezvous point. Cutting through the back streets and regularly checking that he wasn't being followed, he made his way into Queen Square by way of the Redcliffe Bridge and, still having time to spare, he sat for a while in a small café and took time lingering over a mug of tea while pretending to read the newspaper.

Light rain began to fall as he walked down the busy King Street. Standing in a shop doorway, he spotted his contact, the newspaper clearly displayed from his right coat pocket, walking down the opposite side of the road. Bayer's experienced eyes took in each and everyone following him, but he couldn't pick out anyone who resembled being a tail. He decided on caution and waited another thirty minutes, taking the time to scrutinise everyone entering The Old Duke public house before being satisfied it was safe to enter the establishment.

The place was quite busy with lunchtime drinkers, but as he stood at the bar, it didn't take him long to spot the neatly folded raincoat by the side of its wearer, the newspaper easily visible as arranged. Bayer took a few minutes to size the man up. He estimated his age to be around thirty, and he looked to be extremely fit by his build. A force to be reckoned with,

Bayer thought, as he took a drink while watching him over the rim of the glass. He chose a table facing the door, so he could observe the comings and goings of the bar's clientele, all the time keeping a wary eye on his contact opposite. The man's nervousness did worry him, obvious from the constant checking of his watch and rubbing his right fist inside the palm of his left hand, all the signs that showed he was not happy being kept waiting.

Bayer let the minutes tick by, but the bar seemed to have a constant movement of drinkers, and as far as he could see there didn't seem to be anybody that set the alarm bells ringing by their behaviour. Close to time being called, he drank up and left and took up a position where he could see when the other agent left. His patience was soon to be rewarded for, a little after two, he saw him leave and, following him at a discreet distance, tailed him to a residential area along the side of the river. The end of terrace, three-storey house looked to be of the Victorian era, its once elegant rooms now turned into rented apartments.

Crossing the road to give himself a better view of the house, he saw his contact through the window in a room on the second floor on the right as he walked by. Bayer smiled to himself as he kept on walking; how easy it all was for MI5 or the police once they had an agent pinpointed. The rendezvous point and who they were meeting, the road and house and even the apartment where he or she lived; he had got it all within a short period of time. Taking a roundabout route to waste time, he eventually made his way back to the café he had used earlier and ate a reasonable meal, after which he steadily made his way back to the house to await nightfall.

Shielded by the darkness and mist that swirled off the river, he opened the gate quietly and made his way to the front door, only to find it could only be opened by a key.

Frustrated, Bayer had just been about to turn away to rethink another means of entry when he heard the sound of laughter from inside and the shape of two figures appear when the door was opened. Standing to one side, he acknowledged two women coming out with "good evening, ladies" while holding the door for them in a polite, gentlemanly fashion. The hallway and stairs were illuminated by a solitary light that shone on the first-floor landing. He cautiously made his way up to the room in question. Bayer noticed there was a light shining from under the door as he pressed his ear hard against the panel to listen, and with his knife at the ready, he used the blade to tap quietly on the door then stood to one side to wait. With lightning speed, the blade of the knife was held close to the man's throat as he was forced back into the room and told to sit down, Bayer closing the door behind him.

"Who are you?" the agent asked, peering wide-eyed at the blade.

"The *Mail* man."

"But why didn't you show at the Du–"

"Shut up!" Bayer snapped, glaring at the man's stupidity at what he was about to say.

"A bit touchy aren't we, friend? We are both on the same side, you know," the agent sniggered as he made to get up from the chair but quickly changed his mind when he felt the knife blade against his throat for a second time.

"Let's get a few things straight. I'm not your friend, and I'm not on anybody's side, only my own. Also, I don't like the way you operate because you are an unprofessional bastard who will get himself caught before long. You didn't even know that I tailed you all the way here after you left the pub, marked the house and, even the room you were in, all within half an hour … That's why I'm a bit *touchy*," he said, sliding the blade of the knife down the man's right cheek.

"I see, I'm sorry. So what happens now?"

Bayer looked down at the sorry state in front of him, straightened up and folded away the blade. "You get your coat and we take a walk … walls have ears."

Walking side by side, they followed the river in silence until they came to an area of industrial buildings devoid of people, at which point Bayer stopped and leaned against the railings.

"What's your name?" he asked.

"Before I tell you that I have to be sure who you are first. What is your codename?" the agent asked, taking out a pistol from under his coat and levelling it at Bayer's stomach.

Bayer looked down at the weapon with its silencer pointing at him and had to admire the man's forward-thinking, even though he didn't know there was a Walther pistol aimed directly back at him. "My code name is *Das Rabe,* and congratulations on your tenacity, it would have been rather interesting to see who would have fired first," he replied, taking the P38 from his pocket.

The makings of a smile swept across the agent's face as he looked at the Walther. "I'm Gerhard Metzger," he answered, concealing his own weapon under his coat and relieved when he saw Bayer do the same. "Your reputation precedes you within the department in Berlin. Also, the Führer thinks very highly of you, if I may say so."

"I'm very glad to hear that," he replied. "So, where are you from, Metzger?"

"Dessau! My parents and sister are still living there, in spite of the air raids," the agent replied, pulling his collar up against the cold night air.

"Dessau? That is not far from Berlin if my memory serves

me right?"

Metzger nodded.

"I hear the bombing is very bad in Berlin?"

"The Berliners can take it if the Führer can," Metzger replied proudly.

Bayer had to smile to himself at the man's smugness. "Yes, I'm sure they can. So why this meeting?"

"The orders I have got for you had to be delivered in person. They came from the very top, from Adolf Hitler himself."

"What are these orders?"

"You are to take the film you have taken of the British jet to the Führer personally. I was told in no uncertain terms to stress to you the importance that you get back to Berlin at whatever cost."

"And how am I to do this?" Bayer asked, leaning back against the railings.

"You are to make your way to Scotland. To a place called Stracandra Island."

Bayer stared into the agent's eyes for a few moments. "And do what?"

"You will await the arrival of a seaplane which will take you to Norway where there will be an aircraft waiting to take you to Berlin," Metzger replied.

"And this Stracandra Island, where exactly does it lie?" he asked, quickly stopping Metzger from responding as voices were heard coming towards them on the opposite side of the road.

Retreating further into the shadows of the thickening mist, they both waited until the voices receded into the distance. "It lies at the southern end of the Western Isles. Boats sail from Oban to a place called Lochboisdale. From there you will have to make your own way to the island."

"Steal a boat, you mean?" Bayer answered.

"Yes! One equipped with a powerful radio."

"And how far is this island?"

"It is about fifty kilometres from Lochboisdale."

"And is it uninhabited?"

"Yes! One of our gallant U-boats had a little target practice there in the early part of the war, destroying one of the keeper's cottages, the other was left undamaged. Since then, the island has been left unoccupied by the British, probably because of its remoteness. Adjacent to the property, you will see a storeroom; in there, you will find hanging on a hook the keys to open the cottage and lighthouse doors."

Bayer lit a cigarette, shielding it with his hand as he smoked. "And if I make it to this island, how do I make contact with Norway?"

Metzger took from his inside pocket a sealed envelope and handed it to him. "In there is all the information you need to make contact. Memorise it, then destroy it."

After concealing the envelope, Bayer leaned on the railings and looked at the cold dark water. "And what of you, Metzger?" he asked, flicking the part smoked cigarette into the water.

"After I have reported to Berlin that I have made contact with you, I have to proceed to a new assignment in southern England."

Bayer's gut instinct had been to eliminate him and let the body slip quietly into the water and be carried out to sea on the outgoing tide. But that could cause problems for him following Metzger's last remark about him contacting Berlin about their successful meeting. If the agent didn't report back, Berlin could well assume that they both had been captured, and that may well put his escape route in jeopardy, so he decided against it and let Metzger go on living.

Chapter 10

Dave Hamilton's letter had been a first for Will, being the first time a fellow crewmember had kept in touch. He had replied within a couple of days, which turned into a regular correspondence, and it didn't take Will long to realise that he was also finding it difficult to settle down to the humdrum life at Castle Kennedy after being on an operational squadron. It had come as no surprise to read in one of the letters that he had applied to transfer to the air-sea rescue unit at Barra, which had ultimately been granted and, with some clever juggling on his part, he had been able to marry up his leave to fit in with Dave.

Will stood on the open deck in the biting wind and pulled up the deep collar on his greatcoat as he watched the ferry manoeuvre into its berth. When secured, he joined the orderly line of disembarking passengers whose identification cards were systematically checked before being allowed on their way. Dave had been waiting for him as promised and after a quick handshake and brief exchange of greetings, they set off for the short walk to where Dave lived.

"It's bloody perishing up here, Dave. Is it always as cold as this?"

"Aye! It does get a bit raw in the winter, but you get used to it. It's you lot from the south of the border, you've got no stamina. What you need is some haggis, tatties and neeps inside you," he laughed.

"Well, I've heard of haggis, and tatties I presume are potatoes, but what the hell are neeps?"

"*Rutabaga*! It's yellow turnip mashed up. I'll get my mam to make us a Burns supper before you go back, you'll enjoy it."

"Sounds good, it will be a change from some of the mess food we get."

"So, what's it like on these Met flights, Will, boring as hell I should imagine?"

"Well, it beats being stuck in the armoury all day and I am doing what I like doing best, flying. And also, I'm out of the way of Nelson. We'll never see eye to eye, him and I."

"You're not thinking of going back on ops again, are you? Christ, you've done two tours now, let some other sod stick his neck out. I honestly think you've done your share, Will."

"I've been thinking about it. I was wondering if I could transfer on to the Met squadron at Tiree? I've got to know Barfield Walker quite well, he's in charge of flying there, and with me doing these odd trips for him, no doubt he could pull a few strings if I asked him. There is a lot less chance of getting the bloody chop on a Met squadron than there is on Bomber Command. The only thing you have to contend with up here is mainly the weather."

"And the odd flying boat," Dave grinned.

Will looked at him. "And them," he nodded.

"Have you seen any more since the one you wrote and told me about?"

"No, not since that run-in we had with that Blohm and Voss."

"I've heard about these from some of the air-sea rescue boys; apparently, one of our boats operating out of Stornoway was out picking up a crew that had come down in the drink, when they were attacked by one of these flying boats, and a right battle ensued."

"What was the outcome?"

"By all accounts, it scurried off with an engine smoking, but there were several injured on the launch, with one of them dying in hospital a couple of days later."

"They are prickly devils to shoot down when you tangle with them; the Jerry pilots drop them down to wave-top height because like our aircraft, they are vulnerable from underneath, but well-armed topside ..."

"I can never understand why the RAF don't fit ventral ball turrets in our bombers like the Yanks do?"

"Well, you know why, Dave, they sacrificed the defence of the aircraft for a heavier bomb load, our bomb-carrying capacity has always been far greater than the Yanks has. Hell, a Mosquito can carry a four thousand pound bomb load to Berlin, and that's on two engines. But I have heard that some of the Canadian squadrons are unofficially fitting a machine gun in the belly of their kites to take on these night fighters with upward-firing guns."

"Aye! They reckon if you're hit with a burst from those you're a bloody goner."

"Anyway, Dave, that's enough about the war, how far is it to your place?"

"Another five minutes or so. When we get there, we will have a bite to eat then we'll go to the Castlebay Bar for a pint or two. How's that sound?"

"Sounds good to me. Are the rest of your family going?"

"Aye! They'll not pass up a chance to have a drink or two. Mind you, don't be surprised if Isobel is a bit frosty with you, she has a low opinion of RAF bods at the moment," he laughed.

"Why's that?"

"She was going out with this Sergeant Roach from the marine craft unit. Anyway, to cut a long story short he sent her a 'Dear John' from his new camp, saying he had met someone else and he was ending their relationship, so airmen aren't in her good books at the moment. She has even been niggly with me of late."

"Oh!" Will answered.

Will noticed the house had a warm family feel about it as he was shown into the parlour to meet Dave's family.

Duncan Hamilton was a true Scot in every way, tough-looking, sporting a full beard with piercing blue eyes and features resilient from years working the sea and whose handheld Will's like a vice when they shook hands.

"Nice to meet you lad. David often talks about you. This is my wife, Aileen," he drawled, standing aside.

"Pleased to meet you, Mrs Hamilton."

She smiled at his politeness. "Nobody stands on ceremony in this house, lad. Aileen is just fine," she told him, carrying on laying the table.

"And this, Will, is my sister Isobel, who I warned you about."

Isobel Hamilton shot her brother a look of annoyance at what he had said as she came forward and took hold of Will's hand.

Captivated by this handsome woman standing in front of him and looking into her sparkling eyes, he took hold of her hand. "Isobel," he said smiling but only getting the small makings of a smile in return.

"Right, sit yourself down, lad, dinner won't be long. You'll take a drink, will you not, while we're waiting?" Duncan Hamilton asked, setting up the glasses ready for filling.

"I'd be glad to Mr Hamilton – sorry, Duncan," he

answered, taking the seat by the fire as a glass of beer was put into his hand.

"So how are you getting on at Tiree, Will? David tells me that you've been doing the odd flight over the last few weeks, no more encounters with German flying boats, I hope?" Aileen Hamilton asked, her eyes holding his.

"It's not a bad station, and I quite enjoy doing the occasional flight when they are offered. And no, we haven't run up against any more German aircraft since that incident," he said, noticing how Isobel was looking at him from the chair opposite. Trying not to make it too obvious that he found her terribly attractive, he decided to try and not mention the RAF over dinner, knowing what Dave had told him. But try as he may, it was only a matter of time before the conversation eventually came around to flying and the aircraft that were being used.

Duncan Hamilton took a long draw on his pipe and stretched out his legs. "So, Will, what do you think is the best heavy aircraft we've got? David says, without a doubt, it's the Lancaster." Lifting his head, he blew a cloud of tobacco smoke into the air.

"Well, I can't argue with that, the Lanc is a first-class aircraft, reliable as the day is long. Mind you, the Halifax is second to none, it's a very strongly made aircraft and can take a lot of punishment."

"Is that so? You've not flown in them, have you, son?" Duncan asked as another cloud of tobacco smoke filled the room.

"No, I haven't, Dad."

"David tells me it's the Halifax they are using for these meteorological flights."

"Yes, that's right," Will answered as he watched Isobel Hamilton come into the room in a dress that enhanced her figure, carrying her coat over her arm.

"Well, they must be good to stand up to the harsh weather conditions up here."

"So are you three ready to go to the Castlebay Bar? It'll soon be getting full, and Mum wants to get a seat before they are all gone," she said, breaking in on the discussion.

"Aye, we're ready when you two are," Duncan Hamilton replied, getting up.

A biting cold wind blew across the harbour and Will was thankful for the warmth of his greatcoat as he stuck his hands deep into its pockets. The bar was filling up fast by the time they got there. However, they did manage to find a cosy corner where they could have a reasonable conversation and not get drowned out by the piano player, who was hitting the keys with such force that Will wondered if it would survive the night.

With Dave and his father up at the bar getting more drinks and Isobel talking with friends, Will had been left in the company of Aileen, who had picked up through the course of the evening Will's interest in her daughter.

"She's a bonny lass, isn't she?" she smiled.

His first thought was to try and play her remark down. But he knew he had been rumbled. Aileen Hamilton was a lot shrewder than he realised. "Yes, she certainly is."

"You've got your work cut out there, lad."

"I didn't realise I'd been that obvious."

"Maybe not to the others, but I'm her mother, Will. I can read the signs when someone is taking an interest in my daughter, but at the moment, she doesn't rate RAF airmen very highly after Trevor Roach."

"No, I can understand that after what he's done to her."

"Have you got no immediate family, Will? If you don't mind me asking?"

"No. My parents divorced when I was very young. My mother later remarried and now lives in Australia, my sister is married to a Canadian and lives near Calgary, and I've no idea where my father is and, to be honest, I don't much care."

"What do you intend to do when the war is over?" she asked, noticing that Isobel, although in conversation with her friends, was also watching her talking with Will.

"Actually, I was hoping I could stay in the RAF if they'll let me. I've nowhere else to go."

"I should think it would be a good life in peacetime. You could do a lot worse, especially when there will be thousands coming out and looking for work."

"Yes, I had thought of that and, what's more, I do love flying. This war can't go on for much longer. We've got the Germans on the run now. That's why I've been wondering if I could get onto a Met flight. I've got it on good authority that they will carry on collecting weather reports with aircraft after the war."

"But they won't want gunners, will they?"

"Maybe I could become a Met operator. I'm sure the training wouldn't be too difficult. I'm picking up lots of gen from the crews I've been flying with, which could stand me in good stead for the future. If I survive that long."

Aileen Hamilton looked at him and smiled. "I'm sure you will, lad. I'm convinced of that."

Their discussion was cut short by the arrival of Dave and his father carrying two trays loaded with drinks.

"Grab your pint, Will and follow me, there's a lassie over at the bar who wants to meet you."

"Now just a minute, David Hamilton. Who might that be?" his mother asked.

"It's Catriona MacDonald's friend, Flora, she's taken quite a shine to Will here, so I said I would introduce him to her."

Will was steered through the throng to the far side of the bar where two young ladies stood huddled together in a corner. Although he did his best to look interested during the course of the evening, he was glad when they said they had to leave early as they were going on to a private party but promised to meet them the following evening in the Castlebay Bar for a drink.

Dave winked at him as they watched the two girls go. "We're in there tomorrow night, Will, not bad-looking either of them," Dave chuckled, finishing off his pint. "Your round, I think, Will?"

"Right, I'll get them in. Go and see what your mum and dad want?" he answered as he watched Isobel make her way round to where he was, stopping briefly to speak to her brother. "What would you like to drink?" he asked, conscious that he had been making eye contact with her throughout the evening.

"A small beer will be fine," she said, obviously annoyed with him for spending so much time with Flora and Catriona. "Are you seeing them tomorrow night?"

"We are supposed to be meeting them in here," he answered.

"You don't sound too enthusiastic about the prospect. She's a nice girl is Flora. I went to school with her."

"Maybe she is nice, I'm not disputing that," he said. "It's just that I don't fancy her," he had time to reply before her brother arrived. "What are they going to have to drink, Dave?"

"The same as before, Will, a pint and a half. You okay, Issy?"

"I'm fine. And how many more times have I got to tell you to stop calling me Issy … Oh! I'm going over to sit with

Mum and Dad. The company is far better there."

Dave lifted his eyebrows. "What's got into her?"

"I think we had better go over and join them, Dave. We have rather neglected them during the evening."

Chapter 11

After washing and dressing, Will made his way down to the parlour and was surprised to find nobody there. Walking through to the kitchen, he was just about to fill the kettle when Aileen made an appearance from the direction of the shop.

"Morning, Will, did you sleep well?" she asked, spooning a modest amount of tea from the caddie into the teapot.

"Yes, thanks. Aren't the rest of them up yet?"

"No, nary a one, you're the first down, lad, probably nursing hangovers from the amount of drink that they went through last night."

Will gave her a hand to lay out the breakfast table, then was toasting the bread when Isobel came in, looking remarkably refreshed from her night's sleep.

"Morning!" she said coyly, glancing at her mother then in Will's direction.

Her mother gave her a withering look and carried on with what she was doing, so the acknowledgement was left to Will to reciprocate.

"Morning, Isobel, would you like some toast?"

"I will, that's if it's fit for eating," she said, examining the two slices. "Not bad to say a man's done them." Dropping them on her plate.

Will could see by the way her mother looked at her that

she was thinking the same as him. "Well, under the circumstances, I think the best thing for you to do in future is to make your own," he said, drinking down his tea. "I'll not have any breakfast, thanks," he said, looking at Aileen while putting on his greatcoat. "Dave said there was a nice walk around the bay if I walk to the end of town?"

"Aye, that's right, lad, and be careful up there, in places the path runs close to the edge of the cliffs, and it can be dangerous when it's windy."

"Thanks, I will."

Isobel was annoyed at his outspokenness, so she decided to get her mother on her side. "His last remark wasn't very nice, was it? And him being a guest here as well."

Her mother looked at her for a few moments and shook her head. "You only got back as good as you gave, Isobel. There are certain people who you can only push so far, and I think Will is one of them. You were trying to pick a fight with him last night."

"No I wasn't," she answered, annoyed at her mother for taking Will's side.

"Yes, you were, Isobel. You haven't had a civil word to say to him since he arrived. You can't go taking it out on Will for what Trevor Roach did, can you?"

Sounds of footsteps coming down the stairs curtailed any further discussion on the matter, which left an uneasy atmosphere in the room when her father came in, so she decided under the circumstances that a walk would be the best solution.

* * *

Will had reached the point where it overlooked the whole of Castlebay. He stopped to take in the panoramic view that had unfolded around him and needed to shield his eyes from the sun's glare as it shimmered on the surface of the ocean.

"It's a lovely view, isn't it? I often stop here when I'm out walking," a voice said from behind him. Turning to see who had broken in on his solitude, he was surprised to see Isobel walking towards him.

"Isobel, I'm in no mood for arg– "

"I know. I'm sorry about earlier. Mum had a go at me after you left. I've been wrong to take it out on you and that brother of mine for what Roach did."

Will smiled at her and shook his head. "Don't tar us all with the same brush, Isobel. We are not all the same as he was."

"Yes, I know!" she said, removing her mitten to push a strand of her hair back under her woolly hat. "Would you like to see the remains of the *Asrai*. It's a cargo ship that was wrecked when its engine broke down during a storm; it's in a cove along the coast from here?"

"Yes, I would."

"So, what are you going to do about tonight?"

"Tonight? Oh, you mean Flora?"

"Yes."

"If she turns up, I'll tell her the truth."

"That won't go down too well, knowing her as I do. She's a very good-looking girl," she replied, not realising that he had stopped walking behind her.

"She is not as good-looking as the one I'm with now."

His remark stopped her in her tracks. Turning, she smiled at him. "Thank you, that's the nicest thing anybody has said to me in a long time."

"It had to be said." He walked towards her. "So, where's this wreck you were going to show me?"

Once they reached the cove, Isobel led him down a

narrow path to a good vantage point that looked down into what Will could only describe as a pit of hell. Sheer cliffs dropped straight down onto razor-sharp rocks below, battered by centuries of wind and rain and pounding seas and, snared upon them, half-submerged, was the rusting remains of a large freighter.

"How long has it been there?" he asked, looking down at the weather-beaten hulk.

"Since that bad winter of 1928."

"Were there any survivors?"

"The lifeboat managed to rescue a few of the crew. I think it was four? If you go into the lifeboat station, there is the whole story as to what happened. Also, there are photographs taken from here where we are standing the following morning. It must have been terrible."

"The sea has no mercy once it has a hold of you," he said.

Isobel sensed what he was thinking. "David told us that you came down in the sea earlier in the war. Was it very bad?"

He looked at her seriously. "I don't think I have ever been so cold in all my life as I was during those fourteen hours waiting to be picked up."

Isobel could see by the look on his face what he had been through. "It must have been awful to be wet and cold like that for so long," she said, taking the lead up the narrow pathway.

Following the cliff path along for a short distance, it eventually separated, the left-hand path turning back towards the town, which Isobel followed.

"This way will take us back to the path that goes into town. I used to play ball with my dog along here until I lost him."

"What was his name?"

"Bobby. He was a black Labrador. I miss him so much,

even after all this time."

"How long has he been gone?"

"Oh, just over two years now."

"Do you think you will have another one?"

"Maybe, but not until this damn war is over, then I might think about it."

They walked in silence for a few minutes while they negotiated a tricky part of the path that went down a small depression. A stream flowing along its base with stepping stones warranted them walking in single file.

"How do you feel about David going on the air-sea rescue boats?" he asked, catching her up so they could walk side by side.

"Well, I know it can be dangerous, but I think there is less chance of him being hurt on them than flying in bombers. And he is familiar with the workings of a boat, what with my father having one."

"Yes, he told me he used to go out fishing a lot with your father."

"Both of us did, every chance we got. Like David, I love fishing, and even now, I won't pass up a trip if I get the chance, although Dad is a bit nervous about taking me now, with all the strange things that have been going on around this area of late."

Will stopped and looked at her. "What kind of strange things?"

"Strange lights being seen out at sea and around the islands; aircraft engines being heard and reports of submarine periscopes being seen by the fishermen, all sorts of weird things."

"Have the military been told about all this?"

"Oh yes, several times. But you know what they are like, keep everything close to their chest and tell you nothing –

most likely it's our own forces up to something."

"Could be," he said cautiously.

Isobel picked up on his remark and the frown on his face. "Have you seen something unusual while you've been flying?" Her eyes held his until he answered.

"Well, as a matter of fact, I have," he said and went on to tell her about the strange incident with the lighthouse on Stracandra Island.

"You don't think it was lightning reflecting on the lens?"

"I know what I saw, Isobel. And it wasn't that."

"How odd. Do you mind if I tell Dad about it when we get back, he knows those waters well around that area?"

"No, not at all."

When they got back, Isobel was seconded by her mother into helping in the shop, so he found himself wandering down to the harbour to join Dave who was on his father's fishing boat.

"Hiya, Will, had a good walk?"

"Yes, thanks," he shouted over the noise of the boat's engine being started.

"Let go of the bow and stern ropes for us, will you? Then come aboard. Dad has had some work done on the engine so we are taking her out for a spin just to make sure everything is on top line."

He jumped aboard and took up a position by the wheelhouse door and watched as Duncan Hamilton skilfully manoeuvred the boat away from the harbour wall and out into the deep water channel.

"Are you a good sailor, Will?" Duncan asked, meticulously filling his pipe with tobacco.

"I think so, although I've not had a lot to do with boats," he grinned while becoming conscious of the cold wind and spray on his face as they rounded the headland. It made him retreat into the warmth of the wheelhouse as Dave arrived, beaming a smile of satisfaction.

"Everything all right below, David?" his father asked, relighting his pipe.

"Aye, everything seems to be fine, but it will be as well if you check for yourself, then you'll be settled in your own mind before you take her out on your next fishing trip."

"Okay, I'll take a wee look. Here, take the wheel, son."

"Bit different from flying in the tail end of a Halifax, Will?" Dave laughed as a deluge of spray hit the wheelhouse windows.

"It sure is. I was up on the headland with Isobel earlier, and from up there, the sea seemed quite calm, but now I'm on it, I'm amazed how rough it is."

"Aye, it's surprising. So that sister of mine is talking to you, is she? Now that is amazing. She was as moody as hell last night for some reason."

Will didn't mention the little skit Isobel and he had during breakfast. "She was fine with me, Dave. In fact, she took me to see the wreck of a freighter, and we had a good old chinwag while we were walking."

"The *Asrai?* There weren't many rescued off that by all accounts."

"Off what?" his father asked, coming into the wheelhouse and sliding the door closed behind him.

"The *Asrai*, there were four taken off weren't there, Dad?"

"Aye, that's right, only four. It was a wild night. How the lifeboat managed to get them off is a miracle. It was a fine bit of seamanship by Hamish Ballard to get in as close as he did with the sea running like it was. So, what brought up the subject of the *Asrai?*" he asked, patting the used tobacco from his pipe into his hand while switching his gaze between Will and his son.

"Isobel took Will along to see it this morning, he reckons she's mellowed a bit since last night," Dave laughed. "There's the wreck now." Here, take a look," he said, handing Will the binoculars.

Will focused on the distant remains. "I'll bet that was quite a big ship in its day?"

"Aye, over ten thousand tonnes," Duncan Hamilton answered, refilling his pipe. "Better bring her about, David, we don't want to run off too much fuel."

Arriving back alongside the dock, they found Isobel waiting for them with an urgent message for her brother, telling him to report for duty immediately.

"Did they say what it was about?"

"No, only that you had to report there as quickly as possible."

"Right, there must be a bit of a flap on. I'll see you all later."

After securing the boat, Duncan Hamilton suggested a drink in the Castlebay Bar would go down well, but on their return to the shop, they found Aileen on the telephone.

"It's a Flight Lieutenant Fuller from the air-sea rescue base. He wants a word with you, Will," she said, handing him the phone.

"Warrant Officer Madden."

"Can't say much on the phone, but do you fancy making up a crew as a gunner?"

"Yes, certainly."

"Okay, get yourself over here to the marine craft unit as soon as you can. I will meet you at the guardroom when you arrive and take you over to operations."

"What is it, lad?" Duncan Hamilton asked as he watched him replace the receiver on the telephone.

Will frowned. "They want me to make up a crew on one

of the boats, sounds as though they are short of a gunner," he replied, heading for the door, closely followed by Isobel who took hold of his arm and pulled him back gently.

"You be careful out there."

"I will."

* * *

Kitted out against the cold, Will found himself onboard a high-speed launch. Known as the "Whaleback" from its distinctive curved hull and humped cabin, it had a crew of nine and a range of five hundred miles. The boat was being pushed to its maximum speed to rescue the crew of a ditched Wellington of Coastal Command after an encounter with a heavily armed surfaced U-boat.

"Tea, sir?" a voice said, breaking in on Will's thoughts about walking on the cliff path that morning with Isobel and how she had looked at him when he was leaving the house.

"Please," he replied, looking into the eyes of the young medical orderly. "Been on the boats long?" he asked, wrapping his hands around the mug as he took a drink.

"This is my third trip."

"This is my first. I'm usually up there." Will pointed upwards.

"Yes, I heard."

"Did you make a pick-up on the two previous ones?" he asked, bracing himself against the bulkhead as he felt the launch begin to make a high-speed turn to starboard.

"We made a pick-up on the first but no luck on the second, I'm afraid. Some you win and some you lose," he added.

Will nodded. "Yes, that's true."

"How long have you been flying, sir?"

"More or less since the war started, I joined up in thirty-nine."

"So you've seen a fair bit of action then?"

"You could say that," Will grinned.

"I hope we don't run into one of those Jerry flying boats. I heard they are well-armed, them blighters."

Will could see the look of apprehension on the medic's face and knew he was right. They were heavily armed, not only with cannons and machine guns but also bombs. "We can give a good account of ourselves with the Oerlikon and Vickers machine guns," he replied, trying to sound reassuring as Flight Sergeant Nugent came into the galley.

"Is that tea you've got there, *sick note*?" Nugent asked in a light-hearted tone.

"Yes, Flight."

"I could murder a cup of tea, pour us a cup, there's a good chap." He turned to Will. "And the skipper would like to see you up on the bridge."

"Right," Will acknowledged, making his way to the wheelhouse.

"You wanted to see me, sir?" he asked, looking at the seasoned features of Flight Lieutenant Fuller.

"Yes! It was to say thanks for stepping in at the last minute like this and you not being attached to the marine craft unit. It's most appreciated."

"Glad to be of help."

"We were hard pressed to put three boats to sea."

"Three boats?"

"One went out earlier to try and find the crew of the ditched Wellington, but their boat has got trouble with its engine, and they will be out of action for a couple of hours, so a replacement boat was sent out to resume the search for the aircrew."

"So, there will be three boats looking then, sir?" he asked, a little surprised.

"No, we have now been ordered to search for an overdue fishing boat that is missing south of here. It sent a garbled radio message saying it was being attacked, but by what, we don't know as communication was broken during the transmission. So we don't know whether it was an aircraft or a surface vessel."

Will didn't react to the flight lieutenant's remark, but he did wonder if he knew anything about the unexplained things going on in the area that Isobel had mentioned earlier. "I've heard there has been quite a few strange incidents in these waters of late. Do you think it's down to enemy activity?"

"Who knows? Personally, I've seen nothing untoward," Fuller said, turning the boat onto its new course and going no further on the subject, which left Will thinking that he knew more than he was prepared to say.

Nearing the fishing boat's last known position, they closed up to action stations, with Will taking up his allotted position manning the portside twin Vickers machine guns. They searched the area for over an hour but to no avail before moving further south, towards the dark outline of an island that had a high and formidable coastline. Further searching revealed nothing, so after making a wide turn to seaward as dark clouds rolled in, bringing heavy downpours of rain and reducing visibility down to a minimum, the boat was put on a course for home.

They only realised they were under aerial attack when heavy fire arced towards them, hitting the side of the hull, deck and the anti-shrapnel padding forward of the front turret. Turning immediately, Fuller weaved the launch away from its deadly adversary at high speed, lifting its rakish bow clear of the water. Will could see from his position that he was well out of effective range to use the machine guns. He could only stand and watch as another line of hits from the Junkers' machine guns raked across the rear deck, sending up a line of splinters as they tore into the mahogany planking, hitting the gunner manning the Oerlikon.

With the help of two other crewmembers, Will managed to get the wounded man below, then ducked for cover as another line of accurate fire found its mark, bringing down the mast, which intermingled with wires and debris lay strewn across the aft cabin. Pushing to one side the remains of the rescue dinghy, he managed to make it to the unmanned Oerlikon, the only weapon capable of bringing down the enemy aircraft.

Positioning himself in the two curved shoulder braces, he swung the heavy weapon around and, lined up on the circling aircraft and taking aim. He kept up a steady rate of fire until the drum feed was expended. While replacing the ammunition drum, Will felt the dull thud as a shell hit and ricocheted off the protective armoured shield and flew across the deck, embedding itself into the side of the aft cabin. Opening fire, he thought of Isobel and what she had said to him about being careful but hits on the boat's stern quickly brought him back to reality as the aircraft, bomb doors agape, closed in to finish them off.

At least they would go down fighting, he thought, as he watched the enemy aircraft through the gun sight race towards them. His steady stream of fire didn't seem to deter the German pilot or front gunner as a line of machine-gun bullets spurted across the surface of the ocean, hitting the deck aft just behind where he was standing. Sudden evasive action by Fuller made the Junkers' bombs drop wide but close enough for Will to get the full deluge from the last bomb that dropped just beyond the boat's stern. Swinging the Oerlikon round to follow the enemy aircraft's line of flight, he was able to fire one more burst before he was out of ammunition.

Their salvation came in the shape of a Coastal Command Wellington from Benbecula, whose presence was shrouded by the fast-failing light and opened fire on the enemy aircraft from directly astern. The result being that the Wellington's front gunner scored hits on the enemy aircraft's gun position in the rear of the cockpit. Will gave a sigh of relief as he saw the Junkers turn away to seaward, hotly pursued by the Wellington, at least now they had a chance to make it back to Castlebay even though they had been quite badly damaged during the engagement.

The sound of an aircraft returning made him immediately come to action stations and search the darkening sky. His apprehension was soon curtailed as the welcome sight of the Wellington roared over them, climbed and banked to starboard, no doubt asking Fuller if they needed assistance. Relinquishing his hold on the Oerlikon, Will suddenly felt drained of energy as he watched the friendly aircraft circle them several times before heading for its base.

As he turned to go below, he felt the sharp pain in his lower back and realised he had been wounded. Running his hand across the spot, he felt the jagged edges of wood splinters protruding through his blood-soaked clothing. He grimaced at the pain as the boat's speed was increased. He was eternally grateful when he saw Flight Sergeant Nugent appear with his comforting words,

"I've got you, sir," as his arm went around him to give him support, and he was helped below to the sick bay.

Chapter 12

Swinging the office chair gently from side to side, Maynard cupped his hands together behind his head and rested his eyes. With no further development on the *Raven* case either at Filton or from Barrett at Gloucester, his only alternative now was to return to London. He was annoyed at not being able to make any further progress and checked his watch, surprised at the lateness of the hour. Pushing himself up from the chair, he unhooked his coat from the stand and, switching out the light, made his way through to the main office. He had not expected to find anybody still working and had been surprised when he saw the figure of a female huddled over her desk in the partly-lit room and recognised it as being Samantha.

"I thought you would have been gone by now, Sam."

"I think I have found what you are looking for, Mr Maynard."

"What is it?" Maynard dropped his coat over an empty chair, pulling it up alongside her.

"It's Lillian Gilbert's file. There's something that doesn't ring true."

"In what way?"

"It's something she said to me a couple of weeks ago in the canteen. I didn't make much of it at the time."

"What did she say?"

"She said she nearly missed her train the night before due to working late."

Maynard looked at her for a few moments, his eyes encouraging her to bring about a conclusion.

Samantha smiled as she read Maynard's thoughts. "Why would she need a train when her address is given as Horfield, only ten or fifteen minutes away by bus? Take a look at her file."

"Horfield, that's going in towards Bristol, isn't it?" he asked, looking over Gilbert's file.

"Yes, that's right. She came to the Bristol Aeroplane Company from a law firm in Gloucester just prior to the outbreak of war. But the interesting part is her address when she was working in Gloucester: she lived at Primrose Cottage, Coaley. I've checked it on the map and it's only about four miles from Moreton Valence airfield. I was wondering if she still has the place at Coaley and she is in rented accommodation in Horfield. It would be an ideal set-up, wouldn't it?"

"It would indeed. Is there anything on Gilbert before she worked at the law firm?"

"No. But it's not unusual for us just to have an employee's previous employment on file. I see at the interview she produced a reference, which by all accounts was exemplary, so she must have been very highly thought of by her last employer."

"I think it might be wise if we run some background checks on her. I'll give Barrett a ring and see if his team can dig up anything more on Gilbert, I have a sneaky feeling that this just might be the breakthrough we've been looking for. Well done, Sam! Now get yourself home, it's late and I'll see you in the morning."

"Right, goodnight then, sir."

"Goodnight, Sam."

Maynard's first reaction as he slowly read through Gilbert's file was to ring Granville in London, but he decided against it until he had something more concrete to go on. Picking up the telephone, he put a call through to Barrett at Gloucester and was pleased when he came on the line, given the time.

"Good evening, Chief Inspector. I didn't know if I would get hold of you, it being so late."

"You were lucky to catch me, I was just about to leave the office. How can I help you, Mr Maynard?"

"I think for starters, Chief Inspector, seeing as we are working together, we can drop the formalities, don't you? My name is Henry."

"Mine is Leslie," Barrett replied after a few moments of deliberation.

"Good, now we've got that out of the way I was wondering if your department could run a check on a Lillian Gilbert for me, Leslie."

"Yes. I'm sure we can. What details have you got on the woman?" Barrett asked, and Maynard could hear him writing down the details of what Sam had discovered. "It's not a name that I have come across, but I'll run it through our records and see if it turns up anything. If not, we'll have to dig a little deeper, starting with this law firm. What do you want me to do about this address at Coaley?"

"Just hang fire on that at the moment until we see what your investigation turns up. If my hunch is right I wouldn't mind betting it's a blank canvas. How are your enquiries going so far?"

"Not very good I'm afraid, without a description of the man we are after, it's hard going. We are slowly questioning all the known hotels, guesthouses and lodgings in the area but up to now we have drawn a blank."

"I thought you would have a tough time of it without a description. I think what I'll do in the morning is pay this address in Horfield a discreet visit and see what it turns up. After I've seen how the land lies there, I'll then give London a ring and put them in the picture and, on the basis of what I've found out at Horfield, I will then suggest I go back up to Gloucester. I have a feeling we may well be on to something with this Gilbert woman, but we have to be damn sure before we make a move. If our bird is somehow involved with this woman, we don't want him taking flight. But it would be a bonus if we could nab the pair of them."

"I couldn't agree more. In the meantime, I'll put things in motion here in the morning then wait to hear from you."

"Thanks, Leslie. I'll be in touch."

After replacing the receiver, he spent another hour pondering over Gilbert's file, and as he repeatedly read it over, the more convinced he became that Lillian Gilbert held the key. He sat back a few moments to think things over before leaving a message for Sam to check out the times of the trains that stopped at Coaley.

* * *

Adele House lay in a quiet street just off the busy Gloucester Road. Parking at a discreet distance so he could keep the building under surveillance, Maynard sat back to wait. It soon became apparent that none of the female residents leaving the lodgings remotely resembled the photograph he had of Gilbert. Before making enquiries from the proprietor, he decided to ring Samantha to get her to confirm that Gilbert was at work and, after several minutes wait, was told that she was there. Maynard rang the doorbell and came face to face with a rather busty middle-aged woman who, he thought, was highly suited to the role of being a landlady.

"Can I help you?" she said, holding the door back with one hand while resting the other on her hip.

"Good morning. My name is Henry Maynard and I'm with the security service in London. I would like to ask you about one of your guests." He showed the woman his credentials and was shown into a comfortable living room.

"I run a respectable establishment here, Mr Maynard, and have never had any trouble with any of my guests," she said, playing nervously with the crucifix that hung loosely around her neck on a gold chain.

Maynard gave her a few moments to compose herself before answering. "I'm not disputing that Mrs–?"

"Jefferies, Dolores Jefferies."

"Mrs Jefferies, I'm making enquiries about a Lillian Gilbert who I believe may have a room here," Maynard said, trying to put the woman at ease.

"Lillian Gilbert? There is no one here with that name."

"Here is a picture of the woman. Would you take a look at it? She may well be using another name."

"I have nobody staying here that looks like that," she answered, gesturing at the photograph but stopping herself partway to take a closer look. "Wait a minute, I think I do have a vague recollection of this woman. If my memory serves me right, she stayed here the first year of the war. Yes, 1939, if I recall. Just one moment, Mr Maynard, while I fetch the registration books for then, it will tell us exactly when she arrived and left. I'm very strict that all guests register when they first arrive."

"Here we are, now let's see. She arrived here on the 15th of August 1939 and left on the 12th of June the following year."

Maynard wrote down the dates. "Did she, by any chance, leave a forwarding address?"

"No, I'm afraid not."

"Mrs Jefferies, can you remember if she had any callers during that period, male or female, that may have turned up at an unusual hour or maybe had a slight accent?" Maynard knew full well that he may be clutching at straws after this length of time.

"Well, what I remember of her, she kept herself pretty much to herself. But there was one instance when a woman came to the door asking for her, early evening it was, she seemed a nice enough woman, quite friendly and chatty, you know, and she had a slight accent."

Maynard leaned forward in the chair and clasped his hands together, his elbows resting on the arms. "Did this woman give you her name?"

"No, she didn't."

"What happened next?"

"I asked her to come in and I left her sitting where you're sitting now, then went up and told Lillian Gilbert she was here."

"How did she react when you told her?"

"As a matter of fact, I think she was a little surprised. A bit flustered, if you know what I mean, but anyway, she passed it off laughing and followed me down the stairs and from there we went our separate ways, me to the kitchen and her in here."

"Did you notice if they went out together?"

"Yes, they did. I was coming along the passageway to come in here to do the blackout and I saw the pair of them leaving. That would have been about seven o'clock, but I've no idea what time she came back."

"Did you ever see this woman again?"

"No, only the once."

"Did Gilbert have any other callers during the time she was here?"

"Not that I recall, but on the other hand, some may have turned up when I wasn't here. I do like to try and get to the cinema at least once a week if I can … I am a creature of habit."

Maynard smiled at her candidness as he took out his pipe. "Do you mind if I smoke, Mrs Jefferies?"

"No, not at all. I do like the aroma of pipe tobacco, it reminds me of my late husband, Arthur. He was a pipe smoker. Would you like a cup of tea, Mr Maynard?"

"Thank you, that would be very nice." This gave him time to look around at the room's regal furniture and good quality porcelain and silver, securely locked in an early-Victorian display cabinet. He had just been looking over the line of family photographs when his host returned carrying a silver tray. "I do beg your pardon. I was just admiring the lovely furnishings you have. If you don't mind me saying so, Mrs Jefferies, you have some very nice items."

"Most of the things in here are down to my husband, he was a collector of fine things and he ran an antiques business for many years in Bath before we bought this place. This is him just two years before he passed away, fifty-five, that's all he was," she sighed, handing him the photo frame.

"I'm very sorry."

"So, what has Lillian Gilbert been up to, or aren't I allowed to ask that?" she said, settling herself into an easy chair.

Maynard replaced the cup into its saucer and put it down on the table. "I'm afraid I can't tell you that, Mrs Jefferies, Official Secrets Act and all that, and I must stress to you that what we have discussed this morning must go no further than this room."

"I understand."

* * *

Griselda had felt intimidated since Guntram's return from Bristol: his mannerisms towards her had changed, which frightened her. He had said nothing about his meeting with the other agent or what had been discussed, all of which made her feel uneasy. She knew what he was capable of. She decided that when she got back to Coaley that evening to contact Berlin herself, irrespective of what Guntram said. He had made all the transmissions of late and she had found it a little strange that there had been no further instructions for her. Although trained in the art of espionage and having a reasonably good rate of accuracy when it came to shooting, she had never had to put the latter into practice. She had seen the look of satisfaction on his face after returning from Moreton Valence as he sat and cleaned the remainder of the dead soldier's blood from the knife. The "silent killer", he had joked, opening and closing it several times.

Leaving her office she made her way to the railway station and was able to get a seat for the whole of the journey to Coaley. However, as the train came to a stop in the station she didn't move as a sudden feeling of foreboding swept over her. She stared at the only other passenger in the compartment who was engrossed in an evening newspaper and paid her no heed. Did she know him? He looked vaguely familiar, most probably she'd seen him travelling on the train before. They could have shared a compartment together if he was a regular user like herself. He caught her looking at him and she automatically turned away. Out of the corner of her eye, Griselda watched him neatly fold up the newspaper and lay it on his lap, then from his inside pocket, take out a silver cigarette case.

"Do you mind?"

"No, not at all."

Silence reigned for a few moments as she watched him take out a cigarette and light it.

"Oh, do excuse my manners, would you like one?" he asked, flicking open the case and leaning towards her.

"Thank you," she answered, taking a cigarette and the light when it was offered.

"The nights are getting colder," he commented as he turned slightly towards her and crossed his legs.

Griselda wasn't sure whether to engage in conversation with him or not but thought it would seem odd if she didn't reply to his remark, and she was curious to know if he was a regular commuter.

"Yes, they are," she replied, taking a long draw on her cigarette, which had a calming effect. "Do you use the line often?" she said, trying to sound casual.

"No, business meeting tomorrow morning in Gloucester."

"Oh, I see. It's just that you seem rather familiar, that's all. And with me using the train every day for work, I thought I might have seen you before."

"No, I'm afraid not. I can't remember the last time I used this line."

"I'm sorry, my mistake."

"That's quite all right. Do you live in Gloucester?"

Griselda had been ready for this remark when it came. "My husband and I have a small cottage there."

"Sounds very nice. Have you got any family?"

"No, I'm afraid not. How about you?" she asked, wanting to throw the ball back into his court.

"I have a son in the merchant navy, but God knows

where he is at the moment."

Griselda sensed the man's anxiety but inwardly hoped his son was lying at the bottom of the sea with his ship, courtesy of one of Karl Dönitz's U-boats. "Yes, it must be a very worrying time for you when he's at sea."

"It is. He is all I've got, what with his mother now passed on," the man confided.

Griselda felt no remorse as she felt the train start to slow as it approached the station at Gloucester. Her main concern was her ticket, which was only valid to Coaley, as she watched him get up and take down his small travelling bag from the luggage rack above.

"Well, it's been nice talking with you," he smiled as the train came to a halt.

"Likewise."

Chapter 13

Lillian Gilbert not getting off at Coaley had been a surprise for both Maynard and Barrett. Their carefully laid plan to follow Gilbert home with the hope of catching two birds with one stone had come to nothing when the ticket collector at Coaley station had reported that she had not left the train.

"What the hell is she up to, Leslie?" Maynard asked, nodding in acknowledgement at the young constable who handed him a note telling him to ring Clifford Granville in London.

"I don't know unless she is meeting this *Raven* chap somewhere."

"The ticket clerk at Coaley station is sure that the ticket she bought this morning was a return back to there?"

"Positive."

Maynard went quiet for a few moments while he turned things over in his mind. "The train she's on terminates at Birmingham, right?"

"Yes, that's correct."

"Gilbert will be thinking she will most likely get rumbled by a ticket inspector if she stays on the train between Gloucester and Birmingham."

Barrett had been following Maynard's logic closely. "Do you think she will get off at Gloucester?"

"She's got to. But the burning question is why has she done what she's done? It doesn't make any sense putting herself at risk like this?"

"Well, we have a plain clothes man on the train keeping an eye on her and men watching every station between here and Birmingham. If she does try and ride it out to the end of the line, we'll have her under surveillance whatever move she makes," Barrett replied.

"And they all know not to make a move on her?" Maynard asked.

Barrett grinned. "It's taken some organising at such short notice, but Gilbert's description has been circulated to all those involved. The ticket clerk and the inspector have been told to be a little bit lackadaisical when checking her ticket. Although I did wonder, Henry, if she might think it strange if she does stay on the train and doesn't get found out."

"It's a chance we are going to have to take."

"What do you want to do about her place at Coaley?" Barrett enquired before thanking the young policewoman for a file she handed him.

Maynard sat back in his chair and slowly swung it from side to side. "Primrose Cottage, a very English name that could be sheltering a ruthless German spy. How ironic is that?"

Barrett looked up from the file he was reading. "Yes, it is rather perplexing."

"One thing that does worry me, Leslie, is your men having reported that there has been no movement at the cottage all day. I can't help but wonder if the place is empty."

"Well, there's always been that chance we've been keeping watch on an empty house since Gilbert left for work this morning," Barrett concluded, placing the file on his desk.

Maynard thought over the situation for a few moments.

"Your officers, did they say anything about the blackout?"

"The blackout, in what way?"

"Whether it was still in place or taken down when you put the place under surveillance. If it was down when your people arrived and it's up now, there must be someone inside and we know for a fact that it's not Gilbert. You have two teams watching the place, one at either end of the lane, if I remember rightly?"

"Yes, we have a two-man surveillance team in a retired couple's spare bedroom which gives them a good view of the side and rear of Gilbert's place and the lane leading to it."

"And the other team?" Maynard asked.

"They have drawn the short straw, a farmer's barn, but the loft does have a good view of the other side of the property and excellent visibility down the lane from the other direction. We also have backup teams standing by at Cam and Coaley in case he tries to make a run for it across the fields."

"Are all your men armed, Leslie?"

"Yes, they are. Do you want me to enquire about the blackout?"

Their conversation was interrupted by the phone ringing on Barrett's desk.

"Barrett!" His answer was sharp.

Maynard couldn't hear what the conversation was about from where he was but by the look on Barrett's face surmised it was serious.

"I see. And what are the woman's injuries?"

Maynard got up and walked over and stood next to his colleague.

"Facial cuts and bruises and a nasty gash to the back of the head. Where is she now? Right, thank you for letting me know. No, keep everybody in place, Sergeant, until we tell you anything different. Is that understood?"

"Problem?" Maynard asked as Barrett replaced the receiver.

"Our man on the train lost sight of Gilbert on the crowded platform at Gloucester. They think she followed a woman, whose name is Mavis Ross, into the ladies toilet where Gilbert assaulted her, took her hat, scarf and coat and left her unconscious in one of the cubicles. They have taken the woman to hospital where she has been treated for her injuries and they are keeping her in overnight under observation."

"Damn it, that's made things awkward. My gut feeling was that she would try and get off at Gloucester."

"Well, if you want my honest opinion, Henry, I can't see for the life in me what she is trying to achieve. Unless it's as we said earlier. She is trying to meet up with *The Raven.* None of her movements make any sense. I would even go as far as to say they are foolhardy for a professional spy. She is just drawing attention to herself by what she's done."

"Mmm, I wonder. I'll keep an open mind on that for the moment. But first, let's turn our attention to Primrose Cottage and what may be going on there. I suggest we hit the place at first light tomorrow morning and hope we catch our man; if not, the place may well turn up some evidence that could point us in the right direction as to Gilbert's whereabouts or what she's up to. I'll give Clifford Granville a ring and put him in the picture as to what has happened so far and what we are going to do."

* * *

Guntrum Bayer was uneasy with the latest developments as he reassembled the Walther. Too many loose ends, he didn't like that. First, there had been the agent in Bristol – he had a bad feeling about letting him live – and now Griselda had not shown up. He paced the room, scattering laid-out crockery from the dining table onto the floor, annoyed with himself at not eliminating them both earlier. A noise from outside, from where the dustbin stood, made him strain his ears to listen; likely just an animal, but even so, best to check, he thought, picking up the Walther and switching out the kitchen light.

With the door partially ajar, he stood in the darkness for a few moments to watch for any sign of movement outside before he ventured out into the cold night air, the full moon giving him a commanding view of the side and part of the rear garden from his vantage point on the top step. Keeping close to the cottage wall, he walked to the end of the building, where he ran a wary eye around the remainder of the rear garden, taking particular notice that the outhouse lock was still in place.

Satisfied everything was as it should be, he was just about to retrace his steps when he heard what sounded like a car engine running. He stood and tried to listen but was interrupted by the screaming whistle from an express train speeding through Coaley station. Shivering from the cold, which was beginning to penetrate his flimsy attire, prompted him back inside to the warmth of the kitchen.

Not being fully satisfied, however, he made his way upstairs to the main bedroom and gave the garden on that side of the cottage the once over, as far as the bushes that divided the property from the field that ran as far as the junction. Bayer could make out the dark shape of the old barn. A glint of something shiny caught his eye and made him reach for the binoculars that stood on top of a chest of drawers. Focusing, he was able to make out the bonnet of a car and, as he followed the lines of the wooden structure, he also noticed that one of the loading doors at the front was partially open.

Bayer immediately backed away into the darkness. So the bastards had the place under surveillance. No wonder Griselda hadn't turned up; his mind searched for answers: had she been caught and the bitch had talked to save her own neck? Running between each of the upstairs bedrooms he scanned the surrounding area with binoculars which divulged nothing. Trapped wasn't an option for Guntram Bayer; killing was a way of life and if that's what it would take to get him out of his present predicament, so be it – taking the fight to the enemy had always been his way. Dressing quickly in warmer clothes, he then picked up everything he needed for his journey northwards then slipped quietly out of the side door. The garden on that side of the cottage was shaded by trees. Using them for cover, he was able to reach the lane, cross it to a copse of trees on the other side. He screwed the silencer onto the barrel of the Walther, took time to slow his breathing, then set off to follow the hedgerow around to where the two lanes met. Bayer knew that the open road in front of the barn wasn't an option, but a gate to his left was.

Conscious that the rusty hinges may give him away, he climbed over, crossed the lane and into the field opposite through the open field gate, the hedgerow on that side giving him all the cover he needed until he reached the side of the barn.

The sound of muffled voices coming from the interior made him tread carefully. Easing himself gently to the corner of the building, he crouched down to make himself a smaller target. Holding the Walther at arm's length, ready to shoot, should the need arise, he rounded the corner to confront whatever opposition he might encounter. Bayer immediately recognised the distinct lines of the Wolseley police car, its black surface glinting in the moonlight, while above in the loft, its unsuspecting occupants chatted, unaware of the danger that awaited them below. Wisps of straw tumbled down silently from between the creaking boards and settled on the dirt floor as he made his way to the loft ladder.

Testing each rung in turn, he slowly ascended, his eyes burning hatred for the quarry he stalked. The ladder was adjacent to the barn wall made it an ideal killing position: shrouded in darkness, and his victims were easy targets. Their bodies highlighted by the moonlight filtering in through the open loft door. Bayer had to smile to himself at the two men's crude effort to conceal their position behind discarded hay bales as he took aim at the first policeman who sat with his back resting against a bale.

Neither man had time to retaliate as the two deadly shots found their mark, killing them both instantly. Climbing the last few rungs he walked over to where two corpses lay slumped; satisfied with his killing, he unceremoniously dragged the two bodies over onto their backs and, after removing the weapons they were carrying, went about callously rifling through their clothing for anything that might be of use for his journey, including the keys to the police car which he found in the overcoat pocket of the second officer.

Content the dead men had no more to give, he made his way down to the car. Bayer placed his travel bag on the passenger seat then, sliding in behind the wheel, he closed the door quietly behind him. He drove slowly to the open field gate and out into the lane, at which point he turned right and followed the road until it reached the A38.

By daybreak, he was on the outskirts of Stratford-upon-

Avon. With the police vehicle now getting low on petrol and becoming conspicuous in the early morning light, and likely reported as missing, it was becoming obvious that another form of transport was needed. Stealing another car was risky; firstly, he may well be seen and secondly, it could also be low on fuel given the fuel rationing, so the only other alternative was the train. He felt reasonably pleased with his night's work as he parked the Wolseley between several other vehicles in a car park, no one paid him any attention as they drifted off to their places of employment.

* * *

Maynard had not slept at all well in the police cell. The constant singing from a drunk along the corridor had kept him awake until gone two and he had finally been able to get some sleep.

"What time is it?" he asked the desk sergeant as a mug of tea was thrust into his hand.

"Quarter to seven, sir."

"Thanks! Where is Chief Inspector Barrett?"

"I believe he is in the incident room, sir."

Maynard responded with a nod of the head as he got to his feet while massaging his aching back. Carrying the mug of tea, he made his way into the main incident room where he found Barrett replacing the receiver with a look of thunder on his face.

"What's the matter?"

"The two police officers who were watching Gilbert's cottage from the barn have just been found – murdered. Both had been shot from close range. Their car has been taken. Looks like your *Raven's* handiwork, but at least we know now he was in there," Barrett concluded.

"I'm sorry about your two officers, Leslie."

Barrett shook his head in annoyance. "What a waste, both damn good police officers with young families, they didn't deserve that. We've got to stop this maniac one way or another if it's the last thing we do."

"I couldn't agree more. Finding the vehicle is the key – when that's found, it'll give us some indication of which direction he is travelling in. He will no doubt abandon the car now it's light and try for another mode of transport, but in what form that will be, your guess is as good as mine."

"Well, we've a full description out on this Lillian Gilbert and the police car, so I shouldn't think it will be too long before something turns up. Even so, I don't like the state of affairs, Henry. What with this Gilbert woman going to ground here in Gloucester and now this murdering sod has taken off to God knows where, we seem to have a very dangerous situation on our hands at the moment."

Maynard lit his first pipe of the day and made a prominent gesture of putting out the lit match. "Yes, we do, and the first thing I'd better do is give Clifford Granville a ring and tell him about last night's events and see what he has to say."

* * *

Griselda felt tired, cold and used as she sat in the waiting room at Shrewsbury station. She thought over the night's events: Being picked up by the pantechnicon lorry on the outskirts of Gloucester and the slow and uncomfortable night's journey along the roads through Worcester, Kidderminster and Bridgnorth – then the seedy sex in the rear of the van which had been the driver's payment for the lift. She knew she had to get as far away from Guntram as possible, but where? What she needed was help to get her out of the country, but without the means of communication, that wasn't possible unless she made contact with another agent, and Martha had immediately come to mind.

Martha had been her contact when she first arrived from Germany, married to an Englishman called Ronald Warner who was sympathetic to the Nazi cause. They had together set up a small but successful network under the guise of a secretarial agency in Manchester. Their spying activities kept a constant eye on the comings and goings on the Manchester and Salford Docks. It had also been perfect for observing Metrovick, who were in a joint venture with Avro to assemble the Manchester and Lancaster bombers at their factory at Trafford Park. Griselda had, for a short period, been assigned menial tasks under Martha's guidance to prepare her for the more dangerous operations when the time arose, and the training had stood her in good stead when she took up the assignment at the Bristol Aeroplane Company.

"Are you warm enough?" a voice asked, breaking in on her thoughts.

"Not really," she answered, looking up at the gaunt features of the young railway porter.

"I'll get a drop more coal," he smiled, closing the door and returning a few moments later with a bucket that had seen better days.

Griselda watched him place the lumps of coal on the fire and was glad of the warmth as the flames began to take hold.

"What train are you waiting for?" the porter asked, busying himself cleaning the fallen ash from the hearth.

"The Manchester train. Why do you ask?"

"It's just that there's been an incident on the line between Whitchurch and Nantwich so they have been rerouting the Manchester trains via Wrexham and Chester, so you will have a longer journey."

"I see. What was the incident?"

"I'm not sure of all the details, miss, but I believe there's been a problem with the engine on a goods train."

"Nothing too serious then. What time does the refreshment place open?"

"Another twenty minutes," the youthful porter replied, looking at his pocket watch before leaving the room.

To idle away the time, she casually browsed through a couple of the magazines that lay about the waiting room while keeping a watchful eye on the other passengers that had started to congregate and take advantage of the warmth of the fire. Bored with people watching, she eased her way through the waiting travellers and out onto the platform and made her way to the refreshment room, which to Griselda's surprise, was relatively quiet given the number of people on the platform awaiting the arrival of trains. After purchasing something that resembled tea, she sat down at an empty table and started reading a discarded newspaper. Embroiled in the success of a German air raid, she failed to notice the railway police officer make an entrance and cast a slow searching eye around the room before coming over to where she was sitting.

"Good morning, could I ask where you are travelling to?"

Lowering the newspaper, Griselda looked at the rugged features of the mature officer and took a drink of the lukewarm tea before answering. "Manchester."

"Could I see your ticket?"

"Yes, of course, officer, is there a problem?"

"We are just making routine checks. Some people think they can travel on the railway for free, it is my job to make sure they don't."

"Have you caught anybody yet?"

"Not as yet, but the day is young," he grinned, handing back the ticket before moving off to the next table.

Griselda gave a sigh of relief, firstly, to see him leave and secondly, on hearing the arrival of the Manchester train. She walked briskly along the platform, making her way through the crowd and as the train came to a halt she was able to get a seat in a compartment in the last carriage. She began to relax as the train got underway. The previous night's ordeal – and the swaying motion of the carriage – soon lulled her into a state of drowsiness and sleep soon overtook her. Another passenger had woken her as they prepared to leave the train at Wrexham.

The one remaining seat was quickly taken, and Griselda cupped her chin in the palm of her left hand and watched the everyday workings of a busy station. As the platform began to clear, her curiosity was aroused at seeing two men in dark overcoats. They were talking to a uniformed police officer who, after looking at what was either a document or photograph, pointed the two men in the direction of the Manchester train. Griselda had an uneasy feeling. Her assault on the woman at Gloucester would have been reported to the police. Were they now looking for her? She had heard through the grapevine that checks were being made at Filton on all the personnel, and her being absent from work would have now been reported.

She lit a cigarette and began to turn events over in her mind. The personnel checks, the feeling of being followed on and off the train, then there had been the man in the compartment the previous evening who she had foolishly struck up a conversation with. The transmissions to Germany, which no doubt the British had been monitoring. Then there had been the killing of the soldier at the airfield by Guntram, it all seemed to be falling into place, if these two boarding the train were police or MI5, they could well have her description or even a photograph of her and make a search of the carriages. Griselda tried to think rationally. She knew she had to get off the train, but how?

Her only chance would be when they arrived at Chester but there could well be more waiting there to board the train and watch the platform. As the train got underway again, she stared out at farms and fields as they sped by, her mind trying to think of a way to avoid capture. Could she hide, maybe in the toilet? No, they would surely check those as they worked their way along each carriage. Was jumping off an option? She tried to anticipate the train's speed and if she would survive such a jump; time was beginning to run out for her, the distance between the stations wasn't far. She heard the squeal of the train's brakes and it started to slow down; expecting the urban sprawl of Chester to confront her, Griselda was surprised to see green pastureland on either side of the carriage as the train came to a halt.

"Not another damn signal failure. This will be the third time in the last two weeks I will have been late for work," a woman complained, her protest starting a debate among the other travellers.

Griselda knew it was going to be her one and only chance to escape. Excusing herself for the inconvenience she caused, she made for the corridor. With the discussion well underway between her fellow passengers about the hold-up, she slipped unnoticed into the passageway behind the compartment to the carriage door. Lowering the window, she checked to see if the line was clear of any oncoming trains before opening the door and climbing down onto the track bed. She waited until the train got underway and was out of sight before attempting the steep embankment to the fence below. A dilapidated gate gave her access to the field and the lane beyond which, after a few minutes of walking, brought her to a level crossing and the gatekeeper, who from the doorway of his cottage eyed her suspiciously.

"My car broke down on the main road so I set off walking, but I seem to have gone and got myself lost. Could you tell me which way I need to go to get to Chester?" She hoped her explanation for being there sounded convincing as she watched the gatekeeper's steady progress down the path to the garden gate. Leaning on the gate for support for a few moments, he then went through the procedure of rolling a cigarette before answering.

"Chester, you say?"

"Yes, that's right," Griselda answered, eager to get moving.

"So, how far have you come in that motor car of yours before it broke down?"

"I've come from Shrewsbury," she replied.

"Shrewsbury! That's a good bit of travelling you've done this morning."

"I must get to Chester, so if you don't mind ... What direction do I take?"

"Been there once, you know, when I was a youngster."

"Where, Chester?" she said, now growing irritable.

"No, Shrewsbury, didn't like the place much, glad to get home, I was ... Too many people there for my liking."

She closed her eyes and gently stroked her forehead in frustration and decided to try one more time. "Please, which way do I go to Chester?"

"Well, let's see. You want to bear left at the fork yonder, that will take you straight into Chester, mind you. It's a fair stretch of the legs from here if you are walking."

Griselda forced a smile. "It doesn't look like I've got any choice but to walk?" she answered before heading off.

Chapter 14

Will winced as he eased himself into the chair, the cushion giving him some support for his sore back. The second operation had been a long, drawn-out affair with the surgeon having to probe deeper to remove the last of the wood splinters. The winter sun felt good on his face as it filtered through the trees and glass roof of the recreation room that adjoined the hospital.

He reflected as he watched the birds, those that could stand the harsh winters. He thought back on their encounter with the German aircraft and the hard-fought battle that had ensued. It had been a close call and if it hadn't been for the timely arrival of the Wellington, the fight may well have gone in the enemy's favour. He closed his eyes and tried to put the engagement to the back of his mind and think of happier times: his leave in the Lake District and walking the coastal path with Isobel, the thoughts of more pleasurable times eventually lulling him into a deep sleep.

"And how are we this fine afternoon, Warrant Officer Madden?" Sister Murray asked.

Still deep in sleep, he cries out in despair.

"Warrant Officer, you have a visitor."

The words being delivered are with authority and sound distant and well-formed. But they have no business being here and he fights to resist any intrusion into his tranquil world. Consciousness is still far away but slowly he endeavours to claw himself back from the depths of sleep, his eyes eventually focusing on the crisp neat uniform of Sister Murray. He is awake; safe from the nightmare. He is staring wild-eyed at the nurse as he tries to moderate his breathing. "Only a dream," he says, wiping the perspiration from his brow.

Sister Evelyn Murray had seen the signs many times before in her long career, having nursed the sick and injured during two world wars. She knows what war can do to these young men. Sitting down in the seat next to him, she rested her hand gently on his arm in a show of comfort. "You are safe now," she whispered. "And what's more, you have a very attractive lady come to see you," she added in a cheerful tone. "So, we had better make you look more presentable," she smiled, easing him forward to plump up the cushions into a more uniform position. "There, is that more comfortable?"

"Yes, thanks."

"She has been quite concerned about you these last few days, rang the ward several times to see how you were getting on. Is she your young lady?"

Will didn't quite know how to answer her, so decided to be tactful. "I'm working on it, Evelyn," he replied, which earned him a look of being told off for using her first name when on duty.

"Well, I had better bring her in so you can work on her some more, the poor girl."

* * *

Isobel realised she had a touch of butterflies in her tummy as she sat waiting in Sister Murray's office. How would he react to her visiting him? Their first meeting had not got off to the best of starts; hostile would be a better word for it. She knew it was down to her own stubbornness after receiving – what did her brother call them? – a Dear John letter, from Roach.

Approaching footsteps interrupted her thoughts and made her look towards the door, only for them to pass by and recede into the distance. She walked over to the side window and took in the rolling landscape. She knew she wanted to get to know Will better, in spite of what she had said to David about having nothing further to do with airmen. She had been hurting then and felt betrayed. However, since being told a few home truths by her mother, the cliff walk together and him being hospitalised, she had realised that he had been constantly on her mind.

At first it had annoyed her, but over time, annoyance had given way to a slight tingle of excitement at the thought that, just maybe, their friendship could blossom. She found she needed walks, each one longer than the last and wishing she had Bobby, her black Labrador, to talk to. The brisk breeze and tang of the salt air had filled her with vitality during her rambles, prompting her into making that first phone call to ask how he was. Isobel was watching the first of the grey clouds rolling in from the sea, heralding the arrival of the heavy rain, when the door opened and Sister Murray came in.

"He is awake and waiting to see you."

"Before I see him, Sister, could I ask you if the operation to remove the rest of the splinters was successful?"

"Yes, it was. The surgeon was very pleased with how the operation went. He will, of course, need plenty of rest until it heals, after that, he should be fine."

"To go back flying?"

"I don't see why not if that is what he wants to do. Why do you ask?"

"No reason," Isobel replied as she was gently coaxed towards the door.

The first droplets of rain began to run down the corridor windows as she accompanied Sister Murray to the recreation room where, through the small glass pane in the door, she could see Will watching the deteriorating weather conditions.

"Before you go in to see him, there is something I must tell you. I think he has been having bad dreams since his operation. He may well tell you about them, but on the other hand he may not, so I wouldn't say anything unless he brings the subject up. What you could do is maybe ask him during your conversation together if he has been sleeping okay and see what his reaction is."

Isobel nodded. She had decided earlier to take a softly, softly approach at their first meeting and she laid a hand gently on his shoulder and kissed him tenderly on the cheek, but was more than surprised at how he responded to her tenderness.

"I'm sure you can do better than that," he said, smiling broadly.

She sat down next to him. "Yes I'm sure I can," she said, leaning across and kissing him fully on the lips.

"That's better," he said smiling.

"How are you feeling?" she asked, hoping her affectionate tone would encourage him to open up to her.

"I am a bit sore but I'm getting there."

Isobel could tell from his expression that there was something he was not telling her so decided to try another tact. "Sister Murray seems very nice?"

"Yes, she is. But she does get rather cross with me when I call her Evelyn, especially in front of the junior nurses."

"I'm not surprised, a Sister is quite a senior grade in a hospital, Will."

He grinned mischievously. "And what about the nurses?"

"There is one that is a bit stuffy, Imogen. We can't get any rapport going with her, but the rest of them are okay. One of them even knows you."

"Oh! And who might that be?" Isobel asked suspiciously.

He decided to take on a vacant stare. "Can't remember her name off hand."

"Yes, you do. Come on, tell me her name, or I'll not visit you anymore."

"You don't mean that."

"Yes, I do!"

"Her name is Morag."

Isobel thought for a few moments until the name came to mind. "Not Morag Sinclair?"

"Yes, I think that is her last name," he replied, easing himself into a more comfortable position.

"I didn't know she was back on the island."

"She has not been back long, only a couple of weeks or so. She told me you grew up together and that you were a right little tearaway when you were younger. Chasing all the boys at school, kissing them behind the bicycle shed. I got all the lowdown on you, Isobel Hamilton. Whatever would your mother say if she knew?" he said, trying to keeping a straight face.

"It's not true, none of it. Wait until I see Morag Sinclair, she will get a piece of my mind. Spreading rumours like that! I did nothing of the sort."

Will couldn't contain himself any longer and burst out laughing. "Rest assured, Morag never said anything detrimental about you. All she said was that she lived near you and you went to school together."

"You can be very irritating at times, Will Madden," she said, lightly smacking his arm before leaning back in the chair.

"Now, now, no hitting the patients. It's not allowed."

The arrival of the refreshment trolley brought about normality. After a cup of tea, Isobel thought she might try and broach the subject about the bad dreams he had been having.

"So, how have you been sleeping since your operation?"

Will stared at the rain-soaked garden for a few moments before answering. "Not very well. I have been having a lot of dreams of late."

"What kind of dreams?"

"They are bad dreams, Isobel."

"Nightmares?"

"Yes, that kind of thing."

"When did you last have one?"

"Just before you arrived."

"Tell me about it."

"Do you really want me to?" he asked, looking at her.

"Yes, I do."

He went quiet a moment as he reflected back to the earlier encounter with the *Grim Reaper.*

"We are on our way back home in a nearly cloudless sky. What cloud there is, the moon makes it look semi-transparent. There is a deathly silence in the aircraft. No sound of the engines, no cross chatter between the other crewmembers. I call out over the intercom but get no response."

"What happens next?"

"A small speck appears. I immediately bring the turret around to follow its progress but lose it in the moon's glare only for it to reappear directly behind and turning towards us."

"Go on," she said softly.

"I'm breathing heavily into my mask and I can feel the oxygen drying my mouth, I call out again over the intercom to alert the crew of the oncoming danger and to be ready to take evasive action. But my words are met with stony silence. Time seems to stand still as the spectre grows in size, as it races towards me."

"It sounds awful."

"Then comes the frightening part, Isobel. The enemy aircraft's propeller seems to turn in slow motion blotting out everything around me and I can make out the dark shape of its pilot. The terrifying spectacle makes me reel back and push hard against the turret doors behind me, trying to free myself." Will paused a few moments before continuing. "From under a draped black hood, piercing red eyes burn from a featureless skull and the figure's outstretched hand points at me. Screaming abuse, I open fire. I can see the tracer bullets hitting the aircraft, which seem to have no effect."

"Is that the end of the nightmare?"

"No."

"What happens next?"

"I'm looking up at the stars in the moonlight by the side of a large lake; the surface is like a mirror and the moon's rays reflect across its still water, and I have a feeling of inner calm. So assume I must be dead. The strange thing is, it is always the same dream," he said, smiling weakly.

"Have you told the doctor or Sister Murray about them?"

"No, I haven't. But I think Sister has an idea that something is going on. She caught me a bit wild-eyed this afternoon."

Isobel took hold of his hand. "I think you should tell someone, Will. Do you want me to mention it to Sister

Murray before I go?"

"No. I'll have a word with her when I see her. So how are the rest of the family? And has Dave been keeping out of trouble?" he asked, changing the subject.

"Mum and Dad are fine and send their love. David has been out twice while you've been in hospital, but they have had no problems, thank God."

Will nodded. "Glad to hear it," he replied, deliberately keeping off the subject of the air-sea rescue boat's encounter with the German aircraft.

"He has been seeing a lot of Catriona of late. They seem to be getting on quite well together."

"Well, she is an attractive girl, nearly as good-looking as his sister."

Isobel felt a little embarrassed but pleased by Will's remark and leaned towards him. "We were all so worried when David told us that you had been hurt and that you were undergoing immediate surgery. We could see by the look on his face how anxious he was when he told us. You know, Will, he values your friendship above everything else, but he probably wouldn't admit that if you asked him."

"I didn't realise that."

"Well, he does. In all his letters home, when you were flying together, your name would crop up somewhere. You must remember, he was only nineteen when he volunteered for aircrew and it was all a new adventure, but he soon came to realise it wasn't, we could tell that by the tone of his early letters. Then you befriended him and, with all your experience, it brought out an inner strength in him which I don't think he knew he had. He was really disappointed when you were made up to warrant officer and had to move to the officers' quarters. But please don't tell him I told you any of this, will you?"

Taking hold of her hand he smiled at her reassuringly. "I'll not say a thing."

"Do you think you will keep doing these occasional sorties when you get back to Tiree or have you had enough of flying?"

"I will never get tired of flying, there is something about it that gets in your system. You have heard seamen say, 'once the sea gets in your blood', well it's the same for me with flying. The take-off is always exhilarating. That's when you really come alive, then there is the reassuring drone of the engines and the ever-changing sky. I just love it, Isobel."

"Even when you know there is a good chance you could be shot down and killed or drowned in the freezing sea, you still want to go back and do more? Don't you think you've done enough?" She showed a little agitation at his remark.

Will could see the anxiety on her face and the realisation hit him that she was showing signs of having feelings towards him, something he had never known before.

"Does my flying worry you so much?"

"What do you think? I'd be heartless if it didn't. At least with David, we know he has a fairly good chance of coming back, being on the boats. But with you, hundreds of miles out over the sea in all kinds of weather, anything could happen. David has told us that several Met aircraft have never come back – disappeared without trace with their crews. Is that true?"

"Yes, they have lost one or two."

Isobel shook her head, getting slightly angry now. "And by all accounts from what Mum was telling me, you want to keep doing it after the war has finished."

"I've got nothing else, Isobel. No qualifications or trade, so I might as well stay in the air force if they will have me and do what I like doing best – flying. Anyway, why all the concern about me all of a sudden? I thought you had a low opinion of us RAF types at the moment."

Isobel gave him a condescending look. "A girl can change her mind if she wants to, can't she?"

Chapter 15

Griselda heard the car approaching behind her before she saw it and, with the lane not being overly wide, decided the grass verge offered her safer protection as the vehicle passed. It had taken her a little by surprise as it drew level with her and came to a halt, and the figure of a rather distinguished-looking gentleman leaned across and opened the passenger door.

"Are you the lady whose car has broken down and is trying to get to Chester?" a voice asked in a cultured tone.

"Yes, I am," Griselda answered, crouching slightly to look in and seeing what looked like a doctor's bag on the passenger seat.

"Stan told me all about it back at the crossing. Hop in, I'll drop you in the centre, it's on my way to the hospital. I've just got to pop in to see a patient of mine there. So the old jalopy's broken down on you, has it? Bad show, when they do that on you, especially out in the sticks somewhere."

"Yes, it is," Griselda responded as she settled herself into the passenger seat.

"I'm Doctor Roland Freeman, Roly to all the blighters that know me."

"Valerie Turner," Griselda replied on the spur of the moment.

"Do you work in Chester?" Freeman asked, changing

gear rather noisily. "Damn gearbox, can't get the spare parts these days to get it fixed."

Griselda knew she would have to be on her guard and pick her words carefully when she answered. "No. I'm just going up to stay with my sister in Manchester for a few days. It seems an age since I saw her last, what with the war and the petrol rationing."

"Yes, it has made things rather difficult, but I think our chaps will win the day eventually, don't you?" he smiled.

Although it annoyed her, she couldn't do anything but agree. "I hope so."

"What do you do, if you don't mind me asking?"

"Oh, nothing too exciting. I work in an office in the aircraft industry, but that's as much as I can say about it." She hoped her explanation would deter the doctor from probing further.

"I quite understand."

"You know the gatekeeper back there at the crossing quite well?"

"Stan! Yes, he and his wife are both patients of mine. We always pass the time of day together if I'm going into Chester. You wouldn't know it to look at him now, but he was quite highly decorated in the First World War, took out a Hun machine gun post single-handed while badly wounded. Salt of the earth, old Stanley."

"Brave man," Griselda answered quietly as she thought of the death of her father fighting on the Western Front against the British.

"Yes, he was. So where would you like me to drop you, the railway or bus station?" Freeman asked as they began to enter Chester's outer suburbs.

"The bus station will be fine as long as it's not taking you out of your way."

"No, not at all, glad to be of help."

Griselda waved half-heartedly as she watched the doctor drive away while hoping that around the next corner he would be involved in a road accident which would make him late for his hospital visit. The bus station was moderately busy and before crossing the road she ran a careful eye over the proceedings. Satisfied that everything looked normal, she made her way to the information booth to enquire about the time of the bus to Manchester. After purchasing a ticket and, with an hour to wait, she strolled across to a café that lay opposite the bus station which had a good view of the vehicles as they arrived.

She wondered what Guntram was doing and where he was, which brought on a feeling of apprehension, calmed slightly by her tea. Could he be following her? She had told him about her early days in Manchester and working with the Warners. Would he put two and two together and come up with the right answer? She knew he was cunning and ruthless and enjoyed killing. Would he come after her for revenge for running out on him? Panic set in for a few moments, which made her reach for her bag. She felt the smooth lines of the Walther which gave her a feeling of calm. If she had to use it to kill her lover, then so be it.

The bus was full when it left and with frequent stops to let off and pick up passengers, the journey seemed endless, eventually arriving in Manchester's central bus station. Griselda knew she would have to be careful how she contacted the Warners, making contact with other agents was strictly against the rules when on operations unless authorised by headquarters.

She made for the waiting room and, after lighting a cigarette, turned over in her mind what her options were. The easiest choice was to ring but she felt a little uneasy about doing that. One thing her relationship with Guntram had taught her was to never throw caution to the wind, check and double-check before you make a move. That way you'll live longer, he had told her.

Knowing Manchester well, she walked the streets for a while, checking at regular intervals that she wasn't being followed before she caught the tram that would take her to Warwick Road, close to where the Warners lived. Their modest house lay at the end of a quiet cul-de-sac and, surrounded by high trees, it was the ideal property to carry out their clandestine operations if they were still there.

She remembered as she walked the short distance from the tram stop that the large Victorian house on the corner of the road where the Warners lived had been turned into a hotel. She let out a sigh of relief when she saw the name board was still there, if not a little worse for wear, standing defiantly above the garden wall and, hanging in the window, a '*Vacancy*' sign. She had just been about to ring the bell when the door had opened and a rather good-looking man appeared who Griselda estimated was in his late thirties.

"Can I help you?" he asked, flashing her a smile.

"I hope so," she replied rather seductively. "I saw your vacancy sign and I'm looking for a room for two nights."

"Oh, I'm sure I can find you a nice room where you will be comfortable," he answered, guiding her with his hand to the reception desk. "Would you like to be at the back or the front of the house?"

"Definitely the front," she replied, going through the motions of filling in the visitor's book with the name on her identity card – Lillian Gilbert.

"Well, I would recommend room two at the front, it's a very nice spacious room."

"Room two it is then. Would you like me to pay now?"

she asked, conscious that he was running a wanton eye over her full figure.

"In certain cases I do ask for the tariff to be paid up front. But you look very trustworthy, so the morning you leave will be fine," he grinned, reaching for the key. "Have you any luggage?"

Griselda had to think fast for an answer. "No, I haven't. All done in a bit of a hurry this trip, but I'm sure I'll manage for a couple of days," she smiled, hoping her explanation would suffice.

"If you would like to follow me, I'll take you up to your room."

Griselda was both mildly surprised by the size of the room and pleased that it also gave a good view from the bow window of the road below and the entrance to where the Warners lived.

"Is this room satisfactory for you?"

"It's very nice, thank you," she replied as she was handed the keys.

"Breakfast is from seven until nine-thirty, and I lock the front door at eleven. If you are out after that time, you will require a pass key from the reception desk to let yourself in."

She nodded, sitting down on the bed and crossing her legs to reveal their shapely form as she watched him make for the door where he paused before opening it.

"My name is Matthew, or Matt if you prefer. If there is anything you require, you know where to find me. There is also an internal phone on the reception desk with a number on it to ring me after eleven if there's something you may need," he told her, smiling.

Griselda knew exactly what he meant – she had seen that look in men's eyes before and, in truth, it did excite her a little knowing a man was behaving that way towards her. "I'll remember that, Matt," she said, taking out her cigarettes. "Do you, by any chance, have a bar here?"

"Yes, there is a small bar in the lounge which is open all evening to the guests only."

"It sounds very nice and cosy. I'm sorry, would you like one?" she said, offering him a cigarette.

"Not just at the moment, but I would love to partake in one over a drink in the bar with you later if you are there."

Griselda took a long draw on her cigarette and slowly uncrossed her legs and reached for the ashtray. "Oh, I'll definitely be there Matthew, you can count on that."

* * *

She ate in a small café, a fifteen-minute walk from the hotel and, after calling in at a particularly noisy public house to buy cigarettes and have a drink, she arrived back at the hotel by nine. Griselda noted there were five others in the bar who greeted her with the customary "good evening" as she crossed the room and slipped onto the vacant bar stool at the end of the bar. She felt a twinge of pleasant anticipation as Matt finished serving and came over to her, bringing his drink with him and quietly asking her what she would like to drink?

"A small beer would be nice," she smiled.

"My choice exactly," he grinned, taking his own glass to top up. "Did you find the café okay I told you about?" he asked, declining Griselda's offer to pay for her drink.

"Yes, I had a very nice meal there and you certainly have some lively pubs around here. I went into the one just down the road to get some cigarettes. Things were in full swing there."

"Oh, I know the one – yes, it can get rather rowdy in

there, a lot of the factory workers use it," he said, easing closer to her.

Griselda felt the chemistry working between them, and by eleven o'clock, the rest of the guests had retired to their beds, and she was the only one left in the bar. "Well, I suppose I had better make a move," she said reluctantly, hoping her remark would create the response she wanted. Why was she so attracted to him? Hell, she knew why; he was tall, dark, very good-looking and unattached – he had told her that during the course of the evening – and there was the sexual frustration she was feeling. Sex had played a big part in her life while being with Guntram, his insatiable appetite to make love having now ended.

Matt looked at her longingly. "I don't think that is really what you want just yet, is it, Lillian?" he grinned, stroking her leg.

"What had you in mind?" she asked, moving slightly as his hand went under the hem of her skirt.

"Well, we have the bar to ourselves. All the guests are in, so we won't be disturbed. Just give me a few moments to lock up and put out the lights, then we'll have another drink."

"Sounds good to me."

"I won't be long," he said, sliding off the stool.

Griselda took the time while Matt was gone to compose herself. She had a feeling it was going to be a long night.

"Now where were we?"

"I think you were going to get us both another drink," she smiled, gently moving the stool seat from side to side.

"Lillian, can I make a suggestion?"

"I am always open to suggestions," she replied, knowing full well what was coming.

"I've an unopened bottle of malt whisky in my apartment upstairs. We could always go up there and have a nightcap, we would be a lot more comfortable than in here."

Griselda looked into his eyes. "I'm sure we would," she smiled, picking up her shoulder bag and slipping off the stool. "Lead the way!"

His apartment lay at the rear of the hotel and Griselda was more than impressed with the size and décor as she was guided into the lounge area.

"Now, drinks. Oh! I'd better get some water first."

"You have a nice place," she commented, sitting down on the comfortable sofa and took stock of the three paintings of ladies in various stages of undress and the small nude sculpture on a display cabinet.

Matt smiled when he returned and saw her looking at the paintings. "Do you like my ladies? Lovely aren't they? Let me show you Ramona in the bedroom."

Griselda was overwhelmed as the lights were turned on, revealing a bedroom planned to the last detail for seduction. The lights gave off a warm glow that was reflected back by the crimson wallpaper. A large double bed took centre stage, adorned by two stylish bedside cabinets, but the most impressive feature of the room was the large painting above the bed of a beautiful woman in a very enticing pose. Griselda took a sip of her whisky and followed the graceful lines of the woman's body.

"Is Ramona the name the artist gave her?" she asked.

"No. That's the name I gave her, it's a name I've always liked."

"Well, she is very beautiful and I'm sure she gives you a lot of enjoyment when you look at her, but you can only get pleasure from the real thing," she said, turning to face him.

"That's true," he said, softly taking her in his arms and kissing her with intense feeling.

Griselda knew the rules about getting involved in

relationships while on operations. With Guntram it had been different; with them both being on the same side and working for the same cause, their relationship had been inevitable living under the same roof. But she had been attracted to Matt when she first saw him and, although he was the enemy, she wanted him to make love to her. It had been a feeling of need that had grown ever stronger the more she got to know him. She felt her body responding to his touch. She had no will to resist as he pressed firmly against her and she put up no resistance as he slowly unbuttoned and removed her blouse.

* * *

Griselda lay still with her eyes closed. She had a feeling of contentment and satisfaction as she listened to the early morning sounds. She felt her body responding to the thoughts of their lovemaking and resisted the temptation to caress herself. Matt had been the perfect lover – not just because of his staying power but the tenderness he had shown towards her, something Guntram had never done. She felt warm and comfortable within the confines of his bed and didn't want to move, but the sound of footsteps coming up the stairs and along the landing made her open her eyes and focus on the door as it was slowly opened, and Matthew appeared carrying a cup and saucer.

"Good morning. I didn't know whether you were awake or not," he said, sitting down on the bed and placing the cup and saucer on the bedside table next to her.

She eased herself up slightly so she could drink, cautious not to show off too much of her nudity. "You were up early?"

"I had to do the breakfasts. Ruth, the lady that normally makes them, is not too well by all accounts."

Griselda read his thoughts as the cup was taken from her and she was pressed firmly against the pillow and submitted to a series of long lingering kisses. Moving her legs, she murmured as he began to arouse her sexuality. "Come back to bed," she whispered in his ear.

Pulling back gently from her, he stroked her hair, "I wish I could, but I can't. The breakfasts haven't finished yet and there is only the young waitress and myself down there, so I had better get back," he said, breaking loose from her and making for the door.

"You are a let-down, Matthew Raines, arousing a woman like that, then walking away from her."

Matt turned and looked at her. "I wasn't a let-down last night, was I? You were very vocal, if I remember rightly," he grinned, opening and closing the door behind him.

Griselda frowned, she had to admit he had taken her to the heights of ecstasy. Rolling over onto her side, her eyes settling on her underwear and clothing, which had been picked up from the floor and now lay neatly folded on a chair, which made her wonder how many female guests in the past had fallen for Matthew's charm.

After washing and dressing she made her way down to the dining room and found the place quite busy with several late risers. Griselda felt as though eyes were watching her as if the other guests somehow knew she hadn't slept in her own bed. Guilty feelings started to creep into her mind, mainly for betraying her country and sleeping with the opposing side, but what the hell, what Berlin didn't know about they wouldn't worry about, she thought, casting an eye over the menu.

After breakfast she carried her tea into the lounge and, while enjoying a cigarette, kept a constant eye on the Warners' property. To her annoyance, it showed no sign of life. Bored with her watch-keeping – and having Matthew on her mind – she decided to go up to her own room to get her coat then catch the tram into Manchester, taking a chance on making a cash withdrawal. She knew instantly that the arm that slipped tightly around her waist as she reached the top of the stairs, pulling her close, was Matthew's.

"And where do you think you're going?" he asked, rolling her fully in his arms.

"I was thinking of going into Manchester for the day," she answered, hooking her arms under his so their bodies pressed firmly together.

"You will be back tonight?" he asked, with an expression of hope on his face.

Griselda leaned forward and kissed him. "Of course I will, I haven't finished with you yet, Matthew Raines," she winked, their privacy being disturbed by a couple leaving their room.

"I'll see you later then?" he whispered before heading off downstairs.

She wasn't sure why she took one last look from her bedroom window, but she was glad she did when she caught sight of a woman in her early forties. Griselda recognised her instantly. Martha Warner gave her some hope of freedom and getting back to Germany. Snatching her bag, she hurried out, dropping her key off in the box at reception and fell into step behind Martha, a discreet distance between them.

The tram stop was quite busy, so Griselda had no problem joining the end of the queue without being seen. The only seat available on the top deck was three seats behind where Martha was sitting, but as the tram rattled its way towards the city centre, Griselda was able to move behind her as the passengers alighted at their designated stops. Confident that she wouldn't be overheard, she decided to make contact. "Don't turn round Martha. It's

Griselda. I'm in desperate need of your help. Where can I meet you?"

"I'm sorry you must have the wrong person. I don't know of anybody called Griselda," she replied, staring out through the window.

Griselda was surprised at Martha's rejection, but out of sheer desperation, decided to try again. "Please, Martha, I need your help. I'm on the run from somebody who will kill me if he finds me."

"Would you have a light?" Martha asked, resting her elbow on the back of the seat and recognising at once it was who she said she was.

"Yes, of course," Griselda said, taking out a box of matches from her bag.

"Thank you," she acknowledged, turning back to look at the busy streets below.

Griselda knew she had put Martha in a difficult position. Firstly, Martha had no way of knowing if she was still loyal to Germany or if she had been turned and recruited by the British to infiltrate their organisation.

"This is highly irregular, but I will help you for old time's sake. Do you remember the contact place in area three?"

"Yes," Griselda replied, her confidence restored by Martha's response.

"Good. I'll get off at the next stop; you go on to the one after. I'll meet you there at twelve-thirty by the bowling green. I will wait fifteen minutes. If you don't turn up, I shall leave, is that understood?"

"I'll be there, you can count on that."

* * *

Peel Park was noticeably quiet and apart from a dog walker

Griselda saw no one else until she saw Martha sitting opposite the bowling green, who immediately got up and came towards her.

"Embrace me, then start laughing as though you haven't seen me for a while, it's a precautionary measure just in case someone is watching."

They strolled at a leisurely pace, Griselda explained her dilemma, being immediately interrupted when she mentioned the name of Guntram Bayer.

"I've heard of this Guntram Bayer from another agent. Go on, what happened next?"

After narrating the remainder of her plight, Griselda stopped and turned to face her friend. "Now do you see why I'm in extreme need of your help? If he finds me, I know he will kill me."

Martha could see the fear in Griselda's eyes and tried to reverse the role and how she would have reacted if being in the same circumstances. "Where are you staying now?"

"I'm at the Raines Hotel."

"And how are you off for money?"

"I've enough to last me for a couple more days. In fact, I was going to go into Manchester and risk a withdrawal this morning until I saw you coming along the street."

"You mustn't do that. If the British are on to you, that's one of the things they will be watching for," Warner replied sharply.

"I knew it was risky, but when needs must."

"What I want you to do, Griselda, is stay where you are at the Raines until I've contacted headquarters and have some orders for you."

Griselda nodded, pleased that Martha was willing to help her even though it was in violation of Abwehr orders. "So how will you make contact with me?" she asked.

"What time is breakfast in the hotel?"

"Between seven and nine-thirty."

"Perfect. Have your breakfast early and be back in your room by eight and be ready to leave at a moment's notice. I usually walk past the Raines about five past eight to catch the tram into the city centre. Your cue to follow me will be if I stop and adjust the hat I'll be wearing. The trams are very busy at that time in the morning and will work in our favour. Make sure you stay close to me, either in the queue or on the tram, but don't speak to me. Wear the coat you have on now because sometime during that period, I will slip into your coat pocket your instructions as to what you are to do. Is that understood?"

"Yes, I've got all that."

"Now, here is some money. It isn't a lot but it will keep you going until I can arrange some more for you. God help us if ever we get back to Berlin, I'm sure we'll both be shot."

Griselda cringed at the thought. "Thanks, Martha, I'll never forget what you are doing for me."

"Anyway, I must get back to the office now, and you watch your step, okay?"

"I will," Griselda answered as she watched her walk towards the park gates without once looking back in her direction.

Chapter 16

Guntram Bayer's determination to get back to Germany took precedence over everything else; he knew the film and the information he had gathered was of vital importance and went to the very top of high command, to Hitler himself. But the disappearance of Griselda weighed heavy on his mind. It had been his intention to eliminate her before he left for Scotland; he had always prided himself on leaving no loose ends, but with her going to ground, she was now a danger to the entire operation, especially if she was caught and began to talk to try and save her neck from the noose.

The sight of a police car parked in front of the station entrance made him stop and re-think his travel plans. He fared no better at the bus station, which made him think that the police car he had stolen the night before had already been found and that he needed to get away from Stratford-upon-Avon as soon as possible. His chance came in the form of a motorcycle that had been left unattended in an alleyway. Pushing it away from the rear of the house to a nearby street, the two-stroke engine took a little coaxing before finally starting at the third attempt, filling the cool morning air with a cloud of blue smoke. Using a pre-war map, he headed in the general direction of Balsall Common, keeping as much as possible to the side roads. Skirting around Birmingham, he passed unhindered through Coleshill, the motorcycle eventually grinding to a halt on the outskirts of Lichfield, starved of fuel. A farm building in the corner of a field provided the perfect spot to conceal the stolen motorcycle. It took him a further forty-five minutes of steady walking to reach the town centre and the railway station, which was free of a police presence. After purchasing a ticket for Glasgow and with a two-hour wait for the Manchester train, he utilised the time to wash and shave in the gent's washroom and eat in the station café. It had been over thirty-six hours since he last slept and he was in the early stages of sleep as the train made its way northwards when he felt himself being gently shaken, which made him automatically reach for the knife in his pocket, but he released his grasp on it when he saw the ticket inspector looking down at him.

"Ticket please, sir."

Nodding but still not fully alert, Bayer handed him the ticket from his inside pocket.

"Change at Manchester, sir," the inspector stated, having caught a fleeting glance of a pistol in the passenger's waistband.

Manchester's Piccadilly station was bustling with activity when they arrived, and he joined the throng alighting the train. He bought a daily paper and scanned the headlines when a man's behaviour drew Bayer's attention. Keeping the newspaper up, Bayer soon picked out a second man directly opposite, using the same technique as himself to carry out his observation. The man quickly dropped his head when he saw Bayer looking at him.

A smirk spread across Bayer's face. "So you want to play that game, do you? Well, this is no second-rater you're up against here, you *trottels,*" he said quietly to himself as he cast an eye over the arrival and departure board. The Glasgow train, although at the platform, didn't leave for another twenty-five minutes, which gave him plenty of time to carry out his plan.

He made his way to the adjacent platform to the one he wanted. He knew his followers could keep him in sight and there, mingled amidst the tearful goodbyes from wives and girlfriends of sailors boarding the Newcastle train. Bayer noted that the distance between the carriages was only a few feet and the deception would come changing from one train to another without his pursuers noticing.

Reaching the front section of the train, he could hear the sound of carriage doors being closed behind him as the train prepared to get underway. Leaving it until the last minute, making sure he was seen to board by his two pursuers, he eased his way through several naval ratings to the door on the opposite side and waited. The sound of the guard's whistle being blown was the signal to put his plan into action.

"Have you done this journey to Glasgow before?" Bayer asked one of the ratings.

"It ain't the Glasgow train mate, is it, Dixie?" the rating sniggered, turning to his friend for confirmation to his question.

"What's that?" the burly seaman asked.

"This geezer here thinks he's on the bleeding Glasgow train."

"No, mate! This sod's going to Newcastle. That's the train you want, there," he said, pointing at the neighbouring train.

Bayer gave a look of surprise as he felt the train begin to move off. "Well, there's only one thing to do," he answered, dropping the carriage door window and reaching for the handle.

"You can't do that mate, you'll kill yourself!" the ratings shouted.

"Watch me!" he cried out, sitting down in the open doorway, then using the running board for support, he launched himself onto the track bed below. He landed hard but was able to stay on his feet, coming to a stop several yards in front of the stationary Glasgow train.

"You crazy bastard!" the sailor shouted, closing the carriage door.

Bayer sprinted across the lines in front of the train to the ramp and onto the platform, all unobserved by the waiting engine crew. He found a compartment occupied by an elderly couple. Sliding back the door, he asked if the remaining seats were taken, only to be told in a broad Scots accent that they weren't. Bayer was glad they didn't want to engage in conversation as the old man settled down to read a book and the woman to her knitting, giving him time to plan his next move. He couldn't foresee any problems for his onward movement into the Highlands. The difficulty would be stealing a boat and sailing to Stracandra Island before the boat's owner realised it was missing and alerted the authorities.

"Would it be Scotland you're making for?" the old lady asked, taking a respite from her knitting.

"Yes, it is," Bayer acknowledged, looking at the old lady, which brought thoughts of his own mother back in Germany.

"On leave, are you?" she asked, removing her glasses to massage her tired eyes.

Bayer didn't like being questioned about his movements, so he decided to bring the conversation to a close. "You could say that. But if you don't mind, I'd like to try and catch up on some rest as I have been travelling for quite some time," his tone was sharp, which had the desired effect.

The compartment's shaded lights gave off an eerie glow as he woke from his slumber to find the train at a standstill.

The couple in the opposite corner were both asleep, so, cautiously, he eased back the blind. The track ahead curved to his advantage and he could make out in the distance the red stop light glowing in the mist that covered the surrounding landscape.

Bayer had no way of knowing where they were or how long they had been stationary. He calculated roughly that they must be in the Cumbria area. The sound of muffled voices and doors being opened and closed put him on alert; quietly leaving his seat so as not to awaken his fellow travellers, he opened the compartment door. The subdued blue bulbs gave off little light along the corridor, but Bayer's expertise in recognising danger when it was close at hand put him immediately on the defensive as the two men in civilian clothes came towards him.

"Going somewhere, are we?" the lead man asked in a surly voice while blocking the corridor with his large frame.

"I was going to the lavatory if you must know."

"Where did you board the train?" the second man enquired in a more polite manner.

Bayer studied the two men for a few moments before he answered. "What's this all about, and who are you people?" he asked, his hand clasping the knife hilt in his pocket.

"We are with the Railway Police, now just answer the question!"

Bayer knew if push came to shove, he would need an edge if he had to kill the larger of the two men. His heavy build would warrant him killing him as quickly as possible so he could turn his attention on the second man and eliminate him before he could retaliate or raise the alarm.

"I got on the train in Manchester," he answered, then realised through tiredness, he had made a fatal error and should have said Lichfield.

"And where are you making for?" the larger of the two men asked.

"Scotland."

"What station in Scotland?" the second man queried.

"Glasgow."

"And you say you got on the train in Manchester?"

Bayer knew he had backed himself into a corner if they asked to see his ticket. "Yes, that's right,"

"That is rather strange; the ticket inspector on the train from Lichfield reported a man fitting your description being on that train. He described your height, build and even the clothes you are wearing, exactly," the heavily-built officer answered, his face only inches away from Bayer's.

"Well, he must be mistaken, mustn't he?"

"Maybe. But we can soon clear this up, can you show us your ticket?" the smaller man asked.

Guntram Bayer knew the game would be up as soon as he produced the ticket, so now was the time to make his move while the train was at a standstill and he could make good his escape. But he still needed a slight edge, or better still, a distraction.

"Before I show you my ticket, can I see some identification to prove you are who you say you are?" Bayer asked, his hand easing the knife from his pocket.

Neither men spoke but, in unison, reached in their inside pockets to take out their relevant identification cards.

That split second was all Bayer needed as both men were distracted; with lightning speed, he drove the knife blade deep into the large man's chest. Although badly hurt, the man lunged forward with the ferocity of a raging bull. His action made Bayer take several steps backwards, which gave him the space he needed to make a second strike in the area of the man's heart.

The policeman sank slowly onto the carriage floor, clutching his chest. The quick reaction of the second police officer took Bayer by surprise. The officer launched himself over his colleague, his momentum taking Bayer to the floor with the man on top of him, his hand gripping his wrist in a vice-like hold. Unable to use the knife, he struck out in desperation at the man's head with his left fist but with little effect. Bayer couldn't believe the man's strength for his size as he returned stinging blows from his fist and a head butt which burst Bayer's nose, the blood temporarily blinding the vision in his right eye.

Bayer recognised a street fighter when he saw one and knew he had to end this as quickly as possible before help came from either a fellow passenger or the train guard. Pushing upwards but still taking punches, he managed to grip the handle of the Walther and, with his remaining strength, forcing the gun's barrel into the man's stomach, the two shots ceasing the man's fighting spirit.

The fight and shots had brought about a flurry of activity from the other compartments as doors were opened and figures appeared, shocked at what they saw.

"Get back in your compartments before I kill you all!" he shouted in rage, firing a shot at random into the carriage woodwork, sending splinters flying into the air. Moving back cautiously to his compartment, he found the Scottish couple cowering in the corner. He slid back the door to retrieve his bag. Levelling the Walther at them, he had just been about to eliminate them to stop them giving his description to the police when the uniformed figure of the guard appeared, shouting at him to stop. Wiping away the blood from his face, Bayer managed to raise a smile at the guard's audacity as he aimed and fired, the bullet sending him reeling backwards against the wood panelling behind before sliding down onto the floor blood seeping through a neat hole in his white shirt.

Turning his attention back towards the terrified couple, who were now pleading not to be killed, Bayer suddenly had a slight feeling of remorse; the old woman now begging was so much like his own mother in many ways. Did it justify killing them when all the carriage had seen his face and could give the police a good description? Hell, he'd have to kill everyone in the carriage to stop that happening, and he had neither the time nor ammunition to carry that out.

"It's your lucky day," he smirked, closing the compartment door.

* * *

Crossing the down lines, Guntram scrambled up the steep embankment. Stopping at the top to catch his breath, he looked down on the stationary train and listened to the shouts of the panic-stricken passengers. Bayer knew it wouldn't be long before a hue and cry went out, baying for his blood. He needed to put as much distance between himself and the train before the area was sealed off by the authorities. Climbing over a dry stone wall, he dropped down onto pastureland and set off at a steady pace, the wet grass soon penetrating his shoes while the dense mist reduced his visibility to only a few yards.

The sound of movement brought him to a standstill as he strained to hear what direction it was coming from. Drawing the Walther, he crouched down to make himself a smaller target as he slowly swept the area in front of him for any sign of human activity. A movement to his left and centre made him immediately flatten out, the wet grass quickly seeping through his clothing into his tired body. Reluctant to fire at a target he couldn't see, all he could do was wait for whatever materialised. It had been the characteristic bleat of a sheep that he first heard before the black face of the animal appeared, its facial expression showing signs of utter fright which quickly made it dart back into the safety of the mist for protection, unaware how close it had come to getting a bullet between its eyes.

Cursing, Bayer stood up and put the Walther back in the waistband of his trousers. He soon began to realise he was becoming disorientated in the swirling mist, so he decided on a change of direction which brought him to an overgrown hedgerow, its centre entwined with rusted barbed wire. Instinct told him to go left which brought him to a wooden gate and a well-used farm track. A dog barking in the distance helped him decide which direction he should take.

Keeping between the water-filled ruts, Bayer eventually came to a two-lane highway. The lack of any traffic and with no idea where he was, Bayer decided it was safe to keep to the road. It was easier walking, and there was the possibility of finding some form of transport. He passed and ignored several farm entrances – the risk of dogs alerting the sleeping household worried him – and he was close to the limit of his endurance when the dark shape of a small cottage materialised. Adjacent to the garden wall was a crudely erected wooden lean-to and, under it, Bayer could make out the distinctive lines of a van. On closer inspection, he found the driver's door unlocked and the key in the ignition.

"There must be a God," he whispered to himself, throwing his travel bag onto the passenger seat as he slipped in behind the wheel. Turning the key, he pulled the starter knob. The cold engine was reluctant to start, taking its toll on the van's battery, and he thought he was going to have to abandon the idea when the engine suddenly burst into life. Leaving the lights off, he hastily reversed it out onto the road.

He was sure the van's noisy engine would rouse its owner from sleep. Surprised at no movement from within the confines of the cottage, he took his time to locate the switch for the vehicle's lights before moving off and was thankful that the mist was beginning to lift as he eased his way along the road.

He reached a main road. Turning left, he accelerated through the gears and soon caught sight of the single red rear light of a lorry whose driver seemed to be keeping up a good average of speed for the conditions. It wasn't long before the dark shapes of buildings appeared, and Bayer realised he was coming into a large town; it was a small sign above a shop advertising Kendal Mint Cake that tipped him off as to where he was.

Bringing the van to a stop, he studied the map for a few minutes. He knew it would be foolhardy to keep to the main roads: as the police would by now be setting up roadblocks on all the main routes, although he did find it strange that there didn't seem to be any police activity in the town centre. The map showed his choices were limited: the A685 to Low Borrowbridge, then cut across country using the rural back roads to the A66 seemed his best chance to avoid capture.

* * *

The police checkpoint had been strategically placed on a stretch of the road, which had no side roads to escape, so all Bayer could do was sit and wait, using the time to check the Walther for ammunition. As he edged closer to the inspection point, he noticed, set back off the road, an army vehicle.

Soldiers were assisting the police in their searches. With his cover story ready and his coat half unbuttoned for quick access to his weapon, he eased slowly forward, winding down the side window.

"Could I ask you where you have come from, sir?" the police officer asked, stooping to look in the van.

"I've come from my farm near Killington," Bayer answered, the name he'd picked at random from the map while he had been sat waiting.

"What's the name of this dung hole?" the soldier enquired.

Bayer looked at the two men for a few moments to think of a name before responding. "High Vale and I don't care much for your tone," he replied, focusing his attention on the soldier.

"I'm sorry about that, sir," the constable cut in, looking at the soldier, then at Bayer. "It's just that there has been a rather nasty incident on a train and the perpetrator who carried out the act is on foot and somewhere in the area."

"Oh, I see. Anybody hurt?" Bayer asked with a look of concern.

"Yes, I'm afraid there have been some fatalities," the police officer said quietly.

"I'm sorry to hear that."

"So could I ask you where you are making for, sir?"

Bayer knew he'd got the young officer onside with his caring manner. "I'm on my way up to Brough to pick up some bags of cattle food for my livestock."

"I see. Have you seen anybody on foot or trying to get a lift since leaving home?"

"No, I haven't seen anybody."

"Can we check the rear of the van?" the soldier asked in a more agreeable manner.

"Help yourself. I think the back doors are unlocked," Bayer replied, twisting around in his seat to watch the proceedings.

"Thank you, sir. You can be on your way now," the police officer said, switching off his torch after their inspection, conscious of the build-up of traffic waiting behind.

Chapter 17

Maynard's face had a look of weariness on it. The frustration at getting no nearer to catching Gilbert or *The Raven* and the lack of a decent night's sleep was beginning to show. He had been in Manchester interviewing the two railway police officers and the ticket collector from the Lichfield train when he was given the details about the incident at Kendal, which Maynard knew instinctively was *The Raven's* handiwork. It had been early afternoon by the time transport had been organised to Kendal police station and the opportunity to see the carriage where the killings had taken place.

"You have to walk across the field, sir, to where that police officer is to get down to the railway line," the young constable told him, pointing to where he had to go.

"Is Detective Inspector Vines there?"

"Yes, he is, sir."

Maynard reached the top of the banking and was immediately met by a police sergeant accompanied by a constable.

"Can I help you?" the sergeant asked.

He showed the officers his identity card. "I believe Inspector Vines has been told I'm coming."

"He has, sir. If you would like to follow me, I'll show you where he is. It is rather a mess in there."

"Three dead I was told?" Maynard said, noting the look

of revulsion on the sergeant's face.

"Yes, that's right. And by all accounts, it could have easily been more. If you would like to climb aboard here, sir, you will find the inspector in there."

He climbed up to where he was confronted by a tall, lean-looking man in a dark grey suit.

"You must be Henry Maynard from MI5?" he said, holding out his hand for Maynard to shake.

"That's right. So what have we got, Inspector?"

"If you would like to follow me to the next coach, I'll show you. It's a bit of a bloodbath in there. I hope you aren't squeamish?"

"No, not in the least. I've seen what this man's capable of before."

Vines immediately stopped before entering the connecting passageway between the two carriages, turned, and looked hard at Maynard. "You know who the man is that did this?"

"I've a good idea. But I'll probably be able to tell you more when I've seen the bodies. Tell me, Inspector, have all the victims been shot?"

Vines didn't answer straight away but held Maynard's gaze. "Why do you ask that?"

"Because, if it's the man I think it is, he is also quite handy with a knife."

"Well, as a matter of fact, one of the officers has stab wounds."

Maynard filled his pipe, lit it, then flicked the used match through the open carriage window. "That sounds like our man."

"So, how many has he killed?"

Maynard took a long draw on his pipe. "With these three last night, that's six that we know about."

"My God! And do you have a name for this madman?"

"At the moment, we don't. All we have is a code name which we have got through his transmissions to Germany. *The Raven.*"

"So what has this chap been up to, apart from murdering people?"

"I can't divulge that, Inspector, but what I will say is that it is imperative we stop him one way or another before he gets back to Germany with the information he knows."

"That serious, is it?"

"Yes, it is. It could prolong the war," Maynard emphasised.

"Have you any idea where he might be trying to get to?"

"My guess is Scotland and some remote stretch of coast where he can be picked up by submarine, as regards where that could be?" Maynard shrugged his shoulders while taking a few moments to ponder over his remark. "We really need to find this character before he reaches the border and disappears into the Scottish Highlands."

Vines frowned. "We have roadblocks set up on all the major roads around the area and police vehicles patrolling the side roads, so I'm sure something will turn up, given time."

Maynard gave Vines a worried look. "That's something we haven't got. This man is extremely good at what he does and is always that one step ahead of us. He seems to take pleasure in killing, although up to now it's only been people in authority; a soldier, two ordinary police officers and these three last night. What does worry me is how long it will be before some member of the public gets hurt."

"The Scottish couple who he had shared the compartment with came very close to being shot. He levelled his weapon at them. But then for some reason decided against it after shooting the guard."

"Did he say anything to them?"

"As a matter of fact, he did," Vines replied. "He said, 'it's your lucky day', before closing the compartment door. He must have had a change of heart."

"I doubt that, Inspector. It's more likely he was preserving his ammunition. Where are the witnesses being held?"

"We've set up an incident room in the village hall, they are being looked after there. The Scottish couple has really taken it badly, as you would when a gun is pointed at you. The local doctor is keeping an eye on them due to their age."

"I'll speak to them after I've seen the carnage in here."

"Vines frowned in a manner to warn Maynard that what he was about to see wasn't pleasant. And, as distressing as it was, Maynard noted every detail: the positions of the three bodies, the random bullet hole in the woodwork, the compartment *The Raven* had used and the seating positions of its three occupants.

"This is the door he left by?" Maynard asked, standing and looking across the track bed and up the banking, noting the indentations in the flattened grass.

"That's right. We followed the footprints up and over the banking and halfway across the field, then we lost them due to a flock of sheep milling about. There is a gate on the far side of the field that leads to a farm track and eventually to a road, so it looks like that's the route your man took," Vines replied, excusing himself on hearing his name being called. "Yes, what is it, Sergeant?"

"Information has just arrived from Kendal police station that could be connected to what has happened here, sir."

"And that is?" Vines asked, climbing down from the carriage, closely followed by Maynard.

"The station has had a call from a Mr Draper. He has a

smallholding about a mile from here."

"Go on, Sergeant, what about this Mr Draper?" Vines said impatiently.

"He's had his van taken, sir. Sometime during the early hours of this morning."

"Have we got a full description of the vehicle?"

"Here are the details, and it has been passed on to all the roadblocks."

"Thank you," Vines replied, taking the sheet of paper but noticing that the sergeant seemed hesitant to leave. "Is there something else?" he asked sharply.

"I'm afraid there is, sir. A van fitting that description was let through the roadblock on the A685."

"What time was this?" Maynard asked, breaking in on their conversation.

"I don't know that, sir."

"Then bloody well find out!" Vines snapped.

"Right, sir!"

"One moment before you go, Sergeant, with your approval, Inspector?"

Vines nodded in acknowledgement.

"Would you do something for me?"

"If I can, sir!"

"Will you find out from Mr Draper roughly how much fuel was in the van when it was taken and why it took him so long to report the theft? Also, can you find out the particulars of the vehicle, like its engine size, fuel tank capacity, and how many miles to the gallon it does? You know the kind of thing."

"I'll get on to it right away, Mr Maynard."

"Thank you, Sergeant ...?"

"Croft, sir."

"Right off you go, Croft," Vines said in a more amenable

manner.

"Well, Inspector, there's not much more we can do here. Shall we go and interview the witnesses and see what facts we can acquire from them?"

The bulk of the witnesses' information about the incident was sketchy. The Scottish couple was able to provide Maynard with a good description of *The Raven's* appearance and what had been said in conversation between them, albeit only briefly.

Back at Kendal police station and snacking on sandwiches, washed down with a large pot of tea, Maynard eyed the clock on the wall and knew time was running out for them. Losing interest in the half-eaten sandwich, he got up and walked over to the window and stared at the rain as it beat against the glass pane. The sound of a vehicle coming to a stop and the opening and closing of a car door made him turn and focus his attention on the incident room door. A loud, irritable voice barked orders before the door slammed open, banging hard against a filing cabinet.

"Problem?" Maynard asked, retaking his seat.

"You could say that," Vines replied, throwing himself into a chair and stroking his forehead. "A police patrol car has reported seeing a van fitting the description of Draper's on the A66 near Temple Sowerby at around 07.30 and, because it was being driven in a proper manner and it hadn't been reported stolen, the police officer had no reason to stop it."

Maynard made a facial expression of displeasure. "Damn it ... Damn it! Did Sergeant Croft get the information I asked for?"

"Yes, I have it here," Vines replied, reaching into his inside pocket.

"And the reason why Mr Draper didn't report the theft

of his van until mid-morning?" he asked, taking the sheet of paper from Vines.

"There lies another story. By all accounts, our Mr Draper is having a fling with a local widow woman who lives down the road from him at Natland, so he didn't arrive back to his smallholding until after nine and saw his van had gone. His telephone was out of order and he had to cycle back to his lady friend and use hers to contact us, so we didn't receive the call until 09.35."

"By which time our German bird was well on his way."

"I'm afraid so."

"Well, what's done is done, Inspector. What have we got here?" Maynard answered, unfolding the information sheet he had been given and beginning to read it out loud. *"The Fordson E83W has a 10 horsepower engine with a top speed of about 40mph. Its tank holds seven gallons of petrol and it does about twenty-five miles to the gallon."*

"And Mr Draper said the tank was over half-full. He estimates there were about four gallons in it when it was taken," Vines added.

"So, if we say twenty-five to the gallon, four gallons roughly gives *The Raven* a hundred-mile radius. We don't by any chance have a compass, do we, Inspector?" Maynard asked, getting up and walking over to a large map of the area.

"Williams, bring the compass over here, pronto."

"So, Inspector. An inch is four miles according to your map. So six inches is twenty-four miles," Maynard said, spreading the two points to the right length and turning it over four times. "That is ninety-six miles to there," he said, drawing a pencil line to the north of Moffat. "After that, our man has either to steal more petrol or dump the van and find another mode of transport."

"That's if he's using the A74, there are several alternative routes he could use," Vines pointed to the map.

Maynard didn't answer straight away but stood scrutinising the map. "Where would I be making for if I was in his shoes? Scotland is such a large area, it could be anywhere; there's a hundred and one places he could go to meet a submarine. Look at all these remote bays and coves along the coast of Galloway. But you know, Inspector, with all the choices he's got, I still think it will be the Highlands and the coast up there where he is trying to get to … But God help me if I'm wrong!"

Vines sighed. "Well, the Scottish police are on full alert, so it looks like we are back to the waiting game again, I'm afraid."

* * *

Bayer felt quite pleased with himself evading the police roadblock like he had. Driving along the coastal route towards Ruthwell, the road then swung northwards towards Clarencefield, which had, according to his map, several large woodland areas where he could possibly hide the van and make good his escape by way of the railway that passed close by. Driving at a reasonable speed so as not to attract attention and also conserve what little fuel was left in the fuel tank, he eventually saw what he was looking for: a single track road with a bridge over the railway line that ran through a cutting below.

Activity around the farm buildings adjacent to the tracks made him look for another alternative, which he found, but with one drawback. The road ran under the railway line, which put paid to his plan for boarding a passing train. However, it did give good access to the wooded area beyond and the road seemed to have seen little use with grass growing up through its cracked surface. With the end of the road in sight, which gave way to a pathway, and with thoughts of turning the van around, he saw what looked like the remnants of a cart track.

Stopping the van, he ran a careful eye over the entrance. Although overgrown and narrow, it did offer a solution to his predicament. Bayer was surprised how the van made easy work of the difficult conditions as he pressed deeper into the dense undergrowth, the track eventually ending beside a pool of stagnant water. Switching off the engine, he got out and cautiously retraced the route he had taken and was pleased to see the van's entry had left very few visible signs. Returning, he then spent a vigorous half-hour covering the rear of the vehicle completely with small branches. He knew he needed sleep before nightfall so he could undertake the next part of his plan, but he had one necessary task to do before he settled down in the van's interior: to find the easiest way to the edge of the wood and shortest distance across the open ground to the bridge over the railway line. With perseverance, he eventually found a route he could follow in the darkness, which led him to the open field.

* * *

He felt comfortable and surprisingly warm as his eyes became accustomed to the dark surroundings. He had slept for a full eight hours according to his watch. Opening the van door he threw out his travel bag then eased himself out into the cold night air, which quickly revived him from his drowsiness. A clear sky and a full moon made following the route to the edge of the wood easy, there he stopped to take in the open ground he had to cross, looking for any movement in the vicinity of the farm and its buildings on the far side of the bridge. Satisfied all seemed quiet, he set off at a leisurely pace, never taking his eyes off the farm buildings. Reaching the bridge, he set about lengthening the strap on his bag. With it firmly positioned across his back, he peered down, the tracks prominent in the moon's glare. He didn't have long to wait before he heard a train approaching; a south-bound passenger train speeding towards Carlisle, its noise making Bayer wonder how anybody could sleep living so close to the tracks as the farmhouse was.

The first of the up trains was a passenger train which he ignored. The second he recognised as a goods train working hard with its heavy load on the uphill gradient. Crouching behind the wall so as not to be seen by the engine crew, he let the engine pass under the bridge, then standing directly over the centre of the line, he watched the different variety of mixed freight wagons make their steady progress towards him. The three box vans attached to the train were at the end. The second one, Bayer noticed, was coupled to the guard's van, and although blacked out he felt sure it would be occupied.

Quickly positioning himself on the opposite wall, he timed the jump perfectly, landing in the middle of the roof, laying still for a few moments, then easing himself over to the side of the van. He looked down at the doors below. The cold night air stung his face and penetrated his clothing and he knew he had to get inside or freeze to death. The two doors he could see were only fastened by a hinged device that was held together with what looked like a substantial pin on a chain. Although the train's speed wasn't fast, Bayer knew trying to open the door while clinging to the van's side would be highly dangerous. One mistake, and he could fall, even be killed, but he knew he had to try.

He decided, before attempting the risky manoeuvre, to

see if there was an easier way to reach the doors from between the vans. Keeping flat, he pushed himself forwards along the roof until he reached where he could look down over the end and saw there were two large freight doors held in place by a securing bar down the middle. Shivering intensely now from the cold, this way seemed the better of the two options. He slowly let his body slide over the edge of the swaying roof, his right foot eventually locating the central bracket that held the door locking bar in place. The ball of his foot quivered uncontrollably as it took the weight of his body, but it did give him the support he needed to get a better hold, hooking his hands through a gap between the top of the doors and the framework.

Bayer felt the train's speed increase as it reached the top of the gradient, the momentum buffeting him against the cargo doors and as the track raced by below, the noise became deafening from the coupling and buffers as they took the strain of the heavy load. Releasing his grip with his right hand, he reached down to try and grasp the handle to unlock the doors.

He had been within fingertip distance when the inevitable happened. Losing his foothold, he found himself hanging precariously by his left hand. Screaming with the intense pain from his stretched muscles, he knew he couldn't hold on for much longer. Bayer desperately try to find something to grip onto to stop his downward descent to certain death under the wheels.

Cut, bruised and with the weight of the bag on his back pulling him down, Bayer knew he was out of options. So with last thoughts of his family and satisfied, he had done his best for the Fatherland, he let go. Sliding down, he shouted obscenities from the extreme pain as the door hinges ripped his clothes and tore at his skin.

Falling heavily, he came to rest wedged between the buffer and the coupling chain. The travel bag had saved him from falling through onto the tracks below. His saviour came from the door handle that hung downwards and within arm's reach. With a combination of effort and determination, he eventually pulled himself up into a standing position. Bracing himself, he opened the van door that revealed a mixed load of boxed and bagged produce that was for victualling a ship, its name stamped clearly for all to see. After throwing his travel bag into the space between the top of the load and the van roof, he climbed inside, tying the doors together with twine he cut from the boxes.

Chapter 18

Wearing only her underwear, Griselda walked from the bedroom to the bathroom and looked at herself in the mirror. A smile spread across her face as she saw that her breasts were still firm from her lovemaking with Matthew. She had always enjoyed sex whatever time of day, but there was something incredibly relaxing about doing it in the morning.

Matt had brought out the animal in her the night before, which had been intense, but the few hours of sleep, then his gentle caresses, had awakened her womanly passion. She dressed, putting on the silk stockings Matt had given her: "ask no questions and I'll tell you no lies," he had said to her, winking. Most likely from the black market, she thought, smoothing down her skirt, then standing to admire her appearance in the mirror.

There were the usual early morning risers in the dining room who acknowledged her when she entered, plus a young couple who Matt had said were there for a couple of nights of "hanky panky", and by the speed they consumed their breakfast and left the room giggling, Griselda suspected their bed was going to see more action.

Drinking her tea at the table by the window, which Matthew knew she liked, she was beginning to have concerns about the length of time it was taking Martha to make contact. She had told Matt that she would now require the room for the week, but after their first night together he had just grinned and said, "Why? You won't be using it." She had finally been able to persuade him to let her keep the room so as not to arouse the suspicions of the other guests that they were lovers, which he agreed to.

She was up in her room by the allotted time and standing partly concealed by the curtain. She drew on a cigarette as she watched the road for any sign of movement from the Warner house. She was distracted by the sounds of lovemaking coming from the adjacent room, which brought a smile to her face as she thought of her own indulgence earlier. Martha was almost opposite the hotel when Griselda saw her and she nearly missed the pre-arranged signal of her adjusting her hat, which meant she had to follow her. Quickly grabbing her bag and coat, she left the room, closing the door quietly behind her, then descending the stairs in an unhurried manner, hoping she wouldn't see Matthew in reception, who no doubt would want to know where she was going.

She wasn't able to get close to Martha while waiting for the tram, but with standing-room-only on the lower deck, she did eventually, by various means, get close enough for the transfer of information to be made without any exchange of words from either woman. Alighting the tram at the next stop, she kept walking, deliberately paying the passengers no heed as it rattled on its way. Reaching the next tram stop, she was able to get a seat for the ride into the city centre. Buying a morning paper, she then chose one of the larger cafés, purchased a cup of tea and made for one of the quieter tables away from prying eyes. Using the newspaper as a shield, she opened the envelope, which contained a quantity of money and a rail ticket to Southampton and instructions telling her to go to the Tudor House Hotel at the address given where she would be contacted in due course.

Griselda was angry with the orders. She wanted to go home. The strain over the last six-and-a-half years was beginning to show both mentally and physically. "Christ! Haven't I done enough for the Third Reich?" she said to herself while putting the letter and money into her bag. She was just about to get up to leave when she thought of Matthew. Telling him she was going to leave the following morning would be the hardest part.

For the next few hours, she wandered the streets, going in and out of the stores that hadn't been damaged by the bombing while turning things over in her mind. She thought of the many lies she had told him: where she came from, the false name and being in Manchester to visit a sick aunt. They weighed heavily on her mind, but what annoyed her most were the feelings she was now having for him and for a damned Englishman of all people. She made her way back to the hotel sometime in the middle of the afternoon. Matthew was in reception when she got back booking in a new arrival and, on seeing her, he beckoned with his eyes for her to go into the lounge.

"Had a good day?" he asked, closing the door behind him.

"I spent the day with my aunt," she said.

"How is she?"

"A lot better, thanks."

"You will have to bring her over when she has fully recovered so I can meet her."

Griselda smiled weakly, the constant lying irritating her. "I will!"

"Good, that's settled then. Would you like a drink? There's something I'd like to ask you."

Griselda was both surprised and intrigued by his remark. "Bit early for the bar being open, isn't it?" she said, glancing at her watch.

"It's open when I say so," he winked, going behind the bar.

She watched him fill the glasses. "So what is it you want to ask me?"

"Where to begin?" he said, bringing over the drinks and sitting down next to her.

"I think from the beginning."

"Well, you know my wife Helen was killed in one of the early bombing raids."

Griselda was wondering where Matthew was going with this.

"Since her death, I won't deny it, I have had a few relationships with ladies, mostly through them staying here at the hotel."

"Like me, you mean?" she replied. "And I would think it's more than just a few Matthew Raines, by the seductive décor in your bedroom. It's like a bordello in there."

"Yes, I know, but that could soon be altered … if—"

"If what?" Griselda interrupted.

"If … if you would stay here and help me run the place. You must know how I feel about you? I'm crazy about you, Lillian. And I'm sure you must feel the same way."

This was one thing Griselda hadn't anticipated. She knew their relationship over the last four nights had been a fairly torrid affair, but for Matthew to ask her to come and live with him and help run the hotel caught her completely off guard. "It's not possible, Matthew, I have my life back home, my work, I can't just drop everything like that," she blurted out, furious at putting herself into such a situation as this.

"But why not?" Matthew persisted, gently resting his hand on hers.

"Because I can't. And that's an end to it," she said, pulling her hand out from under his. "We've had our fun, in fact, I was going to tell you this evening that I'm leaving in the morning and for you to make my bill up."

"But I don't want you to leave," he said, getting up and standing in front of her before she could reach the door. "I'm in love with you."

Griselda felt herself begin to weaken as Matthew put his arms around her and slowly pulled her towards him. He kissed her; a kiss with such passion that she closed her eyes to hold back the tears. The sound of the reception bell put an end to their embrace, which Griselda was thankful for, at least it would give her a chance to think of a plausible idea to curtail Matthew's enthusiasm for her to come and live with him.

"We'll speak later, now go and see who wants you at reception, it may be someone wanting a room." Going to her own room, she packed the few items of clothing she had bought during her stay into a small second-hand suitcase which she had bought during one of her visits to Manchester. Drawing the curtains, she switched on the bedside light, kicked off her shoes and, laying on the bed, tried to think how to get out of the awkward situation she had got herself into.

In her heart, she knew if it was peacetime, she would have accepted Matthew's offer without any hesitation. But these were no ordinary times. Matthew – although she was beginning to fall for him – was still the enemy. And she had a job to do.

* * *

It was the sound of voices and rail traffic being shunted nearby that woke him. Light streamed in through the crack above the door and Bayer soon realised he was in a busy goods terminal, but where? He had no way of knowing. Cursing his stupidity for falling asleep, he had no option but to wait out the daylight hours until nightfall. Hungry, he snacked on the contents of the ship's supplies, but with the constant threat of detection by the rail staff, he kept the Walther close at hand in case he had to make a break for freedom.

The hours seemed to drag by. To his relief, no attempt was made to unload the rail van he was in, and as the late afternoon light began to fade into darkness, Bayer noticed a drop in noise outside. "Most likely the changeover period," he said to himself, pushing open the door and climbing down onto the buffer where he waited a few moments to listen before jumping down onto the track bed. It took him a good twenty minutes to work his way through the lines of stationary trucks to the side of the goods yard, which, to his annoyance, he found was protected by a high brick wall topped with broken glass to stop intruders. With no chance of making good his escape that way, he had no alternative but to try and find another way out. Keeping in the shadow of the wall and hidden by the lines of goods wagons, he felt his way along in the darkness, which eventually opened out into a large area where the lines branched off into several large freight sheds, their entrances lit by overhead lamps. With the sound of the night staff in the vicinity and engine movement from within one of the sheds, he decided his best course of action was to retrace his steps. But turning, he was confronted by a torch beam being shone in his face.

"Who are you? And what are you doing here?" a voice asked in a broad Scottish accent.

"I work here," Bayer replied, shielding his eyes with his left hand as his right hand went down for the knife in his pocket.

"I've not seen you before. What's your name?"

"Blake … Harry Blake. And I only started tonight," Bayer answered, edging closer to his victim.

"Alastair never said there was anyone new starting tonight."

"Who's Alastair?" Bayer queried, now within striking distance.

"You don't know who Alastair Logan is? He is the night shift supervisor. I think you had better come with me," the Scotsman said.

Bayer's response was both quick and deadly. "I don't think so." He forced the man back against the open door of an empty rail van and drove the knife into the man's heart, covering his mouth to stifle his scream. Keeping the lifeless body upright with his own weight, he managed to lift and roll the corpse into the van and quietly close the door.

Steady rain started to fall as he walked the dark city streets, the dash from the scene of his last murder, hiding from passing trains and the climb up the bridge buttress to the street above had all added to his weariness; he needed a good night's sleep before attempting the final phase of his journey. He knew his only chance of finding somewhere to stay for the night in a place the size of Glasgow was to ask – not his normal way of doing things, but under the circumstances, his only hope. Passengers alighting from a tram gave him the opportunity he was looking for. Knowing the aggressive manner of his last encounter with a Scotsman, he wondered if their women might be more amenable as his eyes lighted on three girls, obviously friends by their chatter as they came towards him.

"Evening, ladies! I've just arrived in Glasgow and wondered if you know of lodgings close by where I could get a room for the night?" he asked politely.

"Aye!" The middle girl answered immediately. "Just walk along Paisley Road here until you come to a major fork. Bear right there, and you are in Edmiston Drive, that's Ibrox. You will see the Glasgow Rangers Football Ground on your right, there are several guesthouses around there."

"Thanks!" Bayer replied, smiling.

"You're welcome," the prettiest of the three girls answered flirtatiously, which set the other two off giggling.

* * *

The glow from the unshaded lightbulb gave the room a dismal feel as it illuminated its sparse contents. Bayer shivered from the cold as he inserted the coin into the gas meter, then sat down on the bed. He turned over in his mind the latest sequence of events. Being so close to where he had committed his last kill didn't sit easily with him, but he knew he needed to rest before he started the final leg into the Scottish Highlands.

Unfolding the map, he spread it out on the bed and studied the terrain and course he would have to take. He could see from the map his objective was Oban on the Sound of Kerrera. From there, he could take a ferry to the Western Isles. But the problem was which route to take. With the police now on full alert, to take the direct route would be suicidal, whichever form of transport he used. His only option was to keep off the main routes and on the back roads as much as possible.

With the room beginning to feel the benefit of the gas fire, he stripped off his clothes and ventured over to the small but adequate sink, where he was surprised to find the water was reasonably hot. After a wash and shave, he dressed, then sat on the edge of the bed and checked the Walther for ammunition. Satisfied, he pocketed the weapon for ease of use, turned off the fire and light, and left the room. He made his way down the dimly lit stairway to the front door and out into the cold night air.

With several cafés to choose from, all within walking distance of the lodgings, he picked one whose window menu price suited the money he had in his pocket – which was now getting seriously low after having to pay upfront for his room. It was while eating that he became aware that he was being smiled at by an overweight, middle-aged man in a shabby black suit who acknowledged him with a nod of the head. Bayer read the signs; he'd been in the dark, seedy world of back street bars and cafés too many times not to recognise when he was being propositioned for sex. He had done many unsavoury things in his life, but that wasn't one of them – he was purely heterosexual when it came to that game. His first reaction was to get up and leave until a thought crossed his mind – these men usually had money to pay for their needs, and money was something he was running short of. Beckoning with his eyes for them to meet outside, he ran his hand along the switchblade in his pocket as he got up to leave, then thought better of it. Two kills in the same area in one night could put him in danger of being discovered.

The detached house lay in a quiet side street, and Bayer bided his time until they were inside. He swiftly rendered the man unconscious with a blow to the back of the head with the Walther while he was pouring them both a drink. Taking the man's identity card and removing what money he had in his wallet, he then systematically went through drawers and cupboards, which yielded a clothing book and quite a substantial amount of money, which he put in his pocket before leaving.

* * *

"It's for you, sir, a Mr Granville," the young policewoman said, handing him the phone.

"Thank you. Maynard speaking."

"We have Lillian Gilbert, Henry! She was arrested this morning."

"Where was this?" Maynard asked, the anger within him beginning to rise.

"At the railway station in Manchester," Granville replied, elation in his voice.

Maynard couldn't contain himself. "Bloody hell, Clifford, why has it taken this long for me to be notified of her arrest? What are we playing here … catch up? I have this *Raven* bastard leaving a trail of bodies halfway across the ruddy country and we have no idea where he is. The only person who could possibly give us some inclination to where he may be heading is her!"

"Calm down, Henry," Granville chuckled.

"Calm down! I've been sat on my backside here in Kendal all day twiddling my thumbs and she's been in custody since this morning. How do you expect me to feel? You know as well as I do, Clifford, if this *Raven* character gets into the Scottish Highlands, we may never get our hands on the murdering sod."

"Yes … yes, I know how you feel, Henry, but we have to give the police a little slack on this one. Gilbert was arrested by all accounts after a heated argument with the clerk in the ticket office. She was taken by the railway police to their office more or less to give her time to calm down, then they were just going to release her."

"What happened?" Maynard asked, his temper receding slightly.

"She asked if she could have a cigarette and it was as her shoulder bag was being handed to her that a woman officer noticed that Gilbert's bag was surprisingly heavy. On further inspection, concealed in a side pocket, they found a P38 Walther. That set the alarm bells ringing and the local constabulary was called."

"So, where is she now?"

"She is being held at Bootle Street Police Station at the moment. In the morning, she is going to be taken by road to the interrogation centre at Latchmere House. Down at Ham Common."

"Christ! You know what that place is like, Clifford?"

"Yes! They will get her to talk there, all right."

"Can you stop it?"

"Why in God's name would you want me to do that? It's information we want from her and the people at Latchmere are the best in the business," Granville replied.

"Because of the time involved getting her down there and getting the information from her. Hell! *The Raven* could be through the Highlands and away by submarine by the time that happens, had you thought of that? And what's more, I would like to have a crack at her first."

"Do you think you could do any better than them at Ham Common, Henry?"

"Well, I'd like to be given the opportunity before they get their hands on her," Maynard answered, almost pleading with Clifford.

There was silence between them for a few moments while Granville thought the situation over. "Alright, leave it with me and I'll see what I can do. I'll get back to you shortly."

"Do you think he will go along with the idea?" Vines asked, who had been sat listening to the conversation.

Shaking his head, Maynard looked at the inspector for a

few moments before answering. "I honestly don't know. He has a lot to say as regards what goes on within the department and some very useful contacts in high places. He also knows that time is of the essence, but whether he has enough clout to get Gilbert brought up here to Kendal? Your guess is as good as mine."

It was nearly midnight, and both men were dozing in their respective chairs when the phone rang on Vine's desk.

"Yes?" Vines asked quietly. "Yes, he is, I'll put him on. It's for you … Clifford Granville," he said, covering the mouthpiece with his hand before passing it to Maynard.

"Hello, Clifford, what's the outcome?"

"Well, I've had to call in a few favours to get what you want, Henry. But anyway, Gilbert is being brought up to Kendal under armed guard. She will be with you early tomorrow morning."

"Has she said anything while she has been in custody?" Maynard asked.

"Not a dicky bird. Maybe you'll have more luck with her. But in my opinion, I wouldn't mind betting she doesn't know where *The Raven* is or where he's making for. Keep me informed, day or night, if you get anything from her, okay?"

"Will do," Maynard answered, replacing the receiver. Resting his elbows on the chair arms, he stroked the underside of his chin with the back of his hands while looking at Vines. "She will be here in the morning," he grinned, gently rocking his chair from side to side.

"So how do you want to play it when she arrives?" Vines asked.

"I think I'm going to have to play this one by ear, it's the first time I've had any dealings with a female spy."

"Well, you could always put the frighteners on her and see what her reaction is when she knows she's facing the death sentence."

Maynard didn't answer, he just listened to what Vines had to say, but in his own mind, he had already decided what course he would take when he met Lillian Gilbert for the first time.

Chapter 19

Will was feeling more like his old self; his wounds were beginning to heal and his strength returning. He had been able to take walks in the hospital grounds in the winter sunshine with Isobel. The more he got to know her, the more he realised that what had started off as a friendship between them was now becoming a little bit more serious. But with no signs of encouragement from her, he had decided not to upset the apple cart by rushing things. "Let things take their course," he had told himself, but an unexpected visit the previous afternoon by Aileen Hamilton had altered his way of thinking.

Aileen had told him how she had seen a dramatic change of late in her daughter. A change that had all the hallmarks of a woman showing the first signs of love for someone. After she had left, he had taken a longer walk than normal and, after sitting for a further twenty minutes turning things over in his mind, he had returned to the ward thoroughly cold. With the nurses getting anxious about his whereabouts, he had been told off on his return.

He had been sat for over an hour in the recreation room watching a game of cards and keeping a constant eye on the clock when he heard the first of the afternoon visitors arrive. Making his way back to the ward, he couldn't help but have a feeling of excitement at seeing Isobel again. However, he was a little disappointed when he saw her brother sitting in the chair next to his bed. His first thought was to ask him where Isobel was. But in view of his friend's enthusiasm at seeing him, he decided against it.

"How are you feeling?" Dave asked, unbuttoning his tunic top and making himself comfortable. "You certainly look a lot better than the last time I saw you, Will."

"I'm feeling a lot better, and it's good to see you, Dave," he answered, trying not to show too much disappointment that it wasn't his sister.

"I'm sorry I haven't been able to get over to see you sooner, but there's been a lot of activity of late over at the base. Nobody seems to know what the hell's going on. Anyway, I hear Isobel's been paying you regular visits? She'll keep you awake if anybody can."

Will smiled. "Well, at least you have a sister to make fun of, Dave. Mine's in Canada. Anyway, your mother came to see me yesterday."

"Did she?" Dave answered, paying more attention to a pretty, dark-haired nurse who had just come on the ward.

"Good-looking, isn't she? If you're interested, her name's Emily."

"Aye, there's no doubt about that. It hasn't taken you long, Will Madden, to find out her name," Dave laughed, giving him a sly grin.

"To be truthful, Dave, I didn't ask her. I overheard one of the other nurses use it. But I hear, through the Hamilton grapevine, that you have been seeing a good deal of Catriona McCullough just lately?"

"That must have come from that sister of mine?"

"It came out in general conversation, Dave, she didn't mean anything by it, so don't go giving her a rollicking. So, what is she doing this afternoon?" Will asked, trying not to sound too inquisitive.

"Isobel? Oh, she is looking after the shop while my mother is visiting someone who is not very well. She told me to tell you that she will come and see you this evening," he answered, with an eye on the pretty young nurse.

Will couldn't help but have a feeling of pleasant anticipation knowing that in the next few hours he would be seeing her again. He realised he was having difficulty concealing it, brought about by the number of times he inadvertently mentioned Isobel's name during their conversation, so decided on another topic of conversation. "What's all this activity you referred to earlier?"

"There have been several sightings of German aircraft in the last couple of weeks. Also reports from Coastal Command of U-boats in the area," Dave said, frowning.

"That sounds a bit ominous. Where's this been going on, around the Western Isles?"

"Aye! Some of it. Three days ago, we went out to a Catalina that had landed in the sea after tangling with a U-boat. It was one of those big sods, Will, you know the type, with the twin-gun platforms behind the conning tower."

"So what happened?"

"According to the Catalina crew, the U-boat didn't dive but decided to fight it out on the surface."

"Did they sink it?"

"Their depth charges straddled it, but they were hit repeatedly on the run-in, some of the rounds puncturing their port fuel tank, so they had to break off the engagement and head for home. The gunners reported seeing it go under, but whether it was from their attack or not, they weren't sure. They managed to get within forty miles of the coast and bring her down in the sea before they ran out of fuel. Fortunately, the underside of the hull hadn't been hit and we were able to take it in tow."

"What about the crew?"

"Two wounded but not seriously."

Will stroked his chin for a moment while he thought over what Dave had said. "What else has been going on? You said there had been several incidents?"

"One of yours on a Mercer flight had a run-in with Junkers 290. No one was injured and it got back to Tiree okay. What else?" Dave paused. "Oh! A crofter on North Uist reported seeing a German flying boat at low level heading towards Monach Island. So you see there's been quite a lot going on while you've been in hospital." Dave smiled as he saw the tea trolley make an appearance through the ward door. "Any chance, Will?" he asked quietly.

"I'll see what I can do," he winked. With a little cajoling, Will managed to get a second cup of tea but only on the understanding from Jean, the tea lady, that Dave took it into the recreation room to drink it.

"How much longer do you think you will be in hospital for, Will?"

"I don't know. The surgeon was supposed to come and see me this morning, but he never turned up. When I asked one of the nurses why she said there was a bit of a flap on. I hope it's not going to be too much longer because I'm getting bored as hell mooching around here all day. I got a telling-off from Evelyn the other day for taking a longer walk than normal around the grounds."

"Who's Evelyn?" Dave asked, pushing his empty cup and saucer under the chair with his foot after not adhering to the tea lady's request when a nurse came on the ward to check all was okay.

"She is the Ward Sister, I only call her by her first name to wind her up a bit."

Dave gave him a look of disapproval. "A Sister is quite well up the ladder. You are going to get another telling off if you keep using her first name like that, especially if it's in front of the junior nurses."

"Yes, Isobel told me that, so I use my discretion now when I use it," Will winked.

Dave grinned at his friend. "You'd better! Have you decided what you are going to do when your rest period is over? Go back flying or stay grounded?"

"I had this same conversation a few days ago with your sister. She thought I'd done enough flying and should pack it up before I get the chop."

"Well, she may have a point, Will. You've done your fair share, you know."

"But you of all people know what it's like when you've been flying, then get grounded. Don't forget, it wasn't that long ago you couldn't leave Castle Kennedy quick enough to get on the air-sea rescue boats."

"Aye! True enough."

"Talking about the boats. How did you manage to wangle it to get on them before your rest period was up?" Will asked, looking at him suspiciously.

Dave didn't answer straight away but looked around the room to see if anybody was listening. "I had a little help from behind the scenes," he replied softly, the conversation ending when they saw the door open and the Ward Sister appear who stood a few moments to cast a critical eye around the ward.

Will immediately recognised the signs. "Look out. Sister Murray's got her official look on," he said, loud enough for her to hear as she came over to them.

"Good afternoon, Sergeant," she said, looking at Dave and not responding to Will's remark.

"Afternoon, Sister," Dave acknowledged.

"And how are you feeling, Warrant Officer Madden?"

Will knew by her expression that he had better choose his words carefully. "I'm feeling fine, Sister. I was going to ask the surgeon when he came to see me this morning when it would be possible for me to return to my unit, but he didn't come on to the ward."

"Yes, I wasn't on duty this morning and I've just been told about that. But he will be doing his rounds after visiting time this afternoon, so you can have a word with him then, okay?"

Will interlocked his fingers together across his stomach and looked up at her, nodding slowly.

"Have you been taking the medication that was prescribed?" she asked.

Will nodded.

"And have you been sleeping alright? No re-occurrence of the problem you told the doctor about?"

"No. I've been sleeping fine," Will replied.

She looked at him for a few moments. "Right then, I'll leave you with your visitor.

Oh, and Sergeant, don't leave that cup and saucer under the chair, will you?"

Dave watched her leave the ward. "What's the medication for, Will?"

"I wasn't sleeping too well after my operations. Had one or two bad dreams to start with. Anyway, whatever it was the doctor gave me seems to have done the trick." Dave began to smile. "What are you smiling about?"

"A few pints is what you need, that'll put you back on top form."

Will pulled a face. "Beer is the last thing I feel like at the moment." He was interrupted by activity on the ward as some of the visitors began to leave.

"Aye, I suppose I'd better make a move. I'm on duty shortly. Don't forget to tell Isobel what the quack said when you see him later, so she can tell me, okay?" he said, getting up.

Will felt a little envious but pleased he had taken the time to come and see him. "Thanks for coming, Dave, it's most appreciated. And keep your bloody eyes open when you're manning them guns."

"I will," Dave said with a wave as he disappeared through the connecting door to the corridor.

* * *

Lifting her handcuffed hands towards her mouth, Griselda drew hard on the cigarette that had been given to her. Not knowing where she was being taken was bad enough, but the continued silence from the driver and the two men escorting her was beginning to take its toll on her nerves. Several times she had tried to engage them in conversation, only to be met by a wall of silence.

Griselda knew very little about the interrogation methods of the British – what she had heard had only been rumours. Those that had been caught had been executed, so she knew her fate would have an inevitable outcome. Leaning her head against the window, she thought back to her arrest at the station. Her eyes became tearful at the thought of home and family and not being able to see them again. Wiping her cheeks with the back of her hand, she watched the darkness gradually give way to the cold light of day and wondered how many more days like this she would see. She had known capture was always likely ever since arriving in Britain, but in wartime, the chance of apprehension increased considerably.

She had heard about the brutality used by the Gestapo in her own country. Could she withstand such methods if they were used by the British? Griselda winced at the thought of being put through such pain and could only hope that the British still held to their rules of fair play. Whether that applied under the present circumstances, she would have to wait and see. She had to endure another forty minutes of silence before the vehicle finally drew up outside the drab-looking building that was Kendal police station.

* * *

"She's just arrived and they are putting her in one of the cells, like you asked," Vines said, coming into the room accompanied by the Duty Sergeant.

Maynard pondered for a few moments. "We will leave her there while we get a bite to eat, then we'll see what she's got to say for herself. Sergeant, just one question, is the light on in her cell?"

"Yes, it is, sir."

"Switch it off, will you? Let us see how she likes solitude in the dark." The Sergeant nodded. "It's one of the methods used by Latchmere House," Maynard added.

"So, how long are you going to leave her like that for?" Vines asked as they made their way to the canteen.

"It depends on how good your food is here, Inspector," Maynard smiled.

Vines gave him a look of encouragement. "It's not bad for wartime rations," he grinned.

Sleep deprivation was a common method before interrogating prisoners, so Griselda resigned herself to the fact that she may well get very little sleep over the coming hours. She was a little surprised that after what seemed a short period of time, the light was switched back on, followed by footsteps coming along the corridor and the sound of her cell door being unlocked. After which, she was told to "get up and come with me" in a rather abrupt tone.

The room she was taken to had only a table and two chairs. Time seemed to pass painfully slowly before the door behind her opened, and a man who Griselda estimated was in his early fifties came and sat down opposite her. Dropping a file on the table, he looked at her for several moments without speaking.

"So, we finally meet at last – Lillian Gilbert. If that's your proper name, of course, which I doubt very much it isn't. My name is Henry Maynard. I'm with the Military Intelligence and you are in very serious trouble, Lillian."

Griselda looked at Maynard. "I don't see why I should be, I haven't done anything wrong," she replied, trying not to let the fear she was feeling show in her voice.

"Don't insult our intelligence. We have a file on you right back to your early days when you were working for a law firm in Gloucester, then your move to the Bristol Aeroplane Company at Filton, where you were strategically placed to gather information to send back to Germany. We also know about your cosy little cottage at Coaley, which you shared with your male counterpart, *The Raven*. It's all in here and a lot more besides, so don't look so shocked. We have known for some time, Lillian, what you've been up to, but as the saying goes 'give a person enough rope and they will eventually hang themselves'. And that is exactly what we have been doing with you."

Hoping his reference to hanging might put the frighteners on her and get her to open up and fill in the blank parts they desperately needed to find and either kill or capture *The Raven* before he left the country.

"I've nothing to say," Griselda answered, determination in her voice.

Maynard sat back in his chair and looked at her. "Have you heard of the 'cages', Lillian?"

"No, I haven't," she replied with a feeling of foreboding beginning to sweep over her. "What are they, cages for prisoners?"

"Not quite. They are Interrogation Centres, there are several of these around the country, the nearest one to us here is at Preston. I can assure you that they are not very nice places."

"What about the Geneva Convention and the British boast that they always play by the rules?"

"I'm afraid these places don't play by the rules, Lillian. Very much like the methods of your Gestapo. And, before you try and deny it, we know all about the brutal methods that the German secret police use. You can't keep things like that a secret for long."

"So why have I been brought here and not to Preston?" Griselda asked.

"Because I asked for you to be brought here. I think you may have some very useful information that could help us catch a vicious killer, a man who will stop at nothing to get where he is going. You know to whom I'm referring – *Das Rabe.*"

"I don't know of anybody by that name," Griselda answered, knowing full well that her reply didn't at all sound convincing.

Maynard shook his head. "Come on, Lillian. You are not doing yourself any favours by protecting the identity of this man. Would he do the same for you if the roles were reversed? I think not. He'd sell you down the river to save his own neck."

Griselda sat quietly for a few moments while she thought things over. What would Guntram do if he was in the same position as she was now? He had no scruples, she knew he would shop his own mother if he was in a tight corner, so why try and protect him? Her whole reason for being where she was now was to get away from him. She was fully convinced that, given the chance, he would have killed her before leaving Coaley. Besides her own life being at risk, if she decided not to talk, there was scopolamine, the truth serum, which no doubt the British would use. If she talked, she would most likely reveal not only her own secrets but that of Ronald and Martha Warner's network – Griselda knew she needed time to think. "May I have a cigarette?"

"Yes, of course," Maynard answered, beckoning to the duty officer. "I want you to realise that for us, time is of the essence. I don't want to have to send a woman who is as pretty as you are to the main interrogation centre but be assured, I will if I have to and it will not be very pleasant. So make things easy on yourself and tell me what I want to know, Lillian."

She felt tired and drained of energy, the past years of living in constant fear of being caught had taken their toll on her, and she no longer knew who she could trust anymore. She was convinced that headquarters had sanctioned for her to be eliminated by Guntram before he left. When that had failed, had the Warners sent her into a trap at Southampton to stop her talking? She only smoked part of the cigarette, then stubbed it out in the ashtray and looked into Maynard's eyes. "What's in it for me – if I cooperate?"

"Well, that depends on how much information you give us," Maynard replied, sensing she was beginning to weaken by her question. If he trod carefully, she might well have the information to where *The Raven* was trying to get to.

"Will I still be taken to one of these 'cages'?"

Maynard could see the frightened look in the woman's eyes and felt a little saddened, knowing what she would have to endure if she was taken to Latchmere. "Tell me all you know and I'll see what I can do for you. I can't promise you anything, that all rests with London. All I will say is, depending on what you tell me, I'll do my best to try and make things a little easier for you."

Taking another cigarette from the packet she lit it and closed her eyes for a few moments. "My name isn't Lillian Gilbert, it's Griselda Zweig."

Chapter 20

Bayer watched the steady build-up of people and traffic in the street below from his bedroom window. He had slept well – too well. Having slept late into the afternoon the previous day, it had curtailed any thoughts he had of making for the remoteness of the Highlands and so due to the lateness of the hour, he decided to spend a second night where he was.

The morning rush hour was at its peak as he left the hotel and mingled with the early morning crowds. He boarded a tram in Argyle Street for Clydebank, and from there, he caught a second tram which terminated at Duntocher on the outskirts of the city.

From the confines of a roadside café he had been watching the driver of a large vehicle change a wheel. With the flat tyre securely fastened in its cradle on the lorry, the driver headed in the direction of the café and a well-earned breakfast. Bayer grinned at the golden opportunity as the driver came in and made a beeline for the counter to order his meal. He waited until the lorry man was tucking into his breakfast before getting up and leaving and making his way to the rear of the vehicle, which was partially obscured by the end of the café.

Unfastening the tailboard, he lowered it down on its chains until it was level with the lorry floor and with very little effort climbed in, pulling the tailgate up behind him and securing it with the two pins. He found a long, substantially made box to sit on and allowed his eyes to become accustomed to his surroundings. Slowly, black stencilled lettering on the side of the box became readable – *Royal Naval Torpedo Testing Station and Range.* He was riding in the back of a vehicle carrying a load of torpedoes.

He didn't have time to deliberate his predicament as the diesel engine started. Bayer knew he was in a precarious position and one he had to get out of as soon as possible, ideally before it reached the military installation where the contents would be checked before being allowed into the establishment for unloading.

The lorry's speed wasn't excessive, but even so, Bayer knew to try and jump from a vehicle of this height while on the move would be highly dangerous. His only hope of escape would be if the vehicle had to make a stop for some reason. Peering through the rear join in the lorry's canvas, Bayer could see a wide expanse of water to his left with several small islands in its centre. Taking out his map from his travel bag, he ran a finger along the route of the A82 and came to the conclusion that this must be the famous Loch Lomond that he was passing.

The sound of gears being changed down brought him back to reality, followed by the brakes being gradually applied, eventually bringing the heavy vehicle to a halt. Bayer could not believe his good fortune as he looked through the canvas and saw an empty road to the rear of the lorry. Taking full advantage of the opportunity, he lowered the tailboard and jumped out, quickly replacing it and slipping into the undergrowth before the driver appeared to check the vehicle's tyres and load.

Waiting until the lorry moved off, he then moved

stealthily into the densely wooded area. Walking became easier as the woodland began to thin out, eventually giving way to open flat ground, which had a single track road running across it. Beyond that lay rolling hills and a plantation of trees.

Unsure of which direction he should take, he walked to the opposite side of the road and cast a wary eye over the surrounding area. With what looked like the roof of a building in the distance to his right, he decided to follow the road in the opposite direction. It was the sound of running water that drew him to the river, its course concealed from the road by woodland. A well-worn track beside the stream eventually brought him to a bend in the river, and in the distance, he heard the familiar sound of a railway. Emerging from the concealment of the trees, Bayer could make out the distinct shape of a railway station of the island type, where trains could come to a halt on either side of the platform. In front of this was a manned signal box, a siding with two empty coal trucks in it and, beyond that, buildings that had the look of being of military use.

Moving to a position for a better view of the surrounding area, it didn't take him long to realise that the area was being used by the British military, possibly to store munitions and, by the shape and position of the structure in the distance, the testing of torpedoes. Taking the map from his travel bag, he carefully marked the building's positions which would be of great interest to the Luftwaffe when he got back to Germany. With all this military activity in the area, he knew to try and move about by day would increase the risk of him being seen, so he decided to wait until nightfall.

He set about finding somewhere he could rest undercover out of the light rain that had begun to fall. He found shelter in a small storage shed housing tools used by the railway men when repairing the tracks, but with no room to stretch out, he spent an uncomfortable few hours sat on the floor with his back against the door.

The rain had got heavier as he ventured out into the evening darkness and worked his way across to the footpath that he had seen earlier that followed the railway line northward to Arrochar. A large house set among several outbuildings stood adjacent to the water's edge, the dark shapes easily visible against the water and the wooded area that lay on the far side of the Loch. Carefully crossing the two sets of lines, he then picked his way through the undergrowth to the main road and made his way to the hedgerow on the opposite side that surrounded the property. Using the hedge and trees for cover he easily covered the short distance to the Loch side, the surface of the water rippling from the effects of the breeze that accompanied the rain.

The shingle crunched beneath his shoes as he took up a position to see if there was any movement within the vicinity of the house and buildings beyond. All seemed quiet, and Bayer wondered if the place was unoccupied. Breaking cover but keeping low, he made his way along the shoreline in the hope that a house of this size and so close to the water may well have the luxury of a boat he could use to reach the opposite bank. Cold, wet and cursing, he reached the far corner of the estate that jutted out into the Loch and, while taking shelter from the driving rain beneath a tree, he made out the lines of what looked like the remains of a stone jetty. But to his disappointment, on closer inspection, it revealed no sign of a boat tied alongside. Unperturbed, he was nearly back to the road when he felt the shingle suddenly give way to a concrete slipway, its surface overgrown with green mould from years of neglect and its constant fight with the

Loch's water. It was what lay to the rear of the slipway that interested Bayer; the shape having all the hallmarks of a boathouse; where there was a boathouse, there was a possibility of a boat for the taking.

The lock proved difficult but, with the help of a discarded steel rod he found, he managed to lever the lock off the door. Not wanting to risk using the interior lights in case they were seen, he used the torch from his travel bag to make a slow sweep of the boathouse. The beam picked out the shape of a sailing dinghy sat on a launching trailer and two canoes which Bayer was familiar with from his days when he was a youth.

He selected the darker of the two and set about pushing it down to the water's edge. He completed the short crossing relatively easily, given the stiff breeze that was blowing, and he was even able to negotiate the canoe up a narrow inlet, which allowed him to beach it and step ashore without getting his feet wet.

Pulling the craft as far as he could into the undergrowth, he set about concealing it from prying eyes. Satisfied with the outcome, he followed the narrow stream that drained into the Loch, which eventually brought him to a long sweeping bend on a main road.

Staying hidden within the bushes, Bayer studied the map with his torch, quickly coming to the conclusion that this must be the main road to Inveraray. "About sixty miles to Oban," he whispered softly to himself, putting the map and torch back in his bag. He set off walking, thankful for the waterproof jacket he had stolen from the boathouse that kept the upper half of his body dry while the hood offered him warmth and protection from the cold rain that drove into his face. With the white line down the middle of the road giving him guidance in the darkness, he was able to make good progress during the first fifteen or twenty minutes, but after that, he soon realised by his laboured breathing and a slight change in temperature that the road had become much steeper as it followed the Glen into the mountains. With the rain now beginning to turn to sleet, Bayer knew it was time to find some sort of shelter for the remainder of the night. He had passed several houses since breaking cover, but none were suitable for the purpose he had in mind. As the road began to get steeper and become more taxing under the conditions, he decided whatever building materialized next from out of the darkness would have to do. With the hood of his jacket pulled snugly around his head, giving him some protection from the elements, Bayer nearly didn't see the unobtrusive structure set back off the road amongst trees. It was only as he followed the gravel track towards it that he realised it was a house, its timber construction giving it the look of an Alpine chalet. Climbing the gate, he moved across the level ground that lay adjacent to the driveway and into the tree line.

Bayer rested for a few moments while he focused his attention on the house and several dark shapes that lay to the rear of the property. He worked his way carefully through the trees to get a better look at the largest of the buildings, which turned out to be a garage. Rubbing the side window with the sleeve of his jacket, he shone his torch into the dark interior, the light immediately picking out the roof of a vehicle. Grinning to himself, he set off to check the contents of the other three buildings. The first being a storage shed, part filled with logs, the second was a workshop housing a workbench, a few old tools and the rusting parts of a car engine. The last contained a quantity of old furniture and two bicycles, both in need of repair.

Sitting in one of the discarded chairs, he thought over his

options. The rear seat of the car would make a comfortable bed for the night and, although it would be cold, at least he would be in the dry and out of the weather. But what he really needed was food, and the only chance of getting that was from inside the house. He ran a careful eye over the silent property for several minutes from the part-open door and wondered what opposition he would encounter if he forced entry. Spurred on by hunger, he decided it was a chance worth taking. The rear entrance was securely locked, and so he turned his attentions to the kitchen window, which also wouldn't allow him access.

Reluctant to go down the route of breaking a window, which would immediately arouse the household, he decided to try down the side of the building. The central lock of the patio door yielded easily to the blade of his knife. The first thing Bayer noticed was how cold the place was, switching on his torch, he made a slow sweep of the room, the beam picking out the ghostly white shapes of furniture covered over with dust sheets. Making his way across the room, he cautiously opened the door that led out into a hallway. The room opposite was being used as a library and the one neighbouring it, a dining room, both of which also had their furniture covered. By what he had seen so far, he was fairly sure the place was unoccupied but, to be doubly sure, he checked the upstairs bedrooms and, with no sign of life, returned to the kitchen to see if there was any food to be had.

The only meagre rations he was able to find were stored in a pantry and consisted of three tins of various types of fruit and two more of soup, all of which he carried through to the kitchen. Pulling out each drawer in turn until he found the one with cutlery in it, he set about searching through the utensils, eventually finding what he was looking for. He poured the chunky liquid into a pan then set off in the direction of the woodshed. Returning with some old newspapers, kindling and several logs, it wasn't long before the kitchen had a warm, cheerful feel about it and with some reasonably hot soup inside him, followed by fruit segments, it wasn't long before he was overcome by sleep.

It was a drop in the room's temperature that woke him. Putting more logs on the fire, he then located the keys to the garage and car and a little after five, he decided to see if the vehicle's engine had enough life in it to give him transport to Oban. What confronted him when he opened the door was a cold, dense fog shrouding the entire area. Also, there had been a heavy snow shower. Edging his way slowly in the general direction of the garage, his foot caught something hard, and he found himself falling, landing heavily against an ornamental flower pot. "*Schweinhund,*" he shouted, pushing the offending object to one side with his foot.

Having dropped both sets of keys during his fall, it took him several minutes to find them among the disturbed snow. Pocketing both sets of keys he was eventually able to reach the garage without further mishap. Opening the door just wide enough to gain entry, he was confronted by a rather drab-looking Singer motor car which Bayer estimated was from the early 1930s. He soon located the light switch, which, to his surprise, was in working order but which he quickly extinguished until he had blacked out the side window using two lengths of wood and some old, discarded sacking he found.

Sliding in behind the wheel, he inserted the key in the ignition switch and pushed the start button on the right of the dashboard but got no response from the engine. After further inspection, he found the battery had been removed. Slamming the bonnet down hard in disgust, he had just been about to give it up as a bad job when he saw what looked like the square shape of a battery covered over under the workbench. With the battery in place and with some gentle persuasion from the choke and throttle, the motor roared into life, filling the garage with grey, acrid smoke.

Pushing one of the doors ajar to let out the fumes, he let the engine warm up for several minutes before switching it off. With the cold beginning to seep through his wet clothing from his earlier fall, he decided the warmth of the kitchen was the best option. It would also give the fog a chance to lift. Shivering from the cold, he put another log on the fire, opened the two remaining cans of fruit, the cold substance doing little to dampen the pangs of hunger he was feeling. With his body thawing out from the warmth of the fire and thoughts of home when he was a boy, the aroma of his mother's baking, the long hot summers playing in the woods and fields near his home, sleep soon overcame him.

Having not heard the sound of the approaching vehicle, the only realisation that someone was about was when there came a knock on the kitchen door. His first reaction was to reach for the Walther. As his mind cleared and he began to think more clearly, he returned it to his coat pocket but with his hand firmly holding the grip ready for use should he deem it necessary. A second knock, louder than the first, prompted him to open the door and confront the early morning caller. The presence of a rather attractive female looking at him took him a little by surprise.

"Oh! I'm sorry. I thought Rowena was back," she said in a surprised tone.

"What made you think that?" Bayer enquired, admiring the woman's fine features and long red hair.

"The postman said he saw smoke coming from the chimney, so I thought she had come back to see if the house was okay, what with her staying in Perth with her mother while Neil, her husband, is away fighting."

"Yes. I know she is. I'm just renting the place for a few days, a bit of peace and quiet while I'm on leave, if you know what I mean," Bayer replied, hoping his explanation would appease the woman's curiosity.

"Oh! I understand," she smiled, taking a step backwards with the intention of leaving.

"And thank the postman for me for being so observant. I'm sure we can all sleep safely in our beds knowing he is keeping a careful eye on things," he added coldly.

"Yes, I will. He doesn't miss much," she grinned before heading back to her car.

He now knew time wasn't on his side, it wouldn't be long before the woman talked and he may well have a visit from the police. After watching the woman leave, Bayer quickly gathered up his things, stuffing them roughly into his travel bag, and made his way to the garage. The Singer's engine started easily this time but as he drove it out into the grey light of day he noticed the fuel gauge indicating the vehicle was low on fuel. At least it was enough to get him out of the area, he thought, engaging first gear and driving the vehicle down the drive and out onto the road.

Chapter 21

"So you are still no nearer knowing where this man Bayer is making for?" Vines said, rubbing the palms of his hands together as he watched Maynard finish reading then put the information he had gleaned from Griselda Zweig in his briefcase.

"You are quite right, Inspector. We are no closer to knowing. But what we do have is his name and what kind of man he is, which isn't much I grant you, but it's a start."

"Do you think she has given you all she knows about Bayer?" Vines asked, while making a letter 'T' with his fingers at the woman police officer, who immediately got the message and headed off in the direction of the canteen.

"I think so. There is no doubt she was terrified of this man and what he was going to do to her before he left their love nest. That's why she went on the run."

"It's hard to believe he had orders to kill her? One of their own?" Vines said, frowning.

"I'm sure he had. What he has found out would be of top priority to the Germans and had to be got back to Germany at all costs. Zweig was of no further use to him, just an obstacle to be got rid of, mainly to stop her talking if she should fall into our hands, which is exactly what has happened. Unfortunately for us, she doesn't know where he is making for."

Vines nodded in agreement.

"But there is still more I want to know about the information she has passed on while she was working at Filton and who her contacts over here are. She's got to have had help of some kind getting established in this country before the war started, so you can bet your life that they are still active."

"Nazi sympathisers, you mean?" Vines added, raising his eyebrows.

This time it was Maynard who nodded in agreement. "She was picked up on Piccadilly station and in possession of a ticket taking her back south. Why? There must have been some reason for her to come all the way up from Bristol to Manchester. My guess is there is someone there she knows she could trust and would possibly help her, even get her out of the country, and this is what I've got to try and find out." Maynard shook his head. "But I can't help feeling we are running out of time with this *Raven* character. I wouldn't mind betting he is well into the Scottish Highlands by now, and we haven't a damn clue where he is or making for. We've got a bloody disaster on our hands, Inspector, if he gets back with what he's found out, months of work handed to the Germans on a plate."

Vines picked up a pencil off his desktop and turned it over with his fingers. "You've never said what this man Bayer has found out, and I've never asked you, but if he gets back with what he knows, could it prolong the war?"

Maynard had come to like Vines during the short period he had known him, and a friendship had grown between them, so he decided, with the room being empty, he would take him into his confidence on how grave the consequences could be. "I don't know about prolonging the war, but it won't help matters," he said, pausing a few moments before continuing. "What I'm about to tell you, Inspector, you must keep to yourself at all costs. If it gets out, it will be both of us for the chop, do you understand?"

"Yes, I think I've got the picture," Vines answered, visibly taken aback by the emphasis on the three words – *for the chop*.

"We have designed and built a new type of turbojet engine; it's called the Welland. Two of these engines have been fitted to a single-seat interceptor fighter aircraft which will reach speeds of over four hundred miles per hour. At the moment, it is undergoing test flights from an airfield near Gloucester."

"Is this what Bayer's got? Information on these aircraft?"

"Unfortunately he has. He got onto the airfield and into the hangar through a window where the aircraft was. Photographed all he wanted to and got clean away. But not before he murdered the guard who happened to be in the wrong place at the wrong time. Poor sod." Maynard immediately brought the conversation to a close when the policewoman entered the room carrying a tray with two mugs of tea for them.

"What are you going to do about Zweig?" Vines asked, taking a sip of tea.

Maynard looked at him. "I'll get back to her in due course. My main concern at the moment is stopping Bayer from getting back. But since he took that van, there's been nothing. No sightings of the vehicle, no reports of any more killings, nothing. It's as if he has vanished into thin air. He must have hidden that damn thing somewhere. We know he can't have got far into Scotland with it by the amount of fuel it had – so where the bloody hell is it?"

Vines walked over to the large wall map and slowly looked over the area in question. "I've just had a theory.

There's a lot of remote places to the north and west of Dumfries where you could dump a vehicle. But the problem after you've done that is getting out of the area, and there are only four ways we know he could achieve that. Firstly, on foot, which to my way of thinking is unlikely, given the weather conditions and the distance to cover. The second and third options are the risky ones, which are for him to either steal another vehicle or hitch a lift, both of which hold a certain degree of danger of him being reported to the authorities."

Maynard got up and walked over to the map to see what area his attention was drawn to. "And the fourth option?" he asked.

Vines tapped the map with his pencil to the west of Annan. "I wouldn't mind betting this is where he has hidden the van, in this area here around Clarencefield. There is plenty of woodland in that area and also a railway line which heads northward to Glasgow. What more could he ask for?"

Maynard folded his arms as he studied Vines' logic. "You know, Inspector, you could be right. It's been staring us in the face all along. Of course, that's what he'd make for – the damn railway. Can you put a call through to the Dumfries police to get them to do a thorough search of the area around Clarencefield for the van and also the police at Glasgow to see if there have been any unusual incidents in the last twenty-four, no, forty-eight hours, like stabbings or shootings, preferably on the south side of the city."

"I'll do that straight away. Bryant, get me the Dumfries police will you, pronto?" he ordered, his hand hovering above the telephone as he waited to be put through.

Maynard sipped slowly on his tea as he listened to the two calls being made, his interest was aroused by what was said during Vines call to the Glasgow police.

"Thank you very much, Detective Inspector. That information has been very helpful. I will contact the Irvine police straight away and see what more they can tell me. And thanks again for your help and cooperation. And don't hesitate to contact us here at Kendal if you need our help at any time," Vines replied, replacing the receiver. "That was DI McKinnon. Sounds a nice chap, very helpful."

Maynard didn't answer but waited patiently for Vines to fill him in.

"A body has been found in an empty rail van at Ardeer, that's near a place called Stevenson, which is in the Irvine area on the coast. By all accounts, it was going to be loaded with explosives from a factory there when the body was discovered. The victim suffered one single stab wound to the heart. But most interestingly, those rail vans had been brought down from a goods yard in Glasgow. McKinnon said it is heavily used by goods trains travelling north to Glasgow, with a lot of the freight bound for the ships in the Clyde docks."

"So where is this goods yard, exactly?" Maynard asked.

"Just off Paisley Road, here," Vines answered, drawing a circle around the terminal.

Maynard stared hard at the area Vines had indicated with his pencil. "And you can bet there's plenty of accommodation to be had around there with it being near the Prince's Dock. Ideal for our man to lie low while he plans his next move."

"My thoughts too."

"And by now, the murdering sod will be well clear of the city and out into the highlands."

Chapter 22

Isobel couldn't help the look of disappointment on her face when she asked when he would be leaving to return to Tiree.

"The doctor said I could be discharged tomorrow, so I'll catch the early boat back on Sunday."

"I see. I don't suppose it occurred to you to ask him if you were fit enough to go back flying?"

Will looked at her and smiled. "As a matter of fact, I did."

"And?" Giving him a questioning look.

"He said he could see no problems with me flying."

"And how do you feel about sitting in the confines of a gun turret for long hours? Don't forget you are just getting over two operations on your back. If you want my advice, Will, I think you should give yourself a little more time."

Will frowned at the thought of spending long, boring hours in the armoury with Nelson watching his every move. "Maybe you're right," he answered, knowing full well that at the first opportunity to get airborne, he would jump at the chance. "Isobel, if I write to you, will you write back? I know you have had a bit of a downer on us RAF types, but I would really like for us to keep in touch. Hell, that didn't come out right, did it, sounded a bit formal?"

"It did a bit," she laughed. "And, of course I'll write back to you."

"Thanks. I've really enjoyed having you visit me while

I've been in here," he paused a moment to choose his words carefully, "I've also grown very fond of you, Issy."

"Isobel," she corrected him.

Taking hold of her hand. "Sorry, Isobel. But do you understand what I'm trying to say?"

"Yes, of course I do. You're hoping our relationship will develop into something more serious if we write to one another. That is what you are trying to say, isn't it?"

"Yes, I suppose I am."

"Do you want to know what I think, Will Madden?"

Will looked at her a few moments before replying. "What's that?"

"I think you are a bit of a romantic at heart," she replied, her eyes holding his.

Will didn't feel embarrassed by her remark. "I suppose I am."

* * *

Although the earlier fog had now lifted, the snow-covered ice made driving conditions treacherous. The Singer's well-worn tyres gave Bayer several anxious moments as the dated motor car made slow progress up Glen Croe and over the summit of the Rest and Be Thankful and through Glen Kinglas to Cairndow. He had been in sight of Loch Awe when the vehicle's engine started to misfire, which Bayer guessed was due to the nearly empty fuel tank.

Driving off the road into the entrance to a field, he managed to switch the car engine off before it ran out of fuel completely. His first thought had been to abandon the vehicle and look for an alternative form of transport, but on getting out, something else occurred to him: it was a common practice for owners of these old cars to often carry a spare can of petrol. Unlocking the rear boot door, he was pleased to see not just one but two cans of petrol, plus a small funnel to fill the tank. Quickly filling the vehicle with the two gallons and with the fuel gauge now showing a healthy reading, Bayer tried the starter. It took a few moments for the engine to settle down to a rhythmic beat before he engaged first gear and pulled out onto the road. Moving smoothly through the gearbox, Bayer felt confident that he would get back to Germany as he headed the Singer towards the Pass of Brander and on to Oban.

There was a lot of military activity going on when he arrived at the port, and the sight of seaplanes moored in the bay opposite did nothing to deflate his confidence as he drove towards the docks and parked next to a large truck whose driver seemed to be in a deep state of sleep. After making enquiries about where to purchase a ticket, he made his way to the booking office and by its empty appearance could only mean two things, that there were no sailings on a Saturday or the boat had already sailed. Bayer had to tap the booking office counter with a pencil, and it was several minutes before a clerk appeared.

"Can I help you?"

"I would like to book a passage to Lochboisdale," Bayer replied.

"Aye, that's no bother at all, but I'm afraid there are no sailings until early next week. That's when the next cargo boat leaves for the Outer Islands."

Bayer had been expecting such an answer and reluctantly nodded in agreement.

"Will you be travelling alone?" the clerk asked. Bayer nodded. "And would that be a single or return, sir?"

"Single," he answered.

"And can I see your ID card?" Bayer slid his fake card

across the counter to the clerk.

With the ticket safely in his wallet and the relevant information about the sailing time, he made his way back to where he had parked the Singer to consider the best method of getting rid of it. Leaving it in the town or on the docks was too risky. Bayer knew it would soon draw the attention of the authorities and create an investigation, so his best option was concealment. He consulted the map again and decided to drive a little way out on the coastal road that ran adjacent to the Sound of Kerrera, a decision that paid dividends by way of a track leading off the road to a derelict building that was surrounded by several old, discarded farm implements.

With the vehicle tucked neatly inside the walled structure and covered over by an old tarpaulin, he then set about the walk back to Oban. Keeping clear of any houses or farms he encountered on the way, he was back in the town in just over an hour, looking for a place to eat and a place to sleep for the night.

After settling himself into the hotel and with time on his hands, he decided to spend what was left of the afternoon seeing what Oban had to offer. Bayer noticed that the hotel proprietor while booking in, had been looking at his untidy appearance, so in the privacy of his room, he took out the stolen clothing book from his travelling bag and counted the unused coupons, grinning to himself at the amount left he headed in search of a clothing shop.

Bayer laid out the new garments on the bed. After washing and shaving, he set about dressing. Woollen shirt, corduroy trousers, jersey and socks all feeling good after what he had been wearing. He laid on the bed with his head cupped in his hands and thought over the journey that had put him where he was now. So close to his ultimate aim of getting back to Germany. He allowed himself some fond memories of walking by the river with Heidi before his departure, which eventually lulled him into a deep sleep.

It was voices in the corridor outside his room that woke him. He instantly felt for and levelled the Walther at the door but soon realised it was the hotel owner showing newly-arrived guests to the room opposite. Lowering the weapon, he placed it on the bedside table and walked over to the window. The streets below were now in darkness. Bored with his surroundings, he put on his coat and, after locking his room, ventured downstairs to the reception area where he was confronted by a man of medium build who Bayer estimated to be in his early twenties.

"Good evening," he said cheerfully.

Bayer eyed the man suspiciously for a few moments before answering. "Evening."

"You look as bored as I am," he grinned, opening the front door. "If you're looking for a decent pub, there's one round the corner if you're interested? There's quite a few of the local lassies get in there tonight," he added.

"Sounds good," Bayer answered, thinking back to how long it had been since he had felt the pleasure of Griselda.

"I'm Steve."

"Andrew," Bayer replied, following him down the steps.

"Waiting for Tuesday's boat?"

"Yes," Bayer answered cautiously.

"Bit of a bind, but at least it gives us the chance to check out the local talent," Steve chuckled.

"I suppose it does. Were you drinking in this pub at lunchtime?" Bayer asked, hoping to deflect the conversation away from the ferry crossing and why he was going to the island.

"I had a few in there just to while away a couple of hours.

The place was quite busy, but most of the drinkers were men. I got into a game of darts with some of them. That's how I found out about tonight and that there's quite a few of the local women go there. By all accounts, there is a local ceilidh dance on and a lot of them stop off there for a drink before going on to the dance later."

Bayer was surprised by the size of the place and the amount of people already there when they arrived. With a little perseverance, they were finally able to get a drink at the bar, after which they moved to a less-congested part of the room where they acquired an empty table with two chairs that were being vacated.

"What do you think?" Steve asked as he slowly consumed his pint of beer.

"Well, there's a lot of RAF here, but it looks promising," he answered, running a careful eye around the crowded room and coming to an immediate stop when he saw a rather older, more mature woman, standing talking with three other women, looking at him.

"They use the hotels here to billet the RAF. But is there anyone that catches your eye?"

"Not at the moment," Bayer lied, keeping a straight face as he held the woman's gaze.

"Well, I think I might be in with a chance. I'll see you later," Steve winked, getting up to leave.

Bayer watched him go, then turned his attention back to pursuing his quarry. The woman was several years older than the rest of the group, probably in her mid-thirties, and, he noticed, was wearing a wedding ring, which only heightened his interest in her more. Husband in the forces, or dead, and she's not had a good seeing to for a while, he thought. He felt a stirring below, watching the provocative way she stood, which enhanced her full figure. He was just about to get up and go across to introduce himself when he saw her speak to the female next to her, who gave him a look and nod as though acknowledging her friend's decision before she walked over towards him.

"Hello! I haven't seen you in here before?" she said in a rather silky voice.

"That's because I haven't been in here before," he smiled, sitting back in his chair. "I see your glass is empty, would you like to join me for a drink, or are you going on with your friends?"

"The trouble with them is they are a little young for me and are after the RAF guys from the Flying Boat Maintenance Unit. I prefer the more mature man, and I would rather have a drink with you," she smiled, coming round the table and accepting the chair which Bayer offered her.

"I'm Andrew," he said as he watched her sit down, her slightly flared skirt riding up over her shapely legs.

"Stella," she smiled, taking a packet of cigarettes and lighter from her bag.

"And what would you like to drink, Stella?"

"Beer, please."

Returning with their drinks, Bayer saw that he had competition in the shape of a slightly inebriated airman; he was glad for his sake that he beat a hasty retreat when he saw him coming. "What did he want?" he asked, setting the drinks down on the table.

"He must have thought I was on my own but, when he saw you coming, he decided he had better clear off. Probably thought you were my husband," she grinned, offering him a cigarette.

"Where is your husband?" he queried, looking firstly at the ring on her finger and then at her.

"God knows," she answered, pausing to take a draw on her cigarette. "Somewhere in the Far East fighting the Japanese. I think it was Burma that the last letter came from. But I don't really care much, our marriage was on the rocks before the war started," she shrugged.

Bayer did feel a pang of sympathy for her husband, being married to a callous bitch like this, fighting a ruthless enemy in the Burmese jungle and whose only thought would be of getting back home in one piece.

"So, Andrew, are you married?" Bayer shook his head. "Haven't you ever been?"

"Never seemed to have found the right one I wanted to settle down with. Then the war came along, and that put things on hold. I can't see the point in wartime marriages, personally."

"You sound a bit like me, live for today and to hell with tomorrow," she grinned, finishing off the remainder of her beer.

"I couldn't agree more," he smiled as he watched her cross her legs, exposing more of her legs and thighs, which she made no attempt to cover up. "Same again?"

"Okay. Shall we have one more, then go and see what this dance is like?" she replied, taking some money from her purse. "Will you get me some cigarettes when you get the drinks? I think it may be a long night, and I can't do without a cigarette – both before and after if you know what I mean."

Bayer gave her a knowing look. "And you behave yourself while I'm at the bar, no talking to strange men."

"I wouldn't dream of it."

With the evening beginning to draw to a close, Bayer felt himself responding as Stella pressed her body hard against him as they slowly danced in the crowded ballroom. "I think it's time we were going?" he said, releasing his hold on her as the band finished its number.

"If we go now, we'll beat the rush," she smiled, linking her arm through his as they left the dance floor.

The mid-row townhouse was in an elevated position overlooking the bay. The dying embers of the fire gave the high spacious room a warm and homely feel about it. "Drink?" she asked, holding up a bottle of Scotch.

"I don't think so," he answered, getting up and going over to her and slipping his arm around her waist while his other hand took the bottle from her and put it back in the cabinet. "It's not a drink I need," he said, sliding the palms of his hands up and down her back several times before they came to rest around her waist, and he drew her firmly against him.

"My, you are in a hurry," she said softly as their lips came together, and their tongues heightened the moments of intimacy. She gently pulled away from him and led him upstairs to the bedroom. Closing her eyes, she felt his naked body press firmly against her. His arms came under hers and gently caressed the fullness of her breasts while his lips kissed her shoulders and neck, making her moan softly and breathe heavily.

Bayer could feel the excitement building within him as she moved against him, but he knew this was a woman of experience, a woman skilled in the art of lovemaking who would need to be taken to the very height of pleasure. He would have to draw on all his sexual prowess to make sure that was achieved. Coaxing her onto the bed, and with the manipulated skill of his hands and mouth, he gently worked his way down her lithe body.

Stella was no stranger to oral stimulation, but this man was very much adept in the art, which made her push upwards to meet his restless tongue while gripping the rails behind her more tightly as the pleasure intensified as he found her sensitive spot.

The physical sensation was beyond anything she had ever felt before as she felt him bring her to a climax. "Seems like I was in a hurry also," she said, sighing contentedly.

"Yes, you certainly were."

"Did you …?" she asked.

"No, I didn't. I wasn't ready." Looking at him, Stella frowned when she saw he was still fully aroused. "And I haven't finished with you yet."

This time the rhythm was at a slow, unhurried pace. Stella let the pleasure sweep over her as the man she knew as Andrew continued to dominate the pace of their lovemaking. She lay on her back beside him while her breathing moderated. "Will I be able to see you again?" she asked quietly.

Her question immediately put Bayer on the defensive, so he decided to choose how he answered carefully. "Why, do you want to?"

"I would have thought that was obvious after tonight."

"And what if your husband should unexpectedly turn up, what then?" he asked.

"If he does, he does. it's over between us," she grinned, while reaching across him for a cigarette. "Anyway, that's enough about him. We have the rest of the weekend to really get to know one another and there is always Monday night after I get home from work, if you've still got the stamina?"

"You've certainly got it all planned out, haven't you?" Bayer answered. "And yes, I'll have the stamina."

Stella drew hard on the cigarette then put it between Bayer's lips to do the same. "I'll also be there to see you off Tuesday morning."

"You will?" he queried, looking at her suspiciously.

"Yes, I work in the dock office. Didn't I say?"

"No, you didn't," he replied sharply.

"That sounded masterful. That's the second quality I like in a man," she said smiling.

"Is it? And what's the first?" Bayer asked.

"Being highly sexed. That kind of man can do whatever he wants with me."

Chapter 23

"Get anything more from her?" Vines asked, looking up from behind his desk as Maynard came into the room.

"She's given me a lot of information about what she was up to at Filton, but nothing as to what she was doing before that. I think she is covering up for someone or something. My guess is there's a cell working an area; the trouble is, I haven't the time to really go to town on her, what with Bayer still on the loose. He is my main concern. All I can do is pass on what information I have so far to London and hand Zweig over to Latchmere and see if they can get more out of her."

"Well, I've received two lots of information that might help. Firstly, the Scottish police have found the van."

"Where?" Maynard queried, walking over towards the wall map.

"Exactly where we thought it might be." Vines continued, "Clarencefield, a forestry worker found it who was making a routine inspection of the woodland in the area."

"Anything in it which could give us a clue to which way he could be heading?" Maynard queried hopefully.

"I'm afraid not. But the second bit of information I've received looks promising."

"Oh. And what's that?" Maynard asked, retaking his seat.

"A Mr Maxwell phoned the Highland police to report the theft of a canoe from his boat shed on the side of Loch Long. Later that day, a passing boat reported seeing something unusual in a creek on the opposite bank. The local police went to investigate and found the canoe, which somebody had tried to camouflage with undergrowth cut from the surrounding area. They think the strong wind earlier in the day must have partly exposed the thief's handiwork which is what the passing boat saw … Here is the report with the details and times for you to read."

"Thanks, now let's see. Loch Long is here. So where on the Loch is this house you say the canoe was taken from?"

"I'll show you, Vines open a more detailed map. There is the house, and directly opposite is the creek where the canoe was found, right next to the A83."

Maynard pondered over the map for a few moments, taking in the surrounding landscape. "We know he isn't going north up the A82 because there would have been no reason for him to cross the Loch. So, if it's our bird, which I have a strong feeling it is, he must be making for the coast from Oban downwards," Maynard replied, running the stem of his pipe along the area in question.

"The other alternative being the Outer Islands. There are sailings from Oban to both the Inner and Outer Hebrides and there are a hundred and one places out there where he could be picked up by submarine," Vines concluded, drawing rings with his pencil around the islands he had mentioned.

"Precisely. I think my best bet is to get up to Oban as soon as possible. Do you think you could lay me transport on and, while I'm travelling up there, contact the main man at Oban police station and put him in the picture? Most of all, tell him to keep a close eye on all the foot passengers that are boarding vessels for the Outer Islands, anything that looks remotely suspicious, do a search." Maynard reached for the telephone.

"I'll get that organised right away," Vines answered.

"In the meantime, I'll give London a ring and bring them up to speed. Also, I think it's time we brought RAF Coastal Command and the Royal Navy into the equation and for them to step up patrols in these areas."

* * *

Shaking hands with Vines and thanking him for the help he had given him, Maynard then settled himself in the back seat of the police car, pulling a woollen blanket over himself for added warmth for the long night's journey ahead. He watched the blacked-out towns and villages speed by and thought over the series of events that had put him where he was now.

Would he be able to stop Bayer before he left the country, taking with him months of secret experimental work? They were on the northern outskirts of Glasgow when he was woken by the vehicle coming to a halt and the driver saying he needed to pay a 'call'. With both men relieved and refreshed by the flask of coffee and sandwiches provided by the Kendal police canteen, the journey resumed. Their only distraction being the passing of an occasional heavy lorry winding its weary way into the Scottish Highlands. With the first streaks of dawn appearing in the night sky, they pulled up outside Oban's main police station and, accompanied by the weary driver, Maynard entered the building. They were confronted by an equally weary-looking constable.

"Morning. How can I help you?" he asked, stifling a yawn.

"My name's Maynard, and I've driven up here overnight

from Kendal to see whoever is in charge here urgently. You should have had a phone call from Inspector Vines at Kendal police station telling you I was on my way and would be arriving this morning," Maynard said in an authoritative tone and showed his identification card.

"Ah, yes, sir, I was told you would be arriving this morning," the constable answered, staring at the military intelligence classification. "Would you like to follow me, sir? The chief superintendent's office is this way."

"Before I do, could you fix up some food and a bed for the driver? He's been driving all night?"

"A bed is no problem, he can use one of the empty cells," the constable replied, looking at his watch. "The canteen doesn't open for another hour I'm afraid, but I can fix you both up with a cup of tea to keep you going for the time being," he answered.

Armed with a rather ominous looking mug, its stained interior as brown as the tea it was holding, Maynard was shown into a room of modest size.

"Pleased to meet you, Mr Maynard. Please take a seat," Crawford said as he rose from behind a neat and highly polished desk to shake hands.

"Thank you," Maynard replied, sitting down and taking out his pipe. "Do you mind?" he asked, holding up the briar.

"No, not at all," Crawford answered as he watched Maynard go through the process of filling and lighting it.

"So, the first thing I must ask you is when is the next vessel leaving for the Western Isles?"

"Seven o'clock, Tuesday morning. There is the route and timetable she will be taking," Crawford replied, handing Maynard the two sheets of data.

"Thanks. So, she leaves Oban, travels to Coll and Tiree, then on to Castlebay at Barra, then to Lochboisdale,"

Maynard said aloud while studying the timetable. Crawford nodded. "And could you show me on your wall map where exactly these islands are?"

"Certainly. These are the four ports in question," Crawford answered, pointing to each one in turn.

Maynard pondered over the area for some time before speaking. "That's a lot of sea and islands the navy and the air force are going to have to cover. I hadn't thought about the Inner Hebrides being on the route," he said, shaking his head before returning to his seat.

"Well, I know there is a lot of air and naval activity going on in the area. Exactly what they get up to, you'll have to ask them when they arrive," Crawford responded with the makings of a grin.

"Yes, I'll do that. What time are they arriving?"

"They said they would be here at nine."

"Okay. How much did Inspector Vines tell you?"

Crawford sat back in his chair and interlocked his fingers together. "Only the very briefest of details. Inspector Vines didn't like to say too much over the phone. He said you would tell me more when you arrived. We have put in place round-the-clock surveillance of the dock area as you requested, but that's all."

Maynard nodded. "Good. So, firstly I'll have a wash and get cleaned up, then I think a bit of breakfast wouldn't go amiss. Afterwards, when our two friends from the armed forces arrive, I'll brief you all about the man we are after and why we need to get our hands on him as soon as possible."

* * *

Group Captain Carlton took out a cigarette and tapped it several times on his cigarette case before lighting it as he thought over what Maynard had said. "Can I ask you, Mr Maynard, what makes you so sure this man, Bayer, is making for the Outer Islands? Let's face it, there are a hundred and one places along the coast of the mainland he could get picked up from without risking detection travelling by boat. If he did chance his arm going by sea, you have only the briefest description of what he looks like from his ex-lover, which doesn't help matters."

"I quite agree, Group Captain, we are 'peeing in the wind', if you'll excuse my turn of phrase. And, as you quite rightly say, we only have a sketchy idea what he looks like or where he's making for, so it's up to you and Commander Trent to be our eyes."

"We'll do our part from the air, but there is a lot of islands and ocean out there to cover, don't you agree, Commander?" Carlton said, looking at his naval counterpart sitting beside him.

"I quite agree, But we'll give you all the help we can from the sea," Trent said.

"Thank you, gentlemen. I can't ask any more than that," Maynard replied, standing up to shake their hands. After they had left, he sat back in his chair and, with hands clasped behind his head, he stared up at the ceiling. "Carlton is right in what he says, we've no firm ID on Bayer, and we haven't a bloody clue which direction he might take."

"Aye. It seems we are back to the old waiting game with a hope this Bayer character will show his hand by making a wrong move," Crawford replied, leaning forward to answer the telephone.

"The bastard hasn't made one yet. He seems to have been one jump ahead of us since leaving Gloucester. He's either exceptionally good at what he does or been damned lucky."

Crawford listened intently to what he was being told on

the telephone. "And when was this?" he asked the person he was talking to. "Early Saturday morning."

Maynard watched with curiosity as Crawford nodded his head several times in response to what he was being told. "And you say the vehicle taken was a Singer? Right, thank you for letting us know."

"What was all that about?" Maynard asked.

"It could be something to do with the man you're after. An empty house at Ardgarten, near where the canoe was found, has been broken into. The local postman saw smoke coming from the chimney and mentioned it to a Christine Weir, who knows the owner and knew the house was empty. Apparently, the owner was away in Perth staying with her mother, and when Ms Weir went to investigate, she was confronted by a man who said he was renting the place from the owner while on leave. Finding this a bit suspicious, she was eventually able to make contact with the owner in Perth, who said she hadn't rented the place out or given anybody permission to use it. That's when Ms Weir called the police and, it turns out the place had been broken into, used overnight and a dark green Singer motor car taken from the garage the next morning, which was yesterday."

"And there has been no sighting of the vehicle anywhere in the area?" Maynard asked.

"The vehicle's particulars have been passed to the traffic division. I'll check with them now to see if they have anything to report," Crawford replied, picking up the telephone. Maynard listened to what sounded like a negative response to Crawford's enquiry. "Aye, well, tell them to keep their eyes open, okay?" Crawford replied, replacing the receiver.

"Nothing?"

"I'm afraid not," Crawford said, frowning.

"He's here, I know it. I can feel it, the murdering sod's in the area, but where? Where is he making for?" Maynard said, surveying the wall map. Turning around quickly, he looked at Crawford. "Do we know how much petrol was in the Singer?"

"I'm sorry, I never thought to ask," Crawford answered and blushed a little.

"Could you find out for me, also what mileage the car will do on a gallon of petrol, that will give us some idea as to what distance he can travel."

"Aye! I'll do it right away."

* * *

Maynard had just put down the phone after ringing Granville in London when a police constable entered the room holding a piece of paper. "These are the details for the Singer motor vehicle that you asked for, sir."

"Thank you. Where is the chief superintendent now?" Maynard asked.

"He's in the control room."

Maynard found Crawford studying the large wall map with a tall, lean man in a rather shabby looking suit who Maynard suspected was from the plain clothes division.

"Mr Maynard, this is Sergeant Baird, he's with the CID. He is going to work with us on the Bayer case because of his knowledge of the Outer Islands. He has worked on quite a few cases over there in the past, so his input will be greatly appreciated.

"Sergeant," Maynard acknowledged, coming between the two men.

"I see you have got the details of the Singer?" Crawford said.

"Yes, thank you."

"So with the petrol that was in the tank and a couple of gallons in the boot, I would think the vehicle could cover about a hundred miles," Crawford said, looking at both men respectively, to which they were both in agreement.

"Now, let's see. It is roughly about sixty miles from where the vehicle was taken from to here, so that gives Bayer forty miles of coastline to play with on either side of Oban. If he goes northward, up the A828, he's got to go up as far as Fort William to get over to the coast, which means he will have to get more petrol somehow or find some more transport – which he is very adept at doing, but it's not without its risks. The second alternative he's got is to follow the A816 south," Maynard concluded.

"Where there are plenty of bays and islands where he could get picked up from by submarine. Or, like you said, Mr Maynard, he's making for one of the Outer Islands," Baird added.

Chapter 24

Bayer rolled onto his back and looked up at the ceiling while his heavy breathing receded to a more moderate pace. "What time is it?" he asked as he turned on his side to watch Stella's visually appealing figure heading towards the bathroom.

"Quarter to eleven," she replied over the sound of running water.

Slipping out of bed, he got partially dressed, then crossed the room to draw back the curtains to see what Sunday morning had to offer. From his high vantage point, he had a clear view of the town, bay and docks. Running a careful eye over the scene below, he was soon drawn to a certain amount of activity that was taking place around the area of the dock office. He stood watching the comings and goings for several minutes when he felt arms slip around his naked waist, and Stella's chin came to rest on his right shoulder.

"What are you looking at?" she asked, kissing his neck several times.

"I was just wondering what was going on down there at the dock office," he said in a matter-of-fact tone so as not to arouse any suspicion. "You work there, Stella. Is that normal on a Sunday morning?"

Focusing on where her lover was looking, she watched in silence for several minutes, intrigued by the presence of people she didn't recognise. "Well, whatever's going on down there, it's nothing I've heard about. Anyway, are you coming down? I'm going to make some breakfast then, afterwards. Maybe you'd like to leave your hotel and come and stay here for the next two nights."

"If that's what you want, who am I to argue?"

"That's what I want," she answered with a wink.

He finished dressing, deliberately leaving his wrist-watch on the bedside table and giving him a reason to go back upstairs after breakfast to retrieve it and take another look at developments on the docks.

Sitting down at the breakfast table, Bayer still had an uneasy feeling about what he had seen as he watched Stella go through the motions of preparing them a meal.

"You're quiet?"

"I'm fine," he said, trying to sound light-hearted about it.

"Breakfast won't be long. There's tea in the pot if you'd like to pour it."

"How have you found working at the docks? Do you get much going on up here?" Bayer asked casually, filling both cups.

"We have had several reports of German submarines being seen off the Outer Islands. They reckon they could be dropping off or picking up agents that might be trying to get on or off the mainland. Fortunately, the navy and air force are pretty active in these parts, and the port authorities keep a watchful eye on who's coming and going. Only last week, they caught an airman trying to get home without a pass, so he was for the high jump."

"Yes, I suppose he would be," Bayer grinned.

"You've never actually said where you're making for, Andrew?" she said, giving him a questioning look.

Bayer looked at her expressionless. "No, I haven't, have I?" he replied.

Stella dropped her gaze back to what she was doing. "I see, like that, is it?"

"I'm afraid so, not allowed to talk about it, you understand?"

"I get the picture," she said, placing the knives and forks on the table.

* * *

After retrieving his watch from the bedroom, he returned to his hotel, telling Stella he would see her later that evening. As the day wore on, a raw coldness began to take over from the less harsh conditions of the morning and, by early afternoon, snow showers began to sweep in across the bay. He had been in the early stages of sleep after his long night of passion when the sound of a ship's horn roused him back to consciousness and sent him to the bedroom window to watch the docking procedure of the freighter.

Bayer noticed that there seemed to be a lot of interest taken in the disembarking passengers by certain parties on the quayside, which made him wonder if what Stella had said was right. Were the authorities on the lookout for someone? He sat down on the bed to think things over but, no matter which way he looked at the situation, it still came back to the same thing: he had to get to the Outer Islands and steal a boat to get to Stracandra Island. Pulling the eiderdown over himself for added warmth, and with thoughts of his predicament on his mind, he drifted off to sleep.

The room was in total darkness when he woke. Getting out from the confines of the warm bed he shivered as he made his way to the window only to see the dark, silent shape of the ship, its superstructure illuminated by several dimly lit security lights. Bayer noted that there didn't seem to be any activity either on the freighter or the quayside and it passed through his mind whether there was a chance of getting aboard without being seen and finding some obscure place to hide. Closing the curtains, he switched on the light, then set about getting ready to go and meet Stella while turning over his latest plan for getting onboard.

The scheme seemed to throw up several difficulties the more he thought it over. Firstly, he had to get across the open expanse of the docks. If he succeeded in doing that, he then had to get on board and find someplace where he could conceal himself for the duration of the voyage. But with the ship making more than one stop, there was always the chance he could be discovered before he reached Barra, and if he had to kill to protect himself, he knew he had only one line of escape, and that was over the side. That, he knew, would be fatal in these cold northern waters in winter. There had to be another way where he wouldn't look so conspicuous. Leaving the room, he went downstairs to reception to pay his bill. The hotelier gave him a sly grin when he gave the reason for his unusual departure time being a lady he had met the previous evening.

Walking the unlit streets in the cold night air to where Stella lived, Bayer thought of an earlier remark she had made. She would be on the dockside to see him off on Tuesday morning. "Yes," he whispered to himself. There was the answer to his predicament. If he could persuade her to come with him, the authorities would be keeping more of an eye on single passengers, especially men. But a couple travelling together would draw less attention from the authorities if they looked like a couple in love off to the Outer Islands to spend some quality time together. It would be no problem to eliminate her and get rid of her body once he reached his objective.

Stella cried out in ecstasy as Andrew's rhythmic movement made her shed her self-control. She lay quiet and still for quite some time. He was the perfect lover with a body to match; strong, handsome, and at all times in complete control while making love. Could she fall in love with him? That, she knew, would be easy by the way he made her feel. She'd had several lovers while her husband had been away; none had come remotely close to making her feel the way she did now.

"Did you?" she whispered, kissing him tenderly.

"Yes," he grinned.

"I can't get enough of you."

Bayer smiled as he looked up at her, he knew the time was right to suggest that she go away with him, but first, he had to take care of her sexual needs.

* * *

"Are you serious?" Stella asked, propping herself up on one elbow to look at him.

Bayer gave her a pensive look. "Of course I am. I wouldn't have said it if I didn't mean it. I still have two weeks leave left. Do you think you can get some time off at such short notice?"

Stella smiled. "I think I can manage that. It's just a case of knowing the right person to ask, especially when that certain married person is having a discreet affair with one of the girls in the office."

"That office of yours sounds a right den of iniquity. Does this person know about your little indiscretions?" Bayer queried.

"I couldn't care less if he does. I've never kept it a secret what I do. He has come on to me several times in the past but I always keep him at arm's length. I just don't fancy him."

"Have you told him that?"

Stella threw her head back and laughed. "It serves my purpose to keep him dangling if you know what I mean. It's surprising what you can get out of a man if he thinks there is something at the end of it."

Bayer smirked inwardly. If only she knew how he was using her and what her fate was going to be, she wouldn't be so complacent. "You certainly have a devious nature. It's surprising you haven't been recruited by the security services," Bayer answered dryly.

Lowering herself back down so she could lay beside him, she draped her arm across his chest and kissed him tenderly on the cheek. "Do you think I would make a good spy?"

"I'm sure you would."

Chapter 25

Will was thankful for the warmth of his RAF greatcoat as he sat in the unheated transport for the short journey from the dockside back to camp. It had been the first time since joining the RAF he had come back from leave with mixed feelings. Saying goodbye to Aileen and Duncan Hamilton had been hard enough – especially after the hospitality they had shown him during his stay and the compassion they had when in hospital. But saying goodbye to Isobel had been particular heart-wrenching.

He thought back to how quiet they had been with one another as they walked down to the harbour to catch the boat. The way they had held each other as they kissed and the lump that came into his throat as he stood and watched her wave as the ferry pulled away from the quayside. They had been emotions he had never felt before.

"The officers' mess, sir," the driver announced, looking at Will in such a manner to suggest that he must be a new arrival to the base.

Will didn't enlighten him that he was no stranger to the camp but just thanked him before heading for the warmth of the mess, where he was immediately confronted by the chief steward, asking him if he would like to eat after his long journey.

"Yes, please," he said enthusiastically at the thought of

some hot food.

"Very good, sir. By the way, sir, you'll find there is a Flight Lieutenant Bishop sharing the room with you now. It was a shame to hear about Pilot Officer Dennison."

Will looked at the man a few moments before speaking. "Why, what has happened to him?"

"It was while you were in hospital, sir. We heard that Pilot Officer Colin Dennison with his crew had been reported missing flying in a Sunderland aircraft. Very tragic, he was a nice gentleman."

"Yes, he was," Will answered sadly. "Do you know what happened?"

"The aircraft that he was flying in went out to relieve another one that was on convoy duty, but his aircraft never arrived to take over. They don't know what happened to it. There was no radio communication from the aircraft, so they don't know where it has gone down."

The room was in darkness when Will pushed open the door. He threw his bag on the bed and set about unpacking. He had just about finished when the door opened and he came face to face with his new roommate.

"Hello, they said you would be coming back today – I'm Clive Bishop," he said, holding out his hand to shake.

Will reciprocated the handshake. "Will Madden, nice to meet you. So, have you settled in okay?"

"Yes, thanks. That's apart from the ruddy weather up here. The wind cuts you in two when it's blowing in from the sea, doesn't it? I don't know how them lads stick it working outside on the aircraft in this weather."

After taking off his shoes and plumping up his pillow to make a headrest, Will took up a comfortable position on his bed and looked at his slightly overweight roommate. "Yes, you've got to take your hat off to the ground crews, they are always hard at it whatever the weather. So what‘s your particular field of expertise?” Will asked, knowing it must be a ground trade as he wasn’t wearing a flying insignia.

“Engines. I replaced Flight Lieutenant Marsh,” Bishop replied while taking up a similar position on his bed.

“So, where were you before you came here?” Will asked.

“RAF Cosford, in a training capacity. And you?”

“Kelstern.”

“That’s in Lincolnshire, isn’t it? Was it operational?”

“Lancs.”

“When I put in for an operational drome, I hoped it might be Lancasters.”

“You sound a bit disappointed?”

“I was, actually. I’ve only been involved with fighters and the medium-range stuff. But that was only for a short period.”

“Well, at least you’ve got on the heavies, albeit not on Lancs. But there’s nothing wrong with the old Halifax. I did my first tour on them, and they are as reliable as the day is long, and they can take a hell of a lot of punishment,” Will answered in a reassuring voice.

There was silence between the two men for a few moments, each with his own thoughts.

“I did hear through the grapevine that you have done a few sorties since you’ve been here?”

“I’ve done one or two, just to keep my hand in.”

“Like shooting down a German sea plane!” Bishop laughed.

Will nodded, remembering the incident.

“And taking on another enemy aircraft while on an air-sea rescue launch?”

“My, we are well informed.”

“Sorry. It was all around the mess when it filtered back what you had done.”

"Yes, I suppose it would be," Will replied, annoyed that his name had been bandied around the mess in his absence.

Bishop could see by the look on Will's face that he had slightly overstepped the mark.

* * *

Snow showers swept across the airfield as Will made his way to the armoury. He was not relishing his first morning back and his first encounter with Nelson. They had never seen eye to eye up to him going on leave, then being hospitalised, so he was sure that nothing would have changed. Closing the door behind him, he was immediately confronted by Flight Sergeant Milroyd, who welcomed him back in his usual dry manner.

"Hello, Flight. I thought you would have been on your gunnery course by now."

"No. I'm still waiting," Milroyd answered as Will was introduced to a new member of the armaments team who had arrived during his absence. With the formalities done, Milroyd then took Will to one side. "Our intrepid leader said he wants to see you," he said in a rather dubious voice.

"I had an idea he might," Will replied, heading in the direction of Nelson's office. Knocking on the door, he was told to enter and, coming smartly to attention, he stood there waiting for the usual sarcastic remarks that Nelson was capable of.

"At ease, Madden. And please sit down."

"Thank you, sir."

"So how are you feeling?" Nelson enquired.

"Fine," Will responded, wondering what had brought about the change in his manner towards him.

"By all accounts, you had rather a rough time of it while

you were in hospital?"

"Yes, I did," he said, not wanting to elaborate too much on his injuries.

"But you are feeling fit and well now?"

"Yes," Will replied, annoyed that he was repeating himself.

"Well, I have some good news for you, Warrant Officer."

"You have, sir?"

Nelson sat back in his chair and clasped his hands together. "You have been awarded a bar to your D.F.M. and promoted to Pilot Officer for your action against the German aircraft. Flight Lieutenant Fuller, the captain of the launch, said in his report that you saved the boat with your constant fire from the Oerlikon."

"Well, I thank Flight Lieutenant Fuller for what he said in his report, sir. But I think our saviour was the Wellington turning up," Will answered, modesty setting in.

"Maybe so. But by manning the Oerlikon like you did, with its heavier hitting power, you were able to deter the enemy long enough until the Wellington arrived, thus saving the boat from probably being sunk." Will just gave a silent acknowledgement with his head as he listened to what Nelson had to say. "You don't seem very enthusiastic about what was said in the report or your promotion, Madden. I know you've never been happy here in the armoury and that you would rather be on operations, but we all have to put up with things we don't like from time to time, including me," Nelson concluded in a poignant tone.

There's nothing wrong with the armoury, it's the person running it, that's the problem, Will thought, as he slowly answered, "Yes sir."

After leaving Nelson's office he walked over to No1 hangar to look at a Halifax that had arrived and was fitted with a radar-directed, automatic gun-laying turret. It was while he was looking over the turret that Keith Stanbury came up to him and took him to one side.

"I heard you were on your way back, Will, when did you get in?" he asked.

"I got back last night, but I was a bit knackered for socialising. I was going to look you up this evening, so we could sink a few pints. I rang operations to see if you were flying before I left to come over here, and they said you weren't."

"How are you feeling?"

"A lot better than I was."

"It's good to see you back in one piece. Anyway, why I wanted to see you, Will. Our rear gunner has just finished his tour, so we are in need of a replacement. I wondered if you would be interested?"

"Normally I would jump at it, as you know. The trouble is, I haven't completed my six-month rest period, so I don't think they would let me go back flying yet. You know what Nelson's like about me doing these little 'jollies', as he calls them. He would soon turn down any request I put in to go back on ops again. I only got away with it last time because of the flu outbreak, and he was told to release me for flying duties."

Keith Stanbury gave him a sly grin. "Leave it with me, Will. You've got to know the right people to approach on matters like this. I'll let you know the outcome later," he said, winking. "I'll see you in the bar about eight. Oh! One thing before I go, what the hell were you doing on an air-sea rescue boat anyway?"

Will gave him a non-committal look. "I'll give you all the gen on that later when I see you in the bar, okay?"

* * *

"So there you have it, the whole story from start to finish," Will said, taking a drink of beer to alleviate the dryness in his mouth.

Keith sat back in his chair and looked at him with a grin on his face for a few moments. "So this girl, Isobel. Are you going to see her again?"

Will put down his glass on the table and thought back to how Isobel had looked when he left her on the quayside. "I hope so. She said she would write, so I'm hoping it will lead to us meeting up again. I do really like her, Keith."

"I can see that. But what about Daphne?"

Will gave his friend a sheepish look. "Yes, Daphne. I've been thinking about her, too. I'm going to have to tell her I've met somebody else. It's the only decent thing to do."

Keith Stanbury took a drink then sat forward so as not to be overheard. "Well, my old mate, I think you might be off the hook in that department."

"Why's that?"

"You know the navigator she was going out with, the one that was shot down?"

Will nodded. "Well, he's been ringing her up quite frequently. Got back home via the French underground by all accounts. A WAAF I have been seeing called Joan, who is in the same section as Daphne, told me that she has been wondering how she was going to tell you when you got back, especially with you being hurt and in hospital. Anyway, it looks like you are going to have the opportunity to sort things out, she has just come into the bar with Joan and they are coming over," he said, looking over at the door.

"May we join you?" Joan asked, her eyes fixed firmly on Keith Stanbury.

"Certainly. What would you both like to drink?" Keith asked, pulling back two chairs for them to sit down.

"A small beer for both of us, please."

Keith knew that Will wanted to have a quiet word with Daphne, so he cajoled Joan into giving him a hand with the drinks to give the pair a little space and time to talk things over.

Sitting down next to him, Daphne gently laid her hand on his arm. "It's so nice to see you back, Will. I was so worried when Keith told me what had happened to you."

"Thanks," he answered, turning the empty glass slowly around on the table. There followed a few moments of uneasy silence between them, which Will knew he had to end before Keith and Joan returned. "Keith told me the good news about your navigator friend doing a home run through enemy lines. Says he's been ringing you up quite often. You must be very pleased?"

"Yes, I am." Will could see she was finding it difficult to end their brief relationship, so decided to make things a little easier for her, but she was a little quicker off the mark than he had expected. "About us, Will ..."

"Don't worry, Daphne, I understand. I know you were very serious about him before he went missing," he said, squeezing her hand gently.

"You don't mind?"

"No, not in the least. In fact, I was in a bit of a dilemma myself and wasn't sure how I was going to resolve it."

"Let me guess? You've met somebody else."

Will looked at her. "You are very shrewd, Daphne."

"I'm very glad for you. So, who is the lucky lady?"

"She is the sister of Dave Hamilton. He was the mid-upper gunner on my last crew. Her name's Isobel."

The conversation was brought to a close with the arrival

of Keith and Joan with their drinks. Will didn't get a chance until later in the evening, when they were at the bar together, to ask Keith whether he had said anything about him going back flying. Keith had just given him a self-satisfied look, then winked.

"It's all in hand," he said, putting two glasses in his hands.

* * *

High winds and rough seas had delayed the sailing to Lochboisdale. Being cooped up in Stella's home for several days had been pleasurable, but Bayer was now eager to get on the move. He had a smug look on his face as he looked through the porthole at the heavy coating of snow that lay across the dock. Not only had Stella been able to get two weeks leave, but her influence with a certain individual had also got them a cabin of a decent size, albeit with up-and-over bunks. Also, she had been able to get them aboard the previous evening when there were no officials or passengers about. Sitting down on the bottom bunk, he gave her backside a light smack which had the desired effect, making her turn over and look at him.

"Do you think anyone will bother us for a while?"

Stella gave him a seductive grin. "I shouldn't think so. Why, have you got something in mind?"

"I think you know what I've got in mind," he whispered.

It had been activity outside the cabin and the starting of the engines that woke him. Supporting himself up on one elbow, he could see shadows under the door as crew members moved along the corridor, making for their respective stations.

"What's the matter?" Stella asked sleepily, his movement having woken her.

"They have just started the engines. They must be about to get underway," he replied, extricating himself from her arms and going over to take a look through the porthole.

"Is that all? Come back to bed. I've got something that will get you started," she said, patting the bunk next to her.

* * *

Bracing himself against the pitching sea, Bayer could just make out the dark outline of South Uist in the distance and flicked the cigarette stub over the side. Being delayed again, leaving Tiree due to bad weather had set him back another two days. Setbacks he didn't need being so close to reaching his final destination on Stracandra Island. But first, he had to plan how to get rid of Stella. She had played her part well, but now she was no further use, just a millstone around his neck, and she needed to be disposed of as soon as possible.

Going below, Bayer found her in the galley, sitting on the edge of a table making jovial banter with several members of the crew. To his surprise, this irritated him.

"There you are, darling. I was just saying to the guys here that you had been gone a long time and I hoped you hadn't fallen over the side," her flippancy bringing about a round of laughter. "Would you like a cup of tea? Mitch here will make you one if you ask him nicely," she said, flashing her eyes in the cook's direction.

"No, I'm fine," he answered, suppressing the anger he was feeling towards her. "I think we should go back to the cabin and get our things together, we'll be docking shortly," he said.

"He can be so masterful at times," she said, loud enough for all to hear as she slid off the table and straightened her skirt.

Reaching the cabin, he slammed the door shut behind him, then grabbing hold of her arm, he swung her around to face him, then slapped her hard across her left cheek. "Don't you ever try and make me look a fool again in front of anybody, you hear?" he snapped. He lifted his arm to give her another but checked himself when he saw her smile as she rubbed her cheek.

"Now I know you love me," she said, coming towards him, putting her arms around him and kissing him long and hard.

Pulling away, he looked at her and tried to search out the hatred he needed to carry out what he had to do when they reached Lochboisdale. But, however hard he tried, as he looked into her eyes, he could not evoke any feeling of anger towards her. For the first time since joining Abwehr, Bayer knew he had let a woman get her claws into him, something he vowed he would never let happen. She had learned how to communicate with him both physically and emotionally in ways no other woman had. He could easily – and without remorse – have killed Griselda and walked away without a backward glance; those had been his orders. Stella was different. Exceptionally good-looking, highly sexed, which suited his own nature; she had all the qualities he liked in a woman. "What am I going to do with you?" he said, taking her roughly in his arms.

"Whatever you want to," she smiled, unaware that her life was hanging by a thread and could soon come to an end in the next few hours.

They stayed below until the boat had finished docking before venturing out into the cold evening air to the disembarkation centre, which, to Bayer's surprise, was relevantly easy due to some cross-chat from Stella with the disembarkation staff.

Once clear of the port facilities he relaxed a little. They walked the short distance to a guesthouse Stella knew. The proprietor there was very discreet and didn't ask any questions. The room was small in comparison to some he had slept in, but the double bed was soft, and the fire soon gave the room a comfortable feel about it. He lay on the bed and listened as Stella filled the bath. She had only once asked him about his final destination when he reached the island, which he had easily passed off as being a need-to-know matter which she had readily excepted under the circumstances, but he began to wonder how much longer could he keep up the deception. She had given him a rather questioning look when he had told the owner when registering that they only wanted the room for a couple of nights. Having planned to spend a week together, Bayer knew it would only be a matter of time before he would have to give a suitable explanation about what he intended to do about accommodation for the remainder of the holiday.

He knew his first priority was to reconnoitre the area for a boat, but he needed to be on his own to do that. Also, he would need a chart of the islands. The road map he carried in his travel bag had served him well so far, but it only showed the islands in brief. What he needed was a detailed chart of the area, which no doubt would be hard to come by unless the boat he acquired had one onboard.

His thoughts were suddenly interrupted by Stella inviting him to join her. After his slow seduction of her body while they bathed together, the inevitable had followed and, as he lay on his side, he stared into the darkness while listening to his lover sleeping. How easy it would be to kill her now, quick and silent and her body wouldn't be found until mid-morning at the earliest, giving him plenty of time to be well clear of the scene.

Rolling onto his back he sighed heavily, knowing the time or place wasn't right to eliminate her; getting a boat was his first priority, but in such a small place it would soon be missed and reported to the authorities. Why in the hell had High Command wanted to bring him out by seaplane? The normal method by U-boat was surely easier.

Getting out of bed, he walked over to the window and eased back the blackout curtain. He looked at the cold waters of the bay with its scattering of boats gently riding at their moorings. He knew why. Speed was of the essence. The information he had collected was of vital importance to the German war effort and needed to be got back as quickly as possible. He stood there several minutes and, with the help of the moonlight, he was able to take in the position of each boat.

But he kept coming back to one boat in particular. It seemed to have all the qualities he was looking for. Its size wasn't excessive, but it looked sturdy enough to cope with reasonably rough seas. The wheelhouse was set fairly well forward and, to its rear, the open deck looked like it was being used for crab or lobster fishing as there were several pots stacked neatly, as high as the gunwale on either side. Bayer knew he needed to take a closer look at both the boat and surrounding area, but he would have to wait for daylight to do that.

With the cold beginning to take effect on his naked body, he let the curtain drop back into place and returned to the warmth of the bed. Cupping his fingers together, he put them behind his head then started to make mental notes of things he had to do.

The first thing he needed to know was, had the boat enough fuel to take him to the island? If not, where was the fuel for the boats kept? A chart of the area he was heading for was a must. But, the more he thought about it, the more convinced he was that a fishing boat of that size would have charts stored somewhere on board. He would need to locate the fishing boat's tender or, if that failed, find another small boat to reach the moored vessel. Then he would have to take care of Stella and get rid of her body. She posed more of a problem. To kill her was the easy part, but to make sure she stayed hidden long enough for him to get clear was more difficult.

A thought struck him, could he somehow get her onto the boat? What made-up excuse could he use that would sound convincing enough to lure her aboard? A smile spread across his face in the darkness as a plan came into his head. What better reason would he need for getting her onboard than if he told her he was taking her away for a few romantic days in a cottage on an island? That way he could do what he had to do and let the sea do the rest.

Chapter 26

Maynard slammed down the receiver after his talk with Clifford Granville. The lack of anything to report hadn't gone down too well with London. In fact, Maynard thought Granville had been rather standoffish with him.

"Things not sitting too well with London?" Crawford enquired discreetly.

"Does it show that much?" Maynard frowned and sat back in his chair. "They are sending someone else up from London on the pretext of giving me a hand. But I think it's exasperation on their part that I haven't tracked down Bayer yet."

"Do you know who it is they are sending?" Crawford enquired.

"His name is Gideon Soames." Maynard had heard his name before but never worked with him and the last thing he wanted was interference from an outsider and the case being taken away from him. Not when he was so close.

Maynard stood up and walked over to the window. "Where is the sod? Is there something we've overlooked? Some small clue we have missed which could tell us which direction he's making for."

"Nary a thing that I can see. We've checked all the passengers going through the port. There's been nothing out of the ordinary reported apart from two men being arrested for fighting and a couple being drunk and disorderly. They were all dealt with accordingly. What about the navy and air force? Have you been in touch with them?"

"The navy had nothing to report. But some good news from the RAF. A Coastal Command aircraft attacked and sank a U-boat running on the surface during the early hours of this morning. By all accounts, the heading it was on, it was most likely making for the North Atlantic, so that's one less our merchant ships have to worry about," Maynard chuckled.

"Aye. I lost my elder brother in the Great War to a German submarine."

"Oh. I'm sorry to hear that. What branch of the services was he in?"

"Merchant navy, he had just had his twenty-first birthday when their ship was sunk. My father did eventually come to terms with the loss, but my mother never really got over the shock of losing him so young."

Their conversation was interrupted by Crawford's phone ringing.

"Excuse me one moment … And where was this? … Can you have my car brought round to the front entrance right away? Thank you."

Maynard leaned forward in his seat in anticipation.

"The Singer motor car that was taken from that house in Ardgarten has turned up," Crawford grinned, walking over to the coat stand. "Shall we go and take a look?"

"Where was it found?"

"A couple of miles down the coast. It was covered over with a tarpaulin sheet in a derelict building which was being used to store old farm implements."

After leaving the outskirts of Oban, they followed the coastal road for a short distance before turning off onto a narrow, unused track that took them to where the Singer had been found. Maynard was struck by the unspoilt beauty of the area as he looked across the dark restless water to the island of Kerrera in the distance. "What a beautiful spot!"

"Aye, it's a bonny place, alright," Crawford replied as the two men stood side by side to take in the view.

It was the crunching of the gravel behind them that made them both turn around, made by what Maynard could only describe as a youthful-looking constable whose smiling face and enthusiastic walk came to a stop in front of them.

"This is Mr Maynard, Nairn, he is with the Security Service in London," Crawford said, as he closely gave the young constable's appearance the once-over.

"Pleased to meet you, P C Nairn. And very well done in finding the vehicle."

"Thank you, sir," he blushed as he answered. "The vehicle is over here if you would like to follow me."

Maynard stood and closely studied the car for a few moments. "Have you been inside or touched anything since you found the vehicle?"

"No, sir. All I have done is remove the tarpaulin sheet that was covering it. I did look through the windows, but there didn't seem to be anything of any consequence to see, although I did note that the keys were still in the ignition."

Maynard nodded, acknowledging Nairn's tenacity as he carefully opened the driver's door and peered in before slipping in behind the wheel to inspect the vehicle's interior more thoroughly. The inside of the car was devoid of any clues – apart from one. Maynard noted that there was still petrol in the fuel tank, which meant only one thing: it had been concealed here, so its occupant was in easy walking distance of the port facilities.

Getting out, he walked to the rear of the car and opened the boot door. "Now we know how he was able to get this far," he said, holding up the two empty petrol cans.

"Do you think the person who took the vehicle is still in the vicinity, sir?" Nairn asked, not fully aware of the seriousness of the situation he was involved in.

Maynard looked first at Crawford then at Nairn. "No, I don't. I think our man is long gone by now," he answered, closing the boot door.

"Well, it looks like your bird has flown. Most likely he was picked up by a U-boat along the coast close to where he dumped the car," Crawford suggested as they made the return journey back to Oban.

Maynard stroked his chin in silence as he stared at the coastline. "I don't think so. The coast around here doesn't lend itself to a submarine pick-up; it would be too easy for a surfaced submarine to be seen. Those murdering sods prefer remote bays away from prying eyes before they show themselves and they also like plenty of open water to be able to manoeuvre in, should they be spotted."

"What are you suggesting? That he's been able to get over to the Outer Islands? If so, how was he able to get through the port authorities undetected? No. I don't buy that theory, we would have picked him up for sure," Crawford answered, annoyed that a shadow was being cast over the way the police was handling the case.

Maynard sensed Crawford's exasperation, so decided to try and cool things down between them. "I'm not trying to belittle either the police or port authorities in any way. Bayer is a ruthless and calculated operator. I should know, I have been dogging his tracks all the way up the country, and all the time he seems to be one jump ahead of me. It's as if he knows what our next move is. It's also surprising how resolute the man is to get back to Germany. He is definitely a thinker and plans things very carefully before making his move, so don't be at all surprised if he has been able to get on board a boat without being seen."

"Aye. But how?" Crawford retorted.

"That we may never know unless we are able to take the man alive, which I think is going to be very unlikely given his nature."

"Do you think it's worth doing another check of the hotels and guesthouses in the area?"

Maynard shook his head. "You can give it a try, but I don't hold out much hope in that quarter, I think our man is well clear of Oban by now."

"The police stations on the Outer Islands have all been notified to be on the lookout for anything or anyone that looks a bit suspicious. You've got the RAF and the Royal Navy involved, so I don't see what more y'can do. If you want my honest opinion, Mr Maynard, I think this Bayer character is on his way back to Germany by now."

* * *

Bayer looked out at the heavy rain being swept in by a strong south-westerly wind. Searching the bay, he was taken aback to see the boat he had got his eye on wasn't there. Cursing quietly to himself so as not to let Stella hear, he washed and dressed, then together they made their way to the dining room, which they found empty. Occupying the table by the window, they were immediately confronted by a waitress who took their order with the minimum of words.

Stella watched the woman leave the room. "God. She's a barrel of laughs," she said, rolling her eyes.

"Maybe she's depressed over something," Bayer suggested.

Stella threw her head back and laughed. "Well, I know a

good cure for depression."

Bayer shook his head as he studied her for a few moments. "Is that all you think about, sex?"

"Is there anything else?" she said, giving him a sulky expression.

After breakfast, they went into the lounge to allow the non-talkative waitress chance to clear their table. With a respite in the rain, Bayer saw his chance to take a closer look around the bay to see what other boats and tenders were on offer. "Fancy going for a walk?"

Stella frowned, her eyes fixed on the menacing dark grey clouds.

"We could have a walk along the waterside," he said, getting up and walking over to the window. "Anything is better than staying in here."

Stella followed suit and came and stood next to him. "And if the heaven's open up, what then?"

"I'm sure there must be a café we can use," he replied, anxious to be on the move.

Leaving the warmth of the guesthouse, they made their way down towards the harbour, passing several other adventurous souls who had been brave enough to endure the harsh winter weather. The road turned immediately left at the end of a row of brightly painted houses and shops, one of which, they noted, was a café. On the opposite side was an open area, which Bayer assumed was the dock, as there were several empty fish boxes stacked neatly in a row.

"Shall we take a look?" he said, beckoning with his head towards the quay.

Pushing back her hair that swirled across her face, Stella shook her head. "You can if you want to. The only place I'm going is back to that café to get warm and have a drink," she shouted over the gusting wind.

"I won't be long," he grinned, glad that he was on his own to do what he had to do.

Not expecting to find anything moored alongside the deserted quay, it had only been when he reached the end of the line of fish boxes that he saw the ropes around the capstan going over the edge of the stonework to a fishing boat below. Looking down, the first thing Bayer noticed was the aerial that linked to a radio mounted in the wheelhouse and below the console, charts stacked neatly on a shelf. The boat was of a decent size and of sturdy construction and well within his handling capabilities. Using his simple road map, he had calculated the distance between Lochboisdale and the island as being roughly thirty-one miles, which he was hoping to cover during the hours of darkness, weather permitting. Once there, he would contact Norway using the radio, then after opening the seacocks, get ashore and hope the boat would drift far enough away from the island and sink in deep water. Then there would follow the waiting game and hoping the weather would stay calm enough to allow the Luftwaffe to land a seaplane to pick him up.

Running a careful eye over the vessel for a second time, it seemed ideal for what he had in mind. His main concern was whether the boat had been refuelled ready for its next voyage; there was no way of knowing that without boarding her and checking, but that wasn't an option in daylight.

He hadn't been aware of anybody approaching from behind and it was only when a voice said, "I cannae see us getting much fishing done in this weather," that he realised there was someone there.

"It certainly is rough," Bayer said, turning to the voice, whereupon he was confronted by a heavily-built man. A well-worn peaked cap sat upon a tangled mass of curly hair that continued down to a full beard, but it didn't hide his weather-beaten features. His broad frame was covered by a heavy woollen jumper, and his black trousers were tucked inside sturdy sea boots. "Is she yours?" Bayer asked, pointing to the boat below.

"Aye, and a fine craft she is. But in these winds, there will be a hell of a sea running once you've rounded the headland."

"What have you been catching?" Bayer asked, being a keen angler before the war.

Sitting down on the capstan, the sea captain took out his pipe and patted out the old tobacco into the palm of his hand, then set about refilling it. "Now let's see. I brought in a good haul of pollock and whiting on my last trip. But y'know there's some nice haddock around. It's just a case of knowing where to look," he winked, sucking contentedly on his pipe.

Bayer smiled and nodded. "That's the name of the game, knowing where to look," he repeated as his mind was carried back to a certain lake near his home in more peaceful times. The early mornings sat by the water's edge with his father, watching the sunrise over the treetops, its warmth making a grey mist rise from the surface of the water like steam. The aroma of hot coffee being poured from a flask, which could suddenly be interrupted by the dipping of the float as a fish took the bait. The playing of the rod and line until it was safely in the holding net. Bayer smiled to himself. They were good days then, days he would repeat again when Germany had won the war, and things got back to normality.

"When do you think you will go out again? Tomorrow?"

The sea captain took his pipe from his mouth and pointed to the sea with it. "Aye. I'll be away on the tide in the morning."

"Are you all ready to go, fuel and suchlike?" he asked in a casual tone.

"Ach aye! I'd have gone this morning if it hadn't been for

this blow, but you cannae fish in this weather. Too dangerous around these waters."

"Yes, I'm sure it is," Bayer replied, pleased with the information. "Well, I'd better be on my way. It's been nice talking with you."

"Likewise, laddie, and good luck t'ye."

"And to you," he said, walking away. "Shame you won't find your boat there in the morning," he said quietly to himself.

He found Stella sitting at a corner table, passing away the time over a cup of tea and a cigarette. "You've been a long time?"

"I've been finalising arrangements," he answered, sitting down next to her.

"What arrangements?" she asked, stubbing out the cigarette end in the ashtray.

Bayer leaned back in his seat and gave her a look of encouragement. "The transport that will take us to an island where there is a cottage I have hired for a few days," he replied, hoping she would readily fall in with his plans.

"An island! Where?"

Chapter 27

Maynard couldn't help wondering what the information was that Gideon Soames had for him as he climbed aboard the waiting aircraft. All he had been told by London was that Soames would already be aboard the aircraft when it landed at RAF Connel at Oban. From there, it would then take them to RAF Stornoway, where the operation would be conducted to either apprehend or eliminate Bayer.

With the fuselage door securely fastened, he made his way to one of the seats. One of which was occupied by a rather debonair-looking man who, on seeing Maynard, got up to shake hands.

"Morning, sir, I'm Gideon Soames."

Reciprocating the gesture, Maynard couldn't help but notice Soames's vice-like grip during the formality and quickly came to the conclusion that outwardly, although there was an ease of manner about him, he looked extremely fit and would be quite capable of taking care of himself if push came to shove. "Morning, had a good trip up?" he asked, sitting down.

"Tiring. I was just about to go on an assignment when I was told I was coming up here, so I haven't had any sleep for several hours," Soames answered.

"Did London brief you before you left as to what this is all about?"

"Not in its entirety, sir. Only that it involved a spy by the name of Bayer and we need to either apprehend or kill him as soon as possible before he gets back to Germany with the information he has. London said you would fill me in with more details when I got here."

Maynard nodded. "Before I do that, I believe you have some information for me?"

Soames nodded. Taking the document from him, Maynard ran a careful eye over the first page. "So Latchmere has turned her," he smiled.

"Griselda Zweig? Yes, she was only too happy to cooperate. An easy option if you are going to get your neck stretched by the hangman," Soames shouted over the noise of the two engines being started.

Maynard looked at him." Where is she now?"

"I'm not privy to that information, sir. All I know is that she is going to feed the Germans with false information for us," Soames replied, stifling a yawn.

"I see." Maynard went back to reading the document he was holding. His attention was drawn to a paragraph partway down the third page. They were the names at an address Zweig had given while under interrogation of those in the Manchester area that had helped her. He had been right; he always thought she was part of a sleeper network that had been put in place long before the war had started. But why had she been picked up on Manchester's Piccadilly station with a ticket to Southampton in her possession?

Looking up to think things over for a few moments, the reason hit him. Griselda had gone to these people for help, most likely hoping they would get her out of the country, that part was obvious. But, after contacting German intelligence, Griselda's request had been turned down. The Warners must have been told to put her on a train to

Southampton where she could be put to work there under another name, or better still, eliminated. Maynard could see that Griselda must have caused a major problem for the Germans while she was free and on the run. Firstly, her making contact with the Warners put them in grave danger should she be arrested and talk, and secondly, her intimate knowledge of the *Raven* and how he operated also posed a threat to his safety.

Maynard sat back in his seat and looked across at Soames. He was fast asleep. The remainder of the page made for disappointing reading. When the Warners' home had been visited by the police, they had found the place empty with no clues as to their whereabouts. The neighbours hadn't been much help either, with most saying that they had seemed a friendly couple and they had gone about their daily business like everyone else.

Putting down the document, Maynard massaged his forehead for a few moments before picking it up and reading on. There was no mention who Griselda's contact was to be when she reached Southampton, just the name of the Tudor House hotel where she had been told to go to and wait until she was contacted. The remaining page-and-a-half had been transcripts of messages sent between Germany and Britain, some of which was appertaining to Bayer and his movements.

Putting the document in his briefcase, Maynard had just settled back to enjoy the remainder of the flight when one of the crew told him that they were nearing Stornoway and would be landing in around fifteen minutes. After making a perfect landing, the pilot then taxied the aircraft to a dispersal bay. Maynard and Soames were then taken to a waiting car that took them to the operations room. Maynard immediately recognised Trent and Carlton, who he had met previously in Oban, plus one other who was introduced as

RAF Stornoway's Commanding Officer.

Maynard sat down at the table and looked at the three men. "Thank you for coming at such short notice. This," Maynard beckoned with his hand, "is Mr Soames, who works for the same department as me in London. He has brought with him a dossier that contains some information that could be vital to the operation. But before we start, I believe congratulations are in order, Group Captain, for the sinking of a U-boat by one of your Coastal Command aircraft."

Carlton leaned back in his chair with a self-satisfied look on his face. "Thank you. That's one less that won't be going back to Germany to gloat over its achievements," he replied, to which they all agreed.

"Right, gentlemen. I won't bore you all with too much detail of how we came by this information we have as it's a long story, but what I will say is this. It is vital that we stop Bayer now. He has got this far north and within striking distance of getting home with the information he's got in his possession. The main routes into this country by enemy agents while we have been at war has been by a night parachute drop or by submarine. The latter you would think being the only means of getting an agent out and back to Germany. But there is another way, not so common, but quite feasible if planned right, and that is by seaplane. With Norway and Denmark now occupied by the Germans, there are plenty of places where they can use these types of aircraft to the best of their ability."

"Does London think this is the way the Germans are going to try and get this man Bayer out of the country?" Commander Trent asked.

Maynard had the makings of a smile on his face as he sat back in his chair and looked at Gideon Soames to answer Trent's question.

"From intercepted communications, it seems very likely. The only thing we don't know is where the pick-up is going to be," Soames answered.

"I see," Trent replied, a perplexed look on his face.

Maynard turned his gaze towards Carlton. "What are your thoughts, Group Captain?"

"Well, German air activity in the area has certainly been on the increase of late, with several encounters between our aircraft and their flying boats. Our air-sea rescue boats have also tangled with these blighters and, being very well-armed, they can give a good account of themselves when we engage them. So, I would think, yes, given good weather and sea conditions for landing, I'm sure the Germans are using these types of aircraft for clandestine operations. But then we come back to the same old question. Where? With so many remote islands in the area, they could make a pick up from any number of places," Carlton answered.

"And you, Wing Commander," Maynard turned to the other man, "have you anything you want to add or ask on the matter?"

"This information that has been intercepted, how reliable do you think it is? Has it specifically mentioned this man Bayer during the transmissions?" the officer asked.

"I can tell you this much. We have only picked up two references to Bayer. At the time of the first intercept, we didn't know who or what '*Das Rabe*' meant. All we had from the second intercept was, '*Das Rabe en route to St Is*', then the transmission ended. We know that '*Das Rabe*' when translated into English means *The Raven*. But it was only after interrogating a young lady we had caught that it came to light that this was Bayer's code name."

"What makes your department think that he is going to be collected by seaplane instead of by U-boat?" Carlton asked.

"Just over fourteen hours ago, one of our listening stations on the east coast picked up a signal sent from Stavanger to the seaplane base at Limfjord near Aalborg in Denmark. It read: *'Dispatch seaplane to Stavanger. Rabe pick-up imminent'*. So now you see why we are pretty sure that's how the Germans are going to get Bayer out." Maynard paused. "The only thing we don't know is what relevance *'St Is'* has in all this. If you have any theories, I would very much like to hear them."

Chapter 28

Since first being told in the café about their trip, Andrew had told her nothing more about where the island was or how long it would take to get there. Stella knew very little about the man she was sleeping with. There was an air of mystery, a dark side to him that she hadn't been able to penetrate, which frightened her at times. So she had left well enough alone and not asked questions. But being whisked away in darkness by boat to an unknown island had cast doubts in her mind. These doubts had been quickly eradicated by their lovemaking during the afternoon, and now all she felt were feelings of excitement.

The wind had dropped considerably as they made their way down to the quayside. With very little talk between them, Bayer had time to think over a problem he could have when they reached the boat and how he was going to resolve it. At least they didn't meet anyone en route. It could have looked suspicious given the late hour and the overnight bags. But his main concern was if the wheelhouse door was locked, how was he going to break in with Stella there?

Stella looked at the *Mary Wade* as it rode gently on the tide. The old car tyres that hung over her side squelched as they were compressed against the dock wall. "It's quite big isn't it, and where's the crew to take us to this island?" she asked.

"We are the crew," Bayer said quietly climbing aboard. "Now pass the bags over," he ordered.

Stella was hesitant but did as she was told, passing them across in turn. "I hope you can handle a boat of this size because I know nothing about these things."

Bayer didn't answer but made his way forward to the wheelhouse, where, to his annoyance, he found the door locked. Looking towards the stern, he could just make out Stella's form deliberating over the best way to get on board. Taking out his knife, he took the pressure of the blade with the palm of his other hand to keep the noise down when it sprung open, then sliding the blade in between the door and the woodwork, he gently pushed upwards. The catch released easily allowing the door to slide open on its runner. Once inside he took stock of the boat's console and in particular the start-up method.

"Shall I put these below?" Stella enquired, holding the two bags.

"Do that while I release the mooring lines."

With the lines untied he returned to the wheelhouse, turned on the ignition key, and pressed the starter button. The engine started on the first attempt, roaring into life and filling the night air with blue smoke. Easing the boat away from the quayside, he made a quick sweep of the surrounding area for inquisitive onlookers; seeing none, he pushed the throttle lever forward to increase speed and headed out towards the deep water channel.

Stella's curiosity had got the better of her when she had carried the bags below. Something hard prompted her to open her lover's bag. Its contents, at first glance, had revealed nothing more than the usual items of clothing and shaving equipment. But further searching revealed a pistol and a road map. She immediately showed visible signs of anxiety. Repacking the bag as she had found it, she contemplated what to do next, but Andrew's voice calling her up to the wheelhouse jolted her back to reality.

"What have you been doing?"

Stella had to think quickly for an answer. "I was in the galley and about to make some coffee," she lied.

"Never mind coffee. Take the wheel and keep it on the course it is on now while I find a chart we need to take us to the island."

Taking the wheel, Stella stared into the darkness while keeping a careful eye on the course indicator as she had been told.

Dropping the charts on the wheelhouse table, he switched on the overhead table light. He then systematically sorted through each chart until he found the one he needed and set about plotting a course to take to reach the island.

"So what is this island called?" Stella asked, trying to keep her tone composed and not show the nervousness she was feeling.

Bayer studied the back of her shapely body while running his hand over the knife in his pocket. It would be so easy to kill her now, he thought and put her lifeless body over the side. She'd given him all the pleasure he'd needed, so why put off what had to be done? She was no further use to him, and by tomorrow, if his luck held and weather permitted, he would be on his way home. Why keep her alive? "Stracandra Island," he answered, straightening up and taking the knife from his pocket.

"I've never heard of that place. How long will it take to get there?" she asked, turning to look at him briefly before turning back to concentrate on keeping the boat on course.

Walking slowly, he came and stood behind her. "Only a few hours," he said quietly, his finger on the release button that would eject the blade from within the handle. One thing he had never been indecisive, he had killed for the love of it in some cases. But as he stood and caught the aroma of her perfume and looked at her perfect figure and thought of the unrelenting satisfaction she had brought him, he suddenly felt neither a willingness nor enthusiasm to take her life. Putting the knife back in his pocket, he put his arm around her waist and gave her a new course to steer.

The weather steadily improved during the latter part of the evening, which continued on through to the early hours. Bayer was pleased with their progress as he took over the wheel and sent Stella below to prepare some food and coffee from the small amount of rations they had been able to bring on board with them.

In the confines of the small galley, Stella got on with the task she had been given, but with the nagging thoughts still playing on her mind. Doubts began to turn to fear and she found her hand beginning to shake as she spooned the coffee into the mugs. She knew nothing about his private life or what he did, or where he came from. She had been too intent on their lovemaking – which he was extremely good at – and it had only been after three days into their steamy relationship that he had disclosed that his last name was Crane.

An impulse made her stop what she was doing and, without hesitating, walk over to the bag, unzip it and take out the gun. She stared at the symbol on the side showing an eagle holding a globe with a swastika. Stella knew nothing about weapons but she now knew enough to know that this one was of German manufacture. What disturbed her most was that it was being carried by her lover. But for what purpose? The only logical explanation she could come up with was that he was a spy or part of one of these fifth column groups she had read about and was now trying to get out of the country.

She turned the pistol over in her hands while wondering what to do. It dawned on her that he was just using her to get to where he was going. After which, she would be no further use to him and her life could be in danger. Stella studied the pistol for a few moments to familiarize herself with its workings. Could she kill to protect herself? She knew she would have to if it meant saving her own life, she thought, slipping the weapon in her coat pocket. She felt a little calmer, knowing she had the means to retaliate if necessary, so after placing the plate of sandwiches and coffee on a rather disgusting looking tray she found, she made her way cautiously up to the wheelhouse.

"You've been a long time?"

"Had trouble with the stove. It's a bit temperamental," she replied, laying the tray down on the chart table. "Is it much further?"

He handed her the binoculars. "That's the island in front of us. Another hour should see us there," he told her, taking a bite from the sandwich.

Stella could make out the distinct line of the island against the lightening sky. The more she studied its high rugged features, the more convinced she became that this was a well-conceived plan her lover had carefully put together for a means of escape.

"Take the wheel, will you? I want to check the chart – make sure you keep her on the course she's on," he ordered in an uncompromising tone.

From the chart, Bayer could see that the lighthouse and buildings and the jetty lay at the most southerly point of the island. He focused the binoculars on the area in question and picked out the tall structure of the lighthouse, standing defiantly against the elements. Lowering the glasses momentarily, he studied the terrain. Satisfied with what he saw, he then refocused the binoculars on the cottages, one of which would give him the much-needed shelter until he was picked up.

Stella could also make out the distant lighthouse with the array of smaller objects off to the right, which she guessed was the cottages that housed the keepers.

"Is that where we are making for, where the lighthouse is?" she asked, looking at his dark features that seemed to look sinister against the side windows of the wheelhouse.

He nodded in response.

"Does anybody else live on the island?" she asked apprehensively.

"No, we've got it all to ourselves."

Alone on an island with a possible killer who could strike at any time, the thought sent a chill through her. How had she been so stupid to let love put her in such a dangerous position, her only salvation being the weapon in her pocket? Taking her right hand off the wheel, she put it in her coat pocket and ran her fingers over the smooth, cold metal, which was reassuring but suddenly brought a thought to mind – was the gun loaded? She hadn't checked it when handling it in the galley, what if her lover had unloaded it in case she found it? She needed to know and the only way she could do that was by making an excuse to go below.

"Can you take the wheel? I need to go below, a bodily function," she grinned, in a tone that had a matter of urgency about it.

"Don't be long. I'll need you to give me a hand to dock when we get there," he replied, taking the wheel from her.

To make things look more natural, she placed the empty plate and mugs on the tray and took them with her and, after leaving them in the galley, she locked herself in the tiny cubicle that served as a toilet. It took her a few minutes to work out that the magazine was in the handle grip and how to get it out. To her relief, she found it contained several rounds of ammunition. Putting the Walther back in her coat pocket, she was just about to make her way back to the wheelhouse when she felt the *Mary Wade* begin to slow down.

Stopping, Stella stared at the narrow stairway in front of her that led up to where her lover was and an uncertain future. Pulling herself together, she climbed the stairs to the wheelhouse that was now bathed in the soft grey light of dawn, which made it easy to pick out the stone jetty that protruded out to sea and rugged features of the keeper's cottages. One of which looked badly damaged.

Picking up the binoculars, she focused them on the remains of the first building. "The first cottage is just a ruin," she said and switched her gaze to the second one.

"Yes, I know," Bayer answered.

"What happened?" Stella asked, lowering the glasses and looking at him.

He adjusted the throttle lever to bring the boat down to a more manageable speed for what he had in mind before answering her. "I believe a German submarine fired at it in the early days of the war. The second cottage wasn't hit so that's the one we will be using," he replied, bringing the boat around in a slow arc until the *Mary Wade's* starboard side lined up nicely with the jetty.

"You know that for sure, do you?"

"Know what?" he asked, concentrating more on the manoeuvre he was trying to undertake than the question.

"That the cottage is fit to live in?"

He glared at her, annoyed at her persistence. "Never mind about the bloody cottage, you stupid bitch. Take the damn wheel so I can get on the jetty and get the ropes through the mooring rings and tied off before we finish up on the rocks!" he shouted.

Expecting to be chastised with a slap to the face like he had done on the way over from Oban, she quickly did as she had been told.

With the boat eventually secure alongside the weathered stonework of the jetty, Bayer shut down the engine then contemplated his next moves. The first was to use the *Mary Wade's* transmitter to contact Norway, followed by scuttling the boat, but he needed Stella out of the way. Thinking back to what Metzger had told him about the location of the cottage key in the adjacent storeroom, he decided to send her on ahead. This would then give him the time he needed to carry out what he had to do. Going below, he brought up their travel bags and dropped them on the deck, then one at a time passed them over to her. "Take them up to the cottage. You'll find the key to unlock the door hanging on a hook in the storeroom next to the cottage. There's no need for you to come back to the boat. As soon as I've made sure everything is secure here, I'll come and join you, okay?"

Stella just nodded. She was still smarting from the abusive way he had spoken to her earlier. Picking up the bags, she turned and made her way along the jetty to the rough-hewn steps that led up to the buildings above.

Switching on the transmitter, Bayer gave it a few moments to warm up. Then, using the details that Metzger had given him, which he had put to memory, he contacted Stavanger and was told to be ready to be picked up at first light the following morning. With the sun beginning to appear through the broken cloud in the east, he knew the fishing boat would now have been reported stolen. He needed to send it to the bottom as soon as possible before it was seen by either a passing ship or aircraft. Well-trained in the art of sabotage, he set about cutting a length of rope from a longer piece he found on deck. Returning to the wheelhouse, he lashed the wheel so the boat would head away from the island and out into deep water. Satisfied, he started the boat's engine then went below to the engine room. Using his knife, he cut the hose and opened the seacock and then did the same with the one in the forward compartment. He grinned to himself as a steady gush of water spread across the floor of the lower deck.

Going back on deck, he knew his timing had to be perfection if his next move was to be successful. With the boat rocking gently against the stonework, he jumped onto the jetty and quickly released the mooring lines and threw them onto the deck. Back on board, he dropped them below through an open hatch cover along with any other loose items he could find before carrying out the final phase of the sinking operation. He knew it would be a leap of faith as he took hold of the throttle lever and slowly eased it forward, and felt the boat gain momentum from the powerful engine.

With the *Mary Wade's* side scraping along with the protruding structure, he stood on the narrow ledge of the gunwale that ran around the boat's side, holding on to a masthead wire for support. The gap between the two was wide, and he fell heavily when landing on the jetty. Slightly winded but with no bones broken, he stood up and took out the binoculars from their case, having had the foresight to hang it around his neck before his hasty departure. He was pleased to see the boat get well clear of the island before it started settling low in the water from the added weight within its hull until its gallant engine finally gave out. Going down by the stern, it gracefully succumbed to a watery grave.

Waiting until the surface had subsided of escaping air

from the stricken vessel, he then spent several minutes scanning the area carefully for any flotsam that may have come up from the wreck. Apart from a patch of fuel oil, which seemed to be drifting out to sea, he could see little sign of any floating debris, which made him wonder if the boat had turned over before hitting the bottom, trapping any loose items inside the hull.

* * *

Stella looked around at the place she was supposed to live in over the next few days. A thick layer of dust covered the whole of the room; pictures hung at odd angles on the walls. A crude attempt had been made to put the curtains back up after the shelling by the U-boat. Dirty crockery lay in an overflowing bowl of filthy water fed from a dripping tap and the discarded remnants of a meal covered over with green mould lay strewn on the table. Broken glass and china from a display cabinet were piled in a corner with the shattered remains of a mirror and, a black damp scar ran down the wall, the hallmarks of a leaking roof.

She hadn't ventured into any of the other rooms. She had seen enough by what she had seen so far. "You must be joking if you think I'm going to stay here in this rubbish dump," she said to herself while turning to go back outside, slamming the door hard behind her as she left. Reaching the cliff edge and the steps that went down to the jetty she suddenly stopped in disbelief. Her only means of getting off the island heading out to sea and sinking while Andrew stood and watched the whole event.

"You bastard!" she shouted at the top of her voice. Taking the pistol from her pocket and holding it with both hands, she took aim and fired several shots at him.

Bayer heard the bullets whistle close overhead and saw them splash harmlessly into the sea on the far side of the jetty. Running for cover and flattening himself against the cliffside, he knew he was in a precarious position if she decided to come down to look for him. Cursing for being too preoccupied with sinking the boat and not taking the Walther from the bag, he desperately tried to remember how many rounds there had been left when he last checked it. The figure five came to mind and, if his memory was right, she still had two bullets left, having fired three, not good odds with only a knife to protect himself with. He needed to make her fire the other two, and the only way he could do that was to show himself and hope she missed when she fired. Working his way slowly forward, using the boulders for cover, he reached the bottom of the steps without being seen. He eased out to take a look. Two shots rang out almost immediately, the first ricocheting off the jetty stonework in front of him. The second found its mark, going through his clothing and tearing a path through the flesh of his upper right arm, which made him cry out from the pain.

"You bitch," he hissed, taking off his jacket, jersey and the belt from his trousers, which he looped around his arm, pulling it tight to stem the bleeding. He then set about cutting a piece of his shirt sleeve into a strip and bound it firmly around the wound. Now feeling a little more comfortable, he slipped his jersey and coat back on and decided to risk another look to see if she was still there. To his surprise, she was standing motionless, arms by her side, her right hand still clutching the Walther with a fixed look on her face staring down at the sea. He moved out from his hiding place and slowly walked forward, keeping the knife out of her view and stopping at the bottom of the steps. Bayer looked up, and he could see that she had begun to cry.

She gave him a long concentrated look. "Why Andrew? Why all this? Whatever have I done to you to deserve it? All I have ever done is give you my love. I know you must be German because of the swastika on the gun and I presume you intend to kill me. But I'd like to know why you have brought me all this way to do it?" she asked, wiping her eyes.

Still a little unsure whether the pistol was empty, he decided on the soft approach. "You were useful, Stella, to get me away from the mainland and over to here. Also, you are a very good lover. I would go as far as saying the best I've ever had. And yes, you are right, I am German, and it's vital I get back to Germany as soon as possible."

Stella studied him for a few moments and wondered whatever she had seen in him. "It's my duty to kill you if I can stop you getting back," she answered, slowly bringing the pistol up and levelling it at his chest.

Grinning, he shook his head. "It's a very hard thing to do, to actually kill a person, Stella. Do you think you have got what it takes to do it?"

"I'm sure I have," she replied, pulling the trigger but getting no response from the weapon. Trying again several times, she realised it was out of ammunition. Dejected, Stella slowly lowered the gun down and, releasing her grip on it, let it fall to the ground.

"You should always check your weapon before you intend to kill. If you had done so, you would have known there were only five bullets left," he told her superciliously, bringing the knife into view so she could see it.

Fearing for her life, Stella turned and ran for the protection of the cottage. But she tripped on the uneven ground, falling heavily and twisting her ankle. She cried out because of the pain and because she hadn't been able to reach the door before his superior speed caught her. His overpowering strength easily brought her down. Rolling her over onto her back and using his body weight to pin her down, he laid the blade of the knife against her throat.

Chapter 29

Hauptmann Bernard Kurtz settled himself into the pilot's seat alongside his radio operator, Oberfeldwebel Herbert Bolling, in the Blohm and Voss flying boat. Starting the three engines, he let them warm up while he checked the crew positions. In the nose turret was Manfred Filor; Walter Myer and Viktor Klingemann manned the rear and upper rear. All reported back that things were satisfactory, then followed the usual, light-hearted banter between the three men who had flown many hours together and came to rely on each other implicitly. Kurtz thought back to the briefing and the annoyance at being told that his regular navigator, Engel, was being replaced for this operation by – Oberleutant Karl Bastion whose navigating skills he knew nothing about.

Getting the thumbs-up from Bolling, indicating they were free to move away from their mooring, Kurtz taxied the flying boat out across the calm waters of Limfjord. While waiting for permission to take off, which was being held up by the late arrival of an Arado reconnaissance aircraft that was making an emergency landing with engine problems, Kurtz's thoughts turned again to the briefing which had been uninformative, to say the least: fly to Stavanger and refuel, after which he would be briefed fully on the operation he was to carry out.

The flight north over the Skagerrak and across the tip of

Norway was uneventful and they landed under clear blue skies at Stavanger ahead of schedule and taxied to their mooring. With the refuelling operation underway and leaving the crew to carry out their own tasks, Kurtz made his way to operations and a meeting that was to bring to the forefront the darker side of the Third Reich.

"Please follow me, sir," the young subordinate said, hastily making his way along the corridor and coming to an abrupt halt outside an office door, whereupon he quickly checked his appearance and adjusted his tie before knocking.

"Come!"

Opening the door, he entered and came smartly to attention. "Hauptmann Kurtz, sir."

"Good, show him in," a voice with authority answered.

On entering, Kurtz immediately saw why the young man had been so uneasy at the door. Sat behind the desk was a thick-set man in a dark grey suit whose features looked to be that of a prize-fighter, and stood next to him in an immaculate black uniform, an officer of the SS.

"You have made good time from Aalborg, Hauptmann. Please, sit."

Kurtz was offered a cigarette, which he took. "It was a good flight, the weather was excellent," he replied, sitting back in the chair to show he wasn't going to be intimidated by their presence.

The man behind the desk drew hard on his cigarette and glared at him for several moments before leaning forward to speak. "We are from Ausland-SD – Department B, our expertise is Espionage in the West. I am SS-Obersturmbannführer Schmitt and this is SS-Sturmbannführer Falk."

Kurtz didn't respond verbally but just gestured with his head in acknowledgement.

"How much were you told before you left Aalborg?"

"Nothing, sir. I was just told that my crew and I were to fly here, refuel and await further orders."

This time it was Schmitt who nodded while stubbing out his cigarette into the ashtray. "Good. Now, what do you know about jet engines, Kurtz?"

"Only what I've read from reviews and books. The English inventor, Frank Whittle, developed the concept of the jet engine in 1928. The turbojet came later, independently by Whittle and later by Hans von Ohain in Germany, and the first operational jet fighter was the Messerschmitt 262. But what I've been hearing is it is difficult to handle by even the most experienced pilots.

"Where have you heard this?" Falk enquired.

"Mainly from other aircrew members. Word soon gets around if there is a problem with an aircraft," he answered casually.

"We do not like loose tongues in the SS, Kurtz," Falk said sharply.

"Is that so? But it is widely known that tongues soon start to wag during interrogation through the methods you people use," he replied. He knew immediately that his remark had touched a nerve by the thunderous look he was given.

"Be careful, Hauptmann. Be very careful," Falk snarled.

"Enough, gentlemen," intervened Schmitt. "We have more pressing matters to discuss. Now, Kurtz, what you have heard, by whatever means, is irrelevant," he said, looking at both men. "The Reich has several projects under mass production and could turn the war in Germany's favour. But that is not why we are here."

"Then why have I been brought here?" Kurtz asked.

A coldness descended for a few moments until Schmitt broke the silence. "The reason is the British. They have developed a new jet engine, which they call the Welland. It has been fitted to a Gloster Meteor and made its first test flight in January, which was very successful. We know, through our operatives, that the British are now building these aircraft and they could be reaching RAF squadrons by as early as mid-summer," he said, abruptly stopping to pick up the telephone to order some coffee.

Kurtz stroked his forehead while he thought over what Schmitt had said. "Do we know the performance capabilities of this new aircraft?"

"Not at the moment, but—" Schmitt immediately stopped as a knock signalled the arrival of the coffee. "What I was about to say before this arrived," he gestured with the coffee cup, "is that this is where you and your crew come in, Kurtz."

He looked at the Obersturmbannführer quizzically. "Us, sir? In what way?"

"Tell him, Falk, while I drink this muck they call coffee."

"Since 1941, our intelligence service has been keeping a close eye on the British experimental jet which flew for the first time on the 15th of May that year. In the early days of its construction and test flights, the British had several problems with the aircraft, which they have slowly overcome, and they have now test flown the fifth prototype at Cranwell airfield in Lincolnshire. This flight was watched and photographed by one of our top agents, who has kept a close eye on its movements during its development stages."

"Where is the aircraft now?"

"It is on an airfield in Gloucestershire. Our agent was able to get on to the airfield and into the hangar where the aircraft was being kept, photograph it and its engines, and get clean away right under their noses," Schmitt boasted.

Kurtz couldn't help but be impressed by Abwehr's

efficiency, even though it was now run by the SS after the removal of Canaris. "So, where is this agent now?"

"He is on a small uninhabited island off the west coast of Scotland, called Stracandra."

"It's not one I've heard of. Where is it located?"

Falk took a folded map from his briefcase and opened it out on the desk. "That is the island there," he said, pointing at the small clump of rock that lay at the southern tip of the Western Isles.

Kurtz ran a careful eye over the area. "Is there anybody living on these other islands in the area?" he asked.

"No. Stracandra Island did have a manned lighthouse until it was attacked by one of our submarines in the early months of the war. Since then, the island has been deserted. The lighthouse and one of the cottages, which our agent is using, survived the attack. We want you there at first light tomorrow morning, collect him and fly him here. On his arrival, an aircraft will be waiting to fly him directly to Berlin for a meeting with the Führer. This mission must not fail, Kurtz. There will be serious consequences for all concerned if it does. That comes from the highest authority. Do I make myself clear?" Falk emphasised, refolding the map and putting it back in his briefcase.

Schmitt scowled menacingly. "You seem bewildered, Kurtz, is there a problem?"

"Well, wouldn't it be easier and safer to pick this man up by U-boat rather than using a seaplane? It is a long way back to the Norwegian coast in daylight. The RAF constantly patrol well out into the Atlantic. An encounter with one of their aircraft is a risk factor."

"We are aware of the dangers, but the need to get this man back as soon as possible far exceeds the risk involved. As you say, a U-boat would have been the safer option, but unfortunately, we do not have a boat in the area. It is down to you and your crew to undertake the operation," Schmitt answered.

Kurtz sighed. "Right, sir."

"Good. I suggest you and your crew now get some rest. You will be called to a briefing prior to take-off. We will see you then."

* * *

Maynard sat back in his chair. Resting his crossed legs on the corner of the desk, he drummed the desktop noisily with the flat end of a pencil in frustration. He stared at the map on the wall; he knew time was running out to stop Bayer from getting out of the country and, looking at it realistically, it probably already had done. Hurried footsteps coming along the corridor outside made him turn as the office door burst open, and Soames came in with the makings of a smile on his face.

"I've just been given some information from the police here in Stornoway. A fisherman who owns a boat at Lochboisdale has reported it missing this morning."

"This morning?" Maynard said, getting up and going quickly over to the wall map.

"Lochboisdale. That's here at the bottom end of South Uist. Bloody hell, why have we only just received this now with only an hour or so of daylight left? We could have had the RAF up doing a search of the area. Now we're snookered until tomorrow morning. Downright incompetence on the police's part; they know how vital it is we get any scrap of information as soon as we can that could help us get Bayer, the murdering sod," he ranted, throwing the pencil onto the desk.

"I'm afraid it gets worse," Soames said. "Apparently, this fisherman told the local police that the day before, he had been talking to a stranger on the quayside about his boat. General run of the mill stuff, the fish he caught, that kind of thing. But one thing this man did ask was if the boat was refuelled ready to go out on his next fishing trip."

"Which it was," Maynard answered.

"I'm afraid so, sir."

"That's our man, Gideon. So where is he trying to get to?" Maynard asked, turning to look at the map again. "We know he has a full tank of fuel, but he has to stay within this area here," he said, drawing an imaginary ring around South Uist. "And wherever he is making for has to be done under cover of darkness."

"Which only gives him seven or eight hours at most, depending on what time he stole the boat," Soames added.

"Right. Contact Carlton at Benbecula straight away and ask him if he can put up one or possibly two aircraft as soon as possible tomorrow morning to do a search of the area. Make sure he gets a full description of the boat as well, so the aircrew has an idea of what they are looking for. Also, have the aircraft on stand-by to fly us down to Benbecula in the morning."

"I'll get on to it right away," Soames replied, grinning. "The RAF boys are going to love us. They have a bit of a crisis on as it is. One of their aircraft is overdue from a sortie."

"Is it one of Carlton's aircraft?"

"No. I believe it's a Met flight Halifax from Tiree. Anyway, I'd better get on to the Group Captain and see what he can do for us tomorrow morning," Soames replied.

"Gideon, just a minute. On reflection, when you speak to him, tell him I will ring him shortly after I've spoken with London."

"Will do."

* * *

Neatly folding the letter to Isobel, Will sealed the envelope and wondered how she would take the news that he was going back flying. Their romance had blossomed during their regular correspondence and he had told her about the strained relationship he was having with Nelson, the armaments officer, and his need to get back on operations. It had been a pleasant walk in the late afternoon sunshine to the station post office and, with Isobel still occupying his thoughts on the walk back, he hadn't been expecting to be confronted by Keith Stanbury when he reached the mess.

"Will, I've been looking for you. There's a flap on!"

"Why, what's up?"

"We've a kite missing and we're down to do a search operation in the morning and we have to report to the flight office immediately."

"Whose crew is it?" Will asked.

"Sergeant Parrish's. The wireless operator radioed in, saying they had problems with two of the engines. After that, there's been nothing heard from them since."

"Two of the engines. Hell, that doesn't sound good, does it?"

"No. It doesn't."

There was a sombre feel in the flight office when Keith and Will arrived. They were told to go and wait in the briefing room with the other members of their crew. However, further waiting ensued while other crewmembers were located around the base. And by the time Squadron Leader Walker arrived, the equivalent of three crews had been assembled.

"Right, are we all here?" he asked, which got him the response he expected. "This is not a full briefing; you will get that at five tomorrow morning. I've assembled you here now to put you in the picture as to what's happening. As you all will have heard by now, Sergeant Parrish and his crew are now overdue from their Met flight. We received a message from the aircraft, saying that their port outer engine had disintegrated, which they thought was caused by an internal seizure. They also reported that debris from the outer engine had damaged the inner one when it broke up, which they had to shut down. They were hoping they could make it back to Tiree on the two starboard engines. Since that message, we have had no further communication from the aircraft and neither have we been able to contact them. We have to assume that the aircraft has either ditched or, the worst-case scenario, they crashed into the sea before they were able to get a message off – any questions so far?" Walker asked, glancing around the room quickly.

"How far from base were they when they got into trouble, sir?" a voice from one of the other crews asked.

"The position they gave us put them 325 miles out on their homeward leg. Which, you'll all appreciate, is a long way out with two duff engines," Walker added.

"What Met flight were they on, sir?" Len Oakes asked, the navigator on Will's crew.

"They were on a Mercer flight," Walker replied, turning to the large map that hung down over the blackboard showing the Mercer and Bismuth operational flight routes. "These are the areas that you will be covering. Aircraft one will search this area here between the Irish coast and the Mercer outward leg. Sergeant Parrish may well have tried to make for Northern Ireland. The second aircraft will search the area within the Mercer triangle. The third aircraft will cover the area between the Mercer homeward leg and the Bismuth outward route. Benbecula is going to put up two Wellingtons to cover the area within the Bismuth triangle. So, the whole area is pretty well covered and, with good weather conditions forecast for the next few days, there is a good chance of finding our chaps. And remember, the regular Met flights will be taking place, so watch out for those aircraft. We don't want any airborne collisions." Looking at his watch, he continued. "After you've eaten, liaise with your ground crews on the status of your aircraft. We don't want any problems before take-off, or during the flights. You will be called at five, a full briefing at six, take-off at seven."

Chapter 30

Watched by Schmitt and Falk, Kurtz walked with his crew to the transport that would take them to their aircraft. He noticed that there was a quietness from the crew, no doubt each man realising there could be a strong possibility of an encounter with a British aircraft during their long flight. As he stood to one side to finish his cigarette, he looked at the Seedrache's unusual shape or the flying clog as it was unofficially called by the crews. Although it was well-armed and had a good operating range, it lacked height and speed, making it vulnerable to attack from allied aircraft.

Flicking the cigarette end into the inky black water, he climbed aboard and took up his position in the pilot's seat. With the engines running and getting the all-clear from the dockside, Kurtz opened the throttles slightly and eased the flying boat away from the mooring and out into the middle of the bay. The noise from the three diesel engines pierced the night air as the aircraft cut a white furrow across the surface of the water before being lifted aloft. On a course of 350 degrees, they climbed steadily to their cruising height, where Kurtz levelled the aircraft off for the flight along the coast to Bergen. With time and fuel consumption to consider, they had debated on whether to take the more direct route between the islands of Shetland and Orkney. But with little room for manoeuvre should British radar pick them up and send an aircraft up to intercept them, the risk was too great. With clear conditions given for the duration of the flight, they had decided to take the northerly route, which would take them between the Faroe and Shetland Islands, the distance being greater but with less chance of detection.

"Beautiful, isn't it?" Kurtz said, looking at the coastline and snow-covered mountains ahead, which were clearly visible.

"Yes, it is. Maybe after the war is over, we could come back and try our hand at skiing," Bolling answered.

"Have you done any?" Kurtz asked, adjusting the aircraft's trim.

"No, I'd probably spend more time on my arse than stood up on the skis," he chuckled. "What about you?"

"My parents liked to ski so we used to holiday in Bavaria in the Oberbayern region during the thirties."

"So, you are pretty good then?" the radio operator said, giving his captain a pretentious stare.

"Well, I might be a bit rusty, but I still think I could get to the bottom of the piste without falling on my backside."

Bolling started to laugh. "I'm not so sure of that. I've seen you on your backside several times when you've been pissed. Remember that night in Aalborg with the two Danish girls?"

Kurtz was just about to respond to his friend's humorous remark but was interrupted by Karl Bastian's voice on the intercom.

"Captain! Come left onto a new course, 290 degrees," he said in a rather brusque tone.

The two men looked at each other without speaking. "Thank you, navigator. Turning on to new course, 290 degrees," Kurtz said.

In the confines of his turret Walter Myer always found night flying monotonous, so it had been nice to listen to the cross-chat between the radio operator and the captain, which had alleviated some of the boredom. He'd had a bad feeling about the flight from the beginning. Having Engle, their regular navigator, replaced hadn't sat well with him and he had voiced his concerns to the captain who had taken him to one side and quietly told him, 'that it was out of his hands'. Looking over the barrel of the cannon in front of him, he felt confident in his own capabilities should they encounter the enemy as he traversed the turret to make another sweep. Even so, it was a long flight with much of it being flown in daylight. Satisfied all was clear, his thoughts turned to his wife, Dagmar, back in Heidelberg. The continuous allied bombing raids weighed heavily on his mind, and he couldn't remember the number of times he had asked her to go to her parents' house in the country where she would be safe, but she always refused. He shook his head in annoyance at her stubbornness, she had always been the same, but in fairness, it had been one of the qualities that he loved about her.

After covering the distance from the Norwegian coast to the mid-way point between the Shetland and Faroe Islands without incident, Kurtz banked the seaplane around sharply onto the new course he had been given. Back on a level flight, he looked down the side of the pronounced features of the front turret as Manfred gently tracked from side to side searching for any signs of hostile aircraft. But even with this threat, Kurtz couldn't help but feel the exhilaration he always got from low flying.

"I wonder how the other flight is making out on its diversionary flight towards Fair Isle?" Bolling said, trying to sound concerned.

"I don't know. The skill with those sort of operations is to get turned around and on your way back before the RAF get up to intercept you, leave it too late, and you can be up the proverbial without a paddle," Kurtz replied, checking their fuel state and hearing the click of the intercom.

"Captain. "New course. Come left onto 200 degrees. That will keep us west of Rona and the Hebrides. Distance to next course change 161 kilometres."

"Thank you, navigator," Kurtz answered, impressed with Bastian's efficiency. "Seems to know his stuff, Herbert."

Bolling didn't reply to the remark about Bastian but just stared down at the sea below. "If operations have got their timings right, the Junkers should be on its way back to Stavanger by now, lucky sods."

"*If* they've got it right. The British are no fools when it comes to the art of deception. They pull the same stunts to keep our fighters away from their bombers. They may well have guessed what we were up to," Kurtz replied, gently reducing height to get as close to the surface as he could to keep below the British radar—knowing that the worst part of the flight was still to come, which would take them very close to the incoming route of the Met flight Halifax's based on Tiree.

Having covered the last hundred kilometres from their last course correction to keep them well clear of the larger islands of South Uist and Barra, they had reached the northern end of Stracandra Island as the first streaks of light were beginning to show in the east. After gaining height, Kurtz decided to run down the dark side of the island to seaward, which would bring them to the headland that housed the cottages, lighthouse, and the all-important jetty.

* * *

Suitably kitted out for the long flight, Will shuffled out with the rest of the crew carrying his parachute, survival rations and other paraphernalia into the surprisingly mild morning air and across to the waiting transport. He grinned at the driver, who he saw stifle a yawn with the back of his hand. "I know the feeling," he said, making his way down the aisle and taking a seat behind Jack Rapier, the wireless operator.

The chat, given they had been called at the God unearthly hour of five o'clock, seemed more intense than normal as they made the journey around the perimeter track to the far side of the airfield to the dispersal where their aircraft, A–Apple, stood with its nose aloof after being lovingly prepared by its ground crew.

"How is she, Flight?" asked Groves, their pilot, taking the form 700 to sign.

"She's spot on, sir!"

"Thanks, Flight. Right chaps, let's get aboard."

* * *

Bayer had been on the walkway that encircled the top of the lighthouse since before dawn and heard the sound of the approaching aircraft before he saw it. Taking the flashlight from his jacket pocket, he held it in readiness. A feeling of gratification, of a job well done, swept over him as he saw the trimotor flying boat with a swastika on its tail unit slowly materialise out of the early morning gloom. After giving the designated three flashes and getting the same response from the aircraft, he stood a few moments to watch it head out to sea before banking around to make a long approach towards the island.

Stella had also heard the distant aircraft and tried desperately to free herself from the ropes that bound her to the chair, but however hard she tried she couldn't. She began to sob as she thought of the previous day and how he had pinned her to the ground and held the knife to her throat. Then, after dragging her to her feet, he had taken her into the cottage where he had forced himself upon her. The sound of him approaching made her look up at the door which was flung open and he stood looking at her in the half-light.

"So, what are we going to do with you?" he smirked, walking over to her and grabbing her by her chin and squeezing it, so it pushed her head back.

"Please, please don't kill me. I won't say anything," she pleaded with tears streaming down her cheeks. "I promise I won't say a word!"

"I'll just bet you wouldn't," Bayer said, scowling at her and keenly aware that time was of the essence as he moved behind her. Stella shrieked as the blade from Bayer's knife flashed open close to her face. "Because you have given me much pleasure, I've decided to let you live," he told her, stroking her cheek with the back of the blade. "But put one foot outside that door before we have left and I will instruct the aircraft's gunners to turn all their firepower on the cottage – is that understood?"

Stella nodded frantically before burbling out a "yes" as she felt the ropes that held her being cut. Free of her bounds, she stayed in the chair and looked up at the man who had once been her lover and despised him for all he had put her through as she wiped away the tears.

"Are you not going to wish me bon voyage, Stella?" he asked. On not getting a reply, he picked up his travel bag and went to kiss her, but she turned her head away.

She sat for a few moments after he had left in utter relief that she was still alive. Standing up, she walked across to the window where she saw him reach the top of the steps that went down to the jetty. There she saw him hesitate and look back, as though troubled by leaving her alive, before disappearing from view.

* * *

From the rear turret, Will watched the grey light of dawn spread across the airfield below. They climbed steadily on a north-westerly course to their designated search height. After test firing the guns and reporting back that all was okay, he settled down to the routine of searching for any sign of enemy activity. As the aircraft levelled off, Will could just make out the dark shape of Tiree in the distance, and he slowly tracked the turret around onto his port quarter.

Thin wisps of transparent white cloud, almost motionless, drifted by above him and seemed to add to the early morning beauty. Depressing the four Brownings down, he felt the seat slowly tilt forward too, a feature he found superior over the Lancaster's Frazer-Nash turret, which made it easier for him to check the lower quarter. In doing so, he saw the distinct shapes of the islands at the southern end of the Western Isles and the one with its prominent lighthouse. Staring at the structure, he recalled the incident on his second Met flight and wondered if it had been a trick of the light. But he knew what he had seen, and no amount of dissuasion would convince him otherwise.

Dismissing it as a closed chapter, he was just about to rotate the turret to do another search when he saw movement below. A bank of low cloud temporarily obscured his vision, so he waited for it to clear. What he saw made him stare in disbelief, a German flying boat – stationary, but with its engines still running – and what looked like two people in a rubber dinghy heading towards the waiting aircraft. Assessing the situation, Will quickly realised the flying boat's vulnerability. The craft was pointing seaward, ready for take-off once the pick-up had been made, but this rendered the two rear gun positions inoperable. It left the aircraft's single front gun as its only means of defence. Alerting the skipper to the enemy's presence and giving him his evaluation on the best line of attack, Flight Sergeant Groves immediately banked the Halifax around in a tight turn to starboard and, given their low search altitude, began a shallow diving attack towards the enemy aircraft.

The German seaplane opened fire with its single cannon. Will saw the enemy's fire pass underneath their tail, while in retaliation, he heard Sergeant Doyle in the nose begin to fire the Vicker's machine gun, who reported scoring hits on the flying boat's hull before being wounded by a cannon shell smashing into the nose section. Undeterred by the damage to the aircraft, Groves pressed home the attack, while Flight Sergeant Oakes, their navigator who was tending the wounded gunner, shouted to Will over the intercom that they were about to overfly the enemy aircraft. Will waited out the few remaining seconds looking into the gun sight. He knew his firing was now the only means of stopping the enemy seaplane from taking off.

Will felt the thud as cannon shells struck the Halifax, and someone shouted that the port wing had been hit as he opened fire on the flying boat, strafing the bow section. His fire hit a crewmember in a dinghy which was tied alongside and a second man – who looked like a civilian – who was climbing into the aircraft through its open forward hatch. Will redirected his fire at the front turret, which stopped firing immediately, and the cockpit. He saw it shatter under the hail of fire from the four Brownings as Groves lifted the Halifax up and made another wide turn to starboard to assess the situation.

Chapter 31

Aboard the flying boat sitting amidst the debris, it had been the sound of the engines still running and a cold breeze on his face that revived Kurtz's senses. Wiping away the blood that ran down his face from the head wound, he watched the Halifax continuing to circle. Looking around at the smashed cockpit, he wondered how he had managed to survive the savage onslaught. The radio operator's position was totally destroyed, putting the radio and wireless systems out of action. The starboard windows had been blown out, and the side of the hull was peppered with jagged holes.

"Can we take off, Captain?" a voice from behind him asked.

Turning around and wiping away more blood, Kurtz saw Karl Bastion, the navigator, looking at him in desperation. "I don't know. Are Myers and Klingemann okay?"

"Yes, Captain," Bastion answered, looking at his captain's head wound.

"Good, at least we've got some means of defending ourselves if we can get airborne," Kurtz replied, still keeping a watchful eye on the enemy aircraft's movements.

"Shall I get the first aid box?"

"Never mind that. You go forward and see what state Filor, Bolling and our passenger are in. Also, see what damage has been done to the forward section of the hull while I check things out here and keep an eye on him," he gestured to the RAF aircraft above them, "to see what he's going to do," Kurtz answered.

Bastian made his way through to the forward compartment and was alarmed at the amount of seawater there was. He found Filor slumped forward over the cannon. Lifting the gunner's head, he checked for a pulse. Satisfied he was dead, he went to check on their passenger, who was lying under the forward hatch, unable to move from wounds to his back and legs. Bastian could see a substantial amount of blood mingling with the cold seawater and knew the wounds were severe.

"Do you think you can move?" he asked, knowing full well what the answer would be.

Looking at the Oberleutant, Bayer shook his head. "But could you make me more comfortable by straightening my legs for me," he asked, his voice all but a whisper.

Bastian nodded. Bayer winced as he was moved and was eventually able to look up at the sky above through the open hatch, his mind drifting back to days past in Germany with family and friends.

Keeping the man's head clear of the water, Bastian asked, "What happened to Bolling, the radio operator?" but he got no reply as he saw Bayer's eyes close. Lowering Bayer's head down gently, he did a quick search outside the hull. Seeing no sign of Bolling, he closed the forward hatch and made his way back to report to Kurtz.

Kurtz knew by their nose-down angle that the aircraft was sinking before Bastian came back and confirmed it. "And what of Bolling, Filor and our passenger?" he asked sullenly.

"All dead," Bastian confirmed, his voice trailing off as he stared hard through the shattered remains of the starboard window. "Take a look at that, Captain."

Coming towards them at high speed, Kurtz saw the rakish bow of an RAF air-sea rescue launch. He knew they were a formidable adversary with the amount of armament they carried. With the forward section now partially underwater, Kurtz knew their chance of taking off was now futile, so, after shutting down the engines, he gave the order to abandon the aircraft.

* * *

Emerging from the rear of the cottage – where she had concealed herself when the gunfire started – Stella cautiously opened the door just wide enough to see why the firing had stopped. Squinting through the narrow gap, she could see nothing but was able to hear what sounded like a heavy aircraft circling above. With curiosity eventually taking over from caution, she opened the door fully and stepped outside, shielding her eyes. She was able to make out the distinct shape of a large greyish-white aircraft. Waving her arms frantically and shouting at the top of her voice to be rescued, she set off running towards the steps that went down to the jetty. But nearing the cliff edge, doubt crept into her mind.

If the aircraft she could see was British, had it attacked the German seaplane before Bayer had got on board? The more Stella thought about it, the more convinced she became that she needed to know. The surface of the sea glinted in the morning sun, while below, she could hear the sound of the waves breaking gently against the rocks. The sound of high-speed engines tempted her to the edge of the cliff where, crouching behind a medium-sized boulder for cover, she looked down at the dramatic scene unfolding below.

* * *

Flight Sergeant Groves knew that, as skipper, the destruction of the enemy aircraft was paramount. But with an injured crewman onboard and damage to his aircraft, he had to make a decision: break off the engagement and head for home or make another run at the flying boat. After a brief discussion with the crew, the outcome had been unanimous, even from the wounded Doyle.

While they were making a wide turn to starboard to make their attack, Will noticed the flying boat's angle in the water and realised that it must be sinking and reported this to Groves. Keith Stanbury also reported the sighting of a rescue launch, but with his line of approach and height set, Groves decided to carry on with the attack. From the damaged nose of the Halifax, Len Oakes and Reggie Doyle watched as the distance between the two aircraft began to close. "We'll finish him off this time, Reggie," Len Oakes winked, patting the injured gunner's shoulder, who responded with a weak grin.

In the rear turret, Will applied pressure to the controls, not expecting any retaliatory fire from the sea plane's front turret. He had decided his aiming point would be the fuel tanks and engines. He stared down at the open expanse of sea behind. The waiting seemed endless, although in real time it would only be a matter of minutes before they would be over the enemy aircraft. His concentration was interrupted by reports over the intercom that four members of the flying boat were taking to the water – this was followed by the skipper telling him to hold his fire. Flying low over the stricken craft, Will saw the four airmen treading water and waving, no doubt terrified that he might open fire. Acknowledging their plea, he elevated his guns and then felt the aircraft begin to climb as they approached the island. A shout came over the intercom. "Who the hell's that waving? Christ! it's a woman down there."

"Maybe she lives there?" Jack Rapier commented from the confines of the wireless shack.

"I wouldn't think so. As far as I know, the island is uninhabited," Groves replied, banking the Halifax round to make another run across the island.

"I was told that," Will answered, looking down at the seaplane that was now partially submerged with only its centre engine and twin-boom tail section still visible.

"Well, whoever she is, she must need help or she wouldn't be waving like that. Jack, make contact with that air-sea rescue boat and tell them they have another passenger to pick up from the island after they've plucked those Jerries out of the drink, will you?"

"Ok, skipper."

"So how's Reggie doing, Len?"

"I've bandaged his wounds for him the best I can and given him a shot of morphine, and he seems quite comfortable at the moment, but the sooner we can get him back to the hospital, the better," the navigator answered, sounding a little concerned.

"Okay, Len. Jack, contact Tiree and tell them we are returning to base and we need an ambulance standing by as soon as we land. Also, tell them the outcome of the attack and about the woman on the island."

* * *

Maynard and Soames had been at RAF Benbecula when they had been given the news of the sinking of the German flying boat off Stracandra Island. Also, four of the aircrew from the aircraft plus a woman from the island were on their way to Lochboisdale aboard an RAF launch and that they would be brought to Benbecula when they arrived under armed guard.

"Well, this will be a first for me," Soames declared, trying to break the silence that had descended on the room.

"What will?" Maynard asked, drawing steadily on his pipe with a contented look on his face.

"Coming face to face with the enemy. I've never met any Luftwaffe aircrew before. Have you, sir?"

"Once. In the early days of the war," Maynard replied, thinking back to the Luftwaffe pilot's attitude as he was led away to be interrogated.

"What was he like?"

Maynard took his pipe from his mouth and grinned. "Cocky sod! Pretty damn sure of himself, but back then, they thought they had the war won having rampaged through Europe practically unopposed."

Soames nodded. "Let's hope these four are a little bit more amenable now that the war isn't going in their favour."

"Don't count on it. With a fanatic like Hitler leading the pack, there's a lot in Germany who still think they can win the war," he replied, as he watched Soames get up and walk over to the window with his hands clasped behind his back. "What's the matter, Gideon? Is something bothering you?"

"Yes, there is. Where does this woman fit into all this? Do you think she could be an accomplice? Was she trying to help him get out of the country and, at the last minute, he abandoned her? We know what a ruthless sod he could be."

"Maybe. But if you want my honest opinion …" his reply was interrupted by a knock on the door. A corporal airwoman informed them that the prisoners and the woman had just arrived at Benbecula and that the commanding officer was waiting for them in his office.

"Thank you," Maynard answered, getting up. "Looks like all could be revealed."

Chapter 32

Crossing Pall Mall, light rain began to fall and, by the time Maynard reached his office in St James's Street, it had turned heavy. After hanging his wet raincoat on the stand behind the door, he sat down and started to sort through the paperwork on his desk; with his concentration fixed firmly on what he was reading, he didn't take any notice of the approaching footsteps which stopped outside his office.

"I always know when you are back," a voice said casually. Amy, Clifford Granville's secretary, was smiling at him in the doorway.

"How's that?" he asked, looking up.

"You always have your office door open when you're in," she answered, coming in and standing in front of his desk.

"I see," he said, leaning back in the chair and clasping his hands together. "So why am I honoured by your presence at this time in the morning?"

"I believe congratulations are in order on your achievement in Scotland."

"Thanks. But it should be that RAF crew who gets the praise, not me, Amy."

"Yes, I know. But you mustn't put yourself down. You played a big part in the operation too, remember that. Anyway, Mr Granville wants to see you," she said, leaving the room.

Sitting down opposite his old friend, Maynard saw Clifford Granville put down his report on the desk, take out one of his cigars and light it, which soon filled the room with smoke. "Excellent outcome, Henry, and I can tell you that the prime minister was over the moon when he was given the news that we had got Bayer."

"Well, it was touch and go at times. Bayer seemed to be always that one jump ahead of us. There's no doubt about it. He was a damn good agent, Clifford."

"Yes. And one for the ladies by what I've read. This woman who was on the island – Stella Grant – I see in your report that she was just another of his conquests. Are you sure about that, Henry? We don't want any loose ends."

"I got the local police in Oban to check out her story thoroughly. Friends at the dance she was with verified that she had deliberately gone out of her way to meet Bayer. Because, as she told her friend, she just fancied him, nothing more than that. And of course, when Bayer found out, through pillow talk I suppose, where she worked–"

"At the shipping office," Granville interrupted.

"I'll bet he couldn't believe his luck."

"Stupid woman."

"A lucky woman. Why he didn't kill her before he left the island is a mystery, knowing his track record," Maynard concluded.

"It was strange that," Granville replied, exhaling a cloud of cigar smoke into the air. "But at least we have confirmation from the flying boat's navigator that Bayer was dead before it sank. Grant was also able to validate Bastian's story by saying that she saw only the four Luftwaffe aircrew in the water – so it was a satisfactory outcome all round, wouldn't you agree?"

"Yes, I would."

"Now, about tomorrow morning, Henry. We have a meeting with the PM at ten, so best bib and tucker. I think you are going to get a pat on the back for what you did, old boy," Granville grinned.

Maynard's face remained neutral. "It's not me he should be congratulating. It should be the crew of that Halifax from Tiree. They were the ones that eventually stopped Bayer, not me."

Granville nodded several times while flicking the ash from his cigar into the ashtray. "Yes, I know that. I believe the pilot will get an award for pressing home the attack like he did. Well deserved, I would think, don't you?"

"Yes, it is. I was told one of the crew was very badly hurt during the attack, have you any news on how he is doing?" Maynard asked.

Granville shuffled uneasily in his chair at being put on the spot. "I haven't, but I'll see what I can find out, and let you know. You mustn't take it to heart, Henry. People get hurt and killed in war, it's inevitable. What you have to remember is that through the combined efforts of all the people involved it has brought about the end of a very brutal killer. If he had got back to Germany, he could have undermined all our work on the development of jet propulsion. And don't forget the capture of Griselda Zweig, which put an end to her escapades at Filton. That was a big feather in the department's cap."

"So where is Griselda now?" Maynard asked, taking out his pipe.

Granville gave him a smug look. "I can't say where she is. All I will say is that she is doing good work for counter-intelligence."

Throwing the near-burnt ember of the match into the ashtray, Maynard sat back in the chair and drew steadily on his pipe. "Good, I'm glad she is being useful."

"She knew she only had two choices, Henry, work with us or the long drop. The choice was hers."

"It would have been a waste if she had chosen the latter. She certainly is an attractive woman."

Granville smiled broadly. "That sounds like you had a bit of a soft spot for the woman, Henry?"

"No, no, I was just making a statement from what I observed when I interviewed her," Maynard replied, getting up to leave, a little embarrassed. "Right, if we have finished here? I'd better get back to the office and get on with some work."

Leaning forward Clifford Granville flicked ash from his cigar. "Yes, I think so."

Chapter 33

It had been the squealing of brakes and clanking of wheels as they crossed the points that woke her. Looking through the grime-covered window, Griselda saw the slope of the platform as the train entered Manchester's busy Piccadilly Station and came to a halt. From the compartment, she sat and watched the exodus of passengers as they alighted from the carriages, all eager to be on their way to whatever life held in store for them now the war had ended.

She drew deeply on her cigarette to calm the uneasy feeling she suddenly felt. What did life hold in store for her now? She knew what she wanted but would it still be on offer? There was only one way to find out. She left the compartment, walked along the corridor to the door and stepped down onto the platform and, with her German pride encouraging her, she made her way to the ticket gate where she smiled at the young ticket collector, who obviously found her attractive by the way he was looking at her as he allowed her through.

Feeling she needed time to think, she ignored the taxis touting for business and set off walking, eventually reaching the tram stop in Stretford Road. When it arrived, the tram was surprisingly full for mid-afternoon, but she did manage to get a seat, given up by a middle-aged gentleman who had insisted when she first declined his offer. Griselda looked through the window as each stop brought her closer to her destination. Could she go through with it when she was stood outside the hotel? What if Matthew had now re-married and he came to the door with his wife, or, if still single, he just out and out rejected her – what would she do then? So many ifs! God, she needed a cigarette, but she couldn't even do that; it wasn't allowed on the lower deck.

The congestion within the tram had eased by the time it reached Warwick Road and, having the added advantage of a seat by the window, Griselda saw the end of the hotel in the distance.

Making her way carefully over the uneven cobbles to the pavement, she stood a few moments to compose herself. She had waited a long time for this moment, all those months in captivity working for British counter-intelligence. She had thought of nothing else but of Matthew. Now reality was only a stone's throw away.

Pushing her blonde hair back onto her shoulders, Griselda set off to walk the short distance, to see what destiny held or didn't hold for her. Closing the gate behind her, she walked up the path. She noticed the *'No Vacancy'* sign in the window and the fresh coat of paint on the ornate door. Pressing the bell, she stood back and waited.

A young girl opened the door and, before Griselda could speak, was told, "I'm sorry, we are fully booked if you are looking for a room. You may find something further along Warwick Road. There are several more guest houses along there."

"I'm not looking for a room," Griselda replied quickly as the door was already shutting. "I'd like to see Mr Raines if that's possible?"

"Oh. Have you come about the vacancy for a waitress?"

"Yes, I have."

"I'm sorry. I thought you were looking for a room. Please come in. I'll get Mr Raines for you. He's in the cellar at the moment, changing over a barrel. If you would like to go into the lounge, you can wait there," the girl said, beckoning towards the room.

Sitting down on the settee, Griselda took in the all too familiar surroundings of the lounge bar where their relationship had begun. She had fond memories of his tenderness during their lovemaking. She must have caused him a great deal of hurt when she told him she was leaving after he had begged her to stay. Her reminiscing was temporarily put on hold by the door partially opening and the young girl's head appeared.

"I've told Mr Raines you are here and he won't be long."

"Thanks. Before you go," Griselda prompted with her hand for the girl's name.

"Laura," the girl replied.

"Is there a Mrs Raines, Laura?"

"No. His wife was killed during the war in an air raid," she replied, closing the door.

Sitting alone, Griselda had time to reflect over the last six years. The loss of life on all sides had been tremendous. Her own country now lay in ruins, destroyed by the allied bombing. And now, paying the price for its failure by being divided up between the victors. What had it all been for? Her eyes became tearful as she thought of her homeland and family.

After locking the cellar door and hanging the key on the hook behind the reception desk, Matthew never expected a former lover to be waiting for him, which rendered him speechless, but for one word – "Lillian?"

Griselda didn't respond to the name but only smiled. "Hello, Matthew. I believe you are looking for a waitress?"

He looked at her bemused. "Yes, I am. But you haven't come about that, have you?" he said, sitting down opposite her. "So, what have you come back for?"

Griselda frowned. "Because I think I owe you an explanation."

"An explanation – I don't understand?" he said, sitting forward and clasping his hands together.

"Why I turned down your offer to stay, and why I had to leave when I did."

"You must have had your reasons. It was wartime."

Griselda forced a weak smile. "But my war was different."

"Different. What do you mean by that remark?"

"All I can tell you is that I was intelligence gathering. I can't say any more than that."

He studied her for a moment to take in what she had said. "You mean MI5 and all that stuff? Are you telling me you were working for them, Lillian?"

Griselda thought deeply, to choose her words carefully, before answering. "Not to start with," she paused before continuing. "I was operating for the other side, Matthew. My name isn't Lillian Gilbert. It's Griselda Zweig – I'm German."

Sitting back in his chair, he looked at her in astonishment. "German?"

"Yes. I came to England before the war started as a sleeper, and when the war began, I was gathering information and sending it back to Germany."

"You were spying on us?"

"I'm afraid so."

"What happened?"

"I was caught here in Manchester by the railway police who handed me over to Military Intelligence. After they interrogated me, they gave me a choice, either work for them or face the alternative. The rest is history, as they say."

"So, have you been back to Germany since the war finished?" he asked.

"No, I haven't, I think I'm too ashamed to," she answered, looking down at the floor.

"What about your family?"

"I've written to my mother and tried to explain. My father's dead. He was killed in the first world war."

There followed a period of silence between them, and Griselda decided maybe it was time to leave. It had been the untimely appearance of Laura entering the room that ended the deadlock.

"Not now, Laura. Knock next time before you come in please," Matthew told her in a raised voice. Griselda felt a little sorry for the young girl who she saw cringe, then apologise and quickly left the room.

"What had you intended doing after you leave here?" he asked, his eyes holding hers.

Not able to hold his stare, she looked towards the window. "I don't honestly know."

Getting up, he went and sat next to her and took hold of her hand. "I think there has been enough hatred and killing on both sides, don't you?"

Turning to look at him. "Yes, I think there has."

"There will always be a home and a future here for you if you want it."

Smiling but tearful, she replied, "Matthew, you don't know how long I've been waiting to hear you say that," she said, laying her head on his shoulder.

Epilogue

* * * SPRING 1946 * * *

"Have you two had enough to eat?"

"Yes, thank you, Doris," they both replied.

"Well, it is a beautiful morning. So what are you going to do today?"

"I'm not sure," Isobel replied, looking at her husband, but he remained quiet on the subject.

"Well, whatever you do, enjoy yourselves. Another young couple will be arriving this afternoon, also on honeymoon, so you will have someone to chat to over dinner," she told them, carrying the tray of breakfast dishes from the room.

After collecting what they needed from their room, they made their way down the stairway, both laughing after commenting on how narrow and quaint it was and in keeping with the rest of the inn. Outside, Isobel took in the aroma of spring as she looked at the lake with its wooded shoreline on the opposite side. The leaves were shimmering in the morning sun.

"So, what do you think of the Lake District, Mrs Madden?"

"It's everything you said it was. It's lovely, Will."

"What would you like to do first?"

"I wouldn't mind having a look around the town," Isobel suggested.

They spent the morning leisurely walking the streets and browsing the shops, some of which were still showing the signs of the continual wartime rationing by their sparse window displays. After a light lunch in the café Will had used on his visit during the war, he gently steered Isobel towards the outskirts of the town. Isobel began to wonder just where she was being taken.

"Where are we going, Will? We seem to have been walking for quite a while. I hope you know the way back?"

Letting go of her hand, he slipped his arm around her waist and gave her a little hug of reassurance. "It's not far now. Just round the next bend, and we should be there."

The finger signpost was still there, if a little bit more dilapidated since the last time he saw it. Climbing over the stile first, he then helped Isobel over, then taking the lead along the single overgrown path, he led her to the place by the lakeside where he had found peace and solitude from the ravages of war.

Standing next to each other, holding hands, neither spoke as they drank in the tranquillity. All that disturbed the peace of the afternoon was the sound of birds singing in the trees above them. But even so, Will couldn't help but wonder what the full story was behind the events that took place on Stracandra Island and why the crew had been told to never talk about it.

No 518 Squadron Motto: Tha An luchair Againn – Ne

Translation: We hold the key

Meteorological Flight Halifax P (Mk 2-1A K9660 of 518 Squadron on Tiree) just before take-off on its historical flight on 1st June 1944. The weather report from that flight was responsible for delaying D-Day from the 5th to 6th June.

Dedicated to all the aircrew who flew on these sometimes dangerous flights.

(Photograph: By kind permission of Peter Allen and An Iodhann – Tiree's Historical Centre.)